# miles from nowhere

## Other books by Amy Clipston

*Roadside Assistance*

*Destination Unknown*

*Reckless Heart*

### *The Kauffman Amish Bakery series*

*A Gift of Grace*

*A Promise of Hope*

*A Place of Peace*

*A Life of Joy*

*A Season of Love*

### *Hearts of Lancaster the Grand Hotel series*

*A Hopeful Heart*

*A Mother's Secret*

*A Dream of Home*

*A Simple Prayer*

### Amish Novellas

*A Plain and Simple Christmas*

*Naomi's Gift*

### *Nonfiction*

*The Gift of Love*

# miles from nowhere



Amy Clipston

ZONDERVAN

*Miles from Nowhere*


This title is also available as a Zondervan ebook.
Visit www.zondervan.com/ebooks.

Requests for information should be addressed to:

Zondervan, 3900 *Sparks Dr. SE, Grand Rapids, Michigan 49546*

ISBN 978-0-310-73670-7



*Cover design: Brand Navigation*
*Cover photography: Getty Images, iStockfoto*
*Interior design: Matthew Van Zomeren*

*Printed in the United States of America*

15 16 17 18 19 20 21 22 23 24 /DCI/ 20 19 18 17 16 15 14 13 12 11 10 9 8 7 6 5 4 3 2 1

*For Jeanne Lampropoulos, my "sister cousin," with love.*

*You're a blessing to our family!*

# chapter one

I cupped my hand over my mouth to stifle a yawn and attempted to get more comfortable in the old wooden theater seat near the back of the auditorium. I wasn't yawning because the auditions were boring. Far from it. In fact, I loved attending auditions, especially since we were gearing up for a big summer musical production of *Grease* at the Cameronville Community Theater. I crossed my legs and smoothed my hands over my colorful skirt.

Summer productions had always been my favorite, since practices could be held five afternoons a week. And that meant my last summer before college would be all theater, all the time. Well, except when I was working the breakfast shift at the Fork & Knife, the restaurant that my boyfriend Todd's parents owned.

"Jimmy, please turn to page one seventeen and read the part of Danny," Jeff Muller, the director, bellowed from his seat near the front of the theater. "And Britney, please read the part of Sandy on the same page."

A tall, dark-haired, muscular boy walked to center stage flanked by a skinny blonde girl—Jimmy and Britney. They'd both graduated with me a few weeks ago, and both of them had played the lead roles in the last musical production at our high school. I'd heard that Britney was planning to go to the university—almost everybody just called it "U"—with me in the fall.

As the actors began reading the lines, I glanced at my phone hoping to find a text from Todd. I'd expected him to meet me here nearly an hour ago, and I couldn't help but worry. It wasn't like him to be late. Normally, he was as predictable as the ocean tide.

"Thank you!" Mr. Muller said when the actors had finished the scene. "Next!"

For the next hour or so, I watched intently as a parade of potential actors read lines for the various parts, two at a time. Eventually, my mind wandered as I envisioned the costumes for each character. Ever since I was in elementary school, it had been a dream of mine to be the lead costumer on a summer production. Now that my dream had finally come true, I was anxious to get started. I decided I'd better write down my ideas before I forgot them.

As two more actors walked onstage and received their instructions from Mr. Muller, I retrieved my sketchbook and a pencil from my bright green messenger bag and turned to a fresh page. I began listing the costumes I'd need to create or assemble for *Grease*: poodle skirts, bobby socks, black leather jackets for the boys, pink denim jackets for the Pink Ladies, jeans, formal dresses for the dance scene, letterman sweaters, cheerleading—

"Hey." A tall body slipped into the seat beside me, interrupting my list making. "How's it going?"

I looked up to see Todd. At five foot ten, he stood over me by nearly five inches. He wore his dark brown hair in a messy but layered style that completely covered his ears and almost his eyes, which reminded me of melted chocolate. He was slender but definitely not weak. I'd seen him carry some heavy pieces of plywood while working on set design back in high school.

When I'd first met Todd two years ago, his nearly constant sullen expressions made him seem aloof. Yet when we worked together on the senior production of *Aladdin* this spring, I'd discovered that Todd is actually shy. He hadn't been ignoring me before; instead, he'd been afraid to talk to me. That part had surprised me quite a bit since I tend to talk to everyone on the cast and crew—even if they aren't all that interested in me.

After our first conversation, Todd and I began talking every day, and pretty soon he worked up the nerve to ask me out on a date to the Dairy Barn to grab a milk shake. Not long after that, he asked me to the prom. We'd been dating since then.

"Hi." I pushed a stray piece of hair behind my ear and leaned toward him, inhaling the aroma of french fries mixed with bacon. "Where have you been?" I asked in a low voice, even though I could tell by the smell that he'd been cooking at his parents' restaurant.

"Working." He slumped lower in his seat and folded his arms over his chest. "Maggie went into labor this morning, so you're looking at the new head cook of the Fork & Knife. Well, head cook in training, really."

"Congratulations. I thought Maggie's baby wasn't due for a couple of weeks yet." I thought back to earlier in the day when I'd been working. "You know, she did look kind of uncomfortable when I saw her this morning."

"Yeah, her water broke soon after you left work."

"Oh my!" I squeaked, prompting Todd to place a finger to his lips as a reminder to keep my voice down. "Did she have the baby yet?" I whispered. "She had a feeling she was having a boy, so she only picked out a boy's name. Since she was prepared to have a boy, she'll most likely have a girl. At least that's what my nana always said."

"I have no idea if the baby's arrived yet or what it is. Last I heard, Maggie was still at the hospital."

"Wow." I tried to imagine Maggie, the meticulous, outspoken cook, holding her baby in the delivery room. Would she criticize the hospital food while she was recovering after the birth? The question lingered in my mind until Todd spoke again.

"I was going to text you, but it got crazy at work." He gestured toward his stained jeans. "I knew I was already late, so I didn't bother going home to shower. I'm sorry I stink."

"You smell just fine to me." I smiled at him, and he shook his head.

"You're crazy, Chelsea Morris."

"That's why you like me," I quipped, and he grinned back at me.

Music director Louise Muller's voice echoed through the auditorium as she instructed Jimmy and Britney, the two actors who'd read for Danny and Sandy earlier. "I'd like to hear you sing 'Summer Nights.'"

"Those two kind of look like Olivia Newton-John and John Travolta," I whispered to Todd.

"I was just thinking the same thing." He moved closer to me.

"Is your dad going to hire another cook?"

Todd grimaced. "No."

"Why not?"

"He told me I'm the cook until Maggie comes back in six weeks." He gave me a look of disbelief.

"What about the musical?" My voice pitched unnaturally high at the end, and I was thankful the piano was playing louder than I was talking. I didn't want Mr. Muller to yell at me before the production even began. Last year, the lead actor, who was also the quarterback of the football team at a nearby high school, got on the director's bad side early on during rehearsals. And Mr. Muller had sent him home in tears more than once before opening night.

Todd held his finger to his lips again, silently cautioning me to keep my voice down. "My dad wants me to pick up more hours not only to fill in for Maggie, but also to earn more money for college. My scholarships for U will only cover so much. And I'm just doing the lighting for *Grease*, so I don't need to be here every day."

I couldn't help but frown at that. "It won't be the same without you here building the sets while I'm tailoring the costumes."

"I promise we'll still see each other this summer." He held my hand. I loved the heat of his skin against mine. "At least we'll still work together at the restaurant. You know I'd go crazy if I didn't see you every day."

"I'm going to hold you to that promise." My mood brightened when he smiled.

We sat in silence while a few more actors took turns singing. But their voices were only background noise as I ran through a mental list of what I'd need to get started on the costumes. First, I'd check my boxes at home and look for any costumes I could modify. After that, I'd start hitting the thrift shops and even a couple of other community theaters in the area.

"Dylan McCormick!" Mrs. Muller called another actor onstage, and her voice broke through my thoughts. "I'd like to hear you sing 'Greased Lightning.' "

A blond young man jogged to center stage, and I surmised he was a college student using the summer production as an internship opportunity. He was taller than Todd, and he was muscular. His handsome face looked confident as he waited for the music to begin. As Dylan bellowed the lyrics of the chorus, his smooth voice drew me in completely.

"He's good," I whispered to Todd. He gave a snort of disbelief while keeping his eyes focused on the stage. "What's that supposed to mean?" I asked.

"I know the type." Todd shifted in his seat. "He thinks he's the hotshot headliner."

I studied Todd's profile. "How can you tell what's he like just by listening to him sing?"

"Trust me. I can tell by his demeanor. He thinks he's all that, but he's a lot of hot air and no substance."

"That's not a nice thing to say about someone. You don't even know him."

"I've been around the theater scene long enough to know how to spot the arrogant ones who think they should have their names up in lights on the marquee."

"Okay, but you used to be afraid to talk to me." I lightly bumped his shoulder with mine. "Your first impression of me was all wrong."

"No, not really." Todd looked at me and his smile was back. "I always get nervous around pretty girls—especially redheads like you."

I felt my cheeks heat up as I turned my attention back to the stage where Dylan was finishing the song. Todd and I sat in silence while the remaining actors completed their musical auditions.

Once it was finished, Todd took my hand in his as we made our way down the aisle toward Mr. and Mrs. Muller as they exited a row of seats near the front.

"Chelsea and Todd," Mr. Muller said. "I'm glad you came by." He focused on me first. "Are you ready to take on the costumes?"

"Absolutely." I nodded emphatically. "I'm so glad you picked me."

"You'll have an assistant." Mr. Muller studied his clipboard. "Kylie Buchanan wants to help you. She'll be a junior at Maywood High this fall."

"Great." I grinned. *I have my own assistant!*

"And you're doing the sound, right, Todd?" Mr. Muller asked.

Todd frowned. "I'm just going to do the lighting this year, if that's all right. I have to work full time this summer." He quickly explained the situation at his parents' restaurant.

"That's fine." Mr. Muller pulled off his glasses and gnawed on one end for a moment, seemingly lost in thought. "I'll just be happy to have you up in the booth, Todd. I'll let you know when we're ready to start the lighting plan."

Mrs. Muller smiled at us. "We'll make the cast announcement tomorrow, so you can get started on the costumes after that."

I rubbed my hands together. "I can't wait."

Todd and I said good-bye to Mr. and Mrs. Muller and made our way to the parking lot where my silver 1985 Nissan Sentra station wagon sat next to his red 2000 Ford Focus coupe.

"Can you believe this is our last production before we leave for college?" I asked. "It seems like only yesterday I was a lowly freshman trying to convince Ms. Cooper that my ideas for Belle's gown in *Beauty and the Beast* were good enough for the Cameronville High School production."

"It is pretty amazing. But we'll be working on productions at the university soon enough."

"Can you come over for supper?" I dropped my messenger bag by the back bumper of my car. "The twins have been asking about you. You haven't played with them in almost a week."

"I wish I could." He leaned against the back of his car. "But I'm exhausted, and I need to be at work early tomorrow. Dad wants to show me how to open the restaurant." He touched my cheek. "I'll take a rain check, though. Tell my little buddies I'll be over as soon as I can, and we'll continue our video game marathon." He leaned down and I closed my eyes as his lips brushed mine, causing my heart to thump against my rib cage. "I'll see you at work tomorrow."

"Sounds good."

As Todd climbed into his car, I scanned the parking lot and spotted Dylan talking with Jimmy and Britney next to a yellow Camaro on the other side of the lot. Dylan met my gaze and nodded. The gesture caught me off guard, and by the time I nodded back, he'd already returned his attention to their conversation.

*Todd must be wrong about Dylan*, I thought, as I tossed my bag onto the passenger seat of the car and climbed in. Dylan seemed like a nice guy. And if he got a part in *Grease*, I wondered if I'd have an opportunity to get to know him better.

♫

"Can you believe it, Mom?" I set a bowl of baby carrots in the middle of the kitchen table as Mom finished making supper. "Mr. Muller called and asked if I'd be willing to do it, and now I'm actually the head costumer for *Grease*! I'm even going to have an assistant!"

"We're proud of you, Chelsea." Mom opened the oven door, and the aroma of baked chicken filled my nose. "Just remember that the musical isn't your only obligation this summer. You have to keep your job at the Fork & Knife. You'll need that money to buy your textbooks and pay for gas when you're away at school. And I need your help with the boys too. I'm counting on you to pick up Justin and J.J. at day camp on Thursday afternoons when I have to work late at the pediatrician's office. They're shorthanded now that one of the assistants quit."

"I haven't forgotten about your schedule or my other obligations, Mom." I retrieved a stack of dishes from the cabinet and began setting the table. "And I won't forget the twins either. I never have in the past."

"I know that, but sometimes you get so wrapped up in your costume designs that you overlook your other responsibilities."

I wanted to defend myself and tell Mom she was wrong about my priorities, but I decided to let it go. I knew I'd never win a debate with her. At least she'd agreed to let me work part time at the restaurant and spend my afternoons working on the production. I was better off than my best friend, Emily Curtis. She had to work full time at the auto body collision repair shop where her dad and boyfriend worked.

Mom placed the chicken on a platter while I set out the silverware next to the place settings. "When will the cast be announced?"

"Tomorrow," I said. "I can't wait to get started on the costumes."

"I love *Grease*," Mom said with a faraway look in her eyes. "When I was in high school, my best friend and I would have sleepovers at each other's houses, and we watched *Grease* and *Grease 2* every weekend. We knew those movies by heart."

I laughed as I tried to imagine my mom as a teenager singing "Beauty School Dropout" while dressed in her pajamas. "The stage production is a little different from the movie."

"Really?" Mom handed me the platter of chicken. "I had no idea." She turned toward the family room, and her bright red chin-length bob swished as she moved. "Justin! J.J.! Dinner!"

"When will Jason be home?" Usually, my stepfather was home by now. I cut up a chicken breast and divided the pieces evenly between the plates of my five-year-old half brothers.

"Any minute now. He said he had to finish a report and put it on his boss's desk before he left." Mom poured three glasses of iced tea. "He's been working on a really big project, and he's hoping it leads to a promotion. He's been passed over so many times now, and the other jobs he's applied for haven't panned out."

Justin and J.J. (whose given name was Jason Jr., after their father) bounced into the kitchen and took their usual seats at the table.

"Chicken?" J.J. clapped his hands. "Yay!"

"Yuck," Justin grimaced. He was identical to J.J. except for a small mole on his right cheek. "I hate chicken."

"That's too bad, Justin," Mom said. "You're going to have to eat it anyway."

I placed the glasses on the table. "Are we going to wait for Jason?"

"I guess we should go ahead and eat," Mom said. "I don't want it to get cold."

"When will Daddy be home?" J.J. asked.

"He'll be home soon." I added some baby carrots to their plates. "Your daddy had to finish up some work."

"That's right," Mom chimed in.

After Mom and I took our seats, I said a prayer for our meal. Then I asked my brothers about their day at camp, and they filled our suppertime with enthusiastic stories about craft projects, snack foods, and kickball tournaments.

My stepfather finally arrived home while we were finishing our bowls of ice cream for dessert. After helping Mom with the dishes, I gave the twins a bath while she folded laundry.

After the twins were settled in front of their video games, I made my way up the stairs to my room, which was located over the attached garage of our brick ranch-style house. While the room had seemed cramped when I shared it with my older sister, Christina, it was fairly spacious now that she'd moved out. I made the room my own as soon as Christina left for college. I painted the walls bright turquoise and peppered them with my favorite pages from the fashion magazines I'd collected since I was a little girl. I found matching urn lamps with paisley shades at the thrift shop and put one on my nightstand and the other on my desk.

Stacks of fashion magazines were littered around the room, and someday, I planned to have the time to sort and organize them into plastic containers. A tall female mannequin dress form wearing a floppy hat stood in the corner on a maple tripod awaiting my next clothing creation.

I'd converted one corner into a sewing area, complete with an old Singer machine that my nana had given to me; a special pegboard that my dad built to hold my spools of thread; and a plastic organizer for pins, needles, rolls of ribbon, and buttons. Half of the large closet now stored costumes and props used during previous productions. Cardboard boxes were neatly stacked in one corner of the room or shoved under my bed, holding costumes, props, and keepsakes from all of the shows I'd been a part of since junior high.

I sat on my twin bed and reviewed the long list of costumes I'd need to provide for the show. Buttons, my orange cat, jumped onto the bed next to me and rubbed his body against my hand repeatedly. When that didn't get the result he was hoping for, he stepped onto my sketch pad and bumped his head against my arm.

"Hey, buddy," I said while he purred. "How was your day?"

He blinked and purred even louder.

"I need to work right now, so you have to get off my pad, please." I gently moved him to the side, and he curled up next to my leg. "Thanks, buddy."

Once I was sure the list of costumes was complete, I searched my room for any items I could use for *Grease*, stopping only briefly to respond when Todd texted me to say good night.

I was deep in thought beside a pile of fabric and props (which my orange cat now sat on top of) when Mom said, "You do realize it's after ten, right?" She stood at the top of the stairs and smiled at me. Her hair was wet and she was wearing her favorite pink terry cloth robe.

"It is?" I looked at the clock on my nightstand and gasped. "I had no idea."

"You'd better get to bed. Mr. Hughes doesn't tolerate late employees."

"That's true." I stretched. "Todd has joked more than once that his dad would probably fire him because he was late to work three times in a row. I'd better take a shower."

"That's a good plan. I'm heading to bed now. Good night, sweetie."

"Good night, Mom." I stood and assessed my pile of possible costumes. Most of them would need to be modified to fit the 1950s setting, but they were a good start.

I fished out my pajamas and headed downstairs. As I stepped into the bathroom, I sent a quick prayer to God, thanking him for the opportunity to work on this new production and asking him to guide me during my last summer before college.

# chapter two

Okay, Mr. Turner," I said, studying my server's notepad the next morning. "You want the Early Bird Platter with extra bacon. And Mrs. Turner, you want the special with extra corned beef hash."

"That's right. I know it's lunchtime, but you have the best breakfast in town. I'm glad you serve it all day long," Mr. Turner said. He and his wife were a gray-haired couple, probably in their midseventies, and they were two of our regulars at the diner.

"How are your brothers doing, Chelsea?" Mrs. Turner asked.

"They're fine." I grinned. "I can't believe they'll be starting kindergarten soon. It seems like only yesterday I was holding them in the hospital."

"I can tell you're a wonderful big sister," Mrs. Turner beamed. "You remind me of my granddaughter. She takes good care of her younger siblings too. Your mother must be thankful to have your help with those little guys."

"Thank you." I pointed toward the kitchen. "I'll get your order in right away."

I nodded at a few customers as I made my way to the register to submit the order to the kitchen. The restaurant was bustling with the midmorning crowd. Families were crammed into booths and around tables, while servers nimbly weaved their way through the sea of chairs, taking orders, delivering food, and clearing dirty dishes off the empty tables for the next round of customers. All of us servers resembled an army thanks to our matching uniforms of khaki slacks, powder-blue collared shirts with the Fork & Knife logo on the upper right corner of the chest, and black aprons tied around our waist. I had once tried to convince Todd's mom to allow me to jazz up the uniform with some color, but she said it was more important to look professional rather than fashionable. Of course, I disagreed, but she owns the business.

I glanced over my shoulder as Janie approached the counter. She was one of Todd's cousins, and she was working at the diner during her summer break from college.

"It's getting busy," Janie said, pushing her long brown ponytail over one shoulder. "There's a line of folks waiting for tables."

"I know." I glanced at the clock hanging over the door to the kitchen. "It's almost eleven. I have to leave soon. The cast for *Grease* is going to be announced today, and I don't want to miss it."

"Todd tells me you make amazing costumes." Janie bumped my shoulder with hers. "My cousin really likes you."

"You think so? Well, the feeling is mutual." My thoughts turned to the absent cook. "Have you heard anything about Maggie and her baby?"

"Oh yeah. I meant to tell you. My aunt and uncle went to see her in the hospital last night. She had a baby girl. Apparently the labor was long and horrible." Janie grimaced. "Anyway, mommy and baby are doing fantastic. I think Aunt Trudy said she named the baby Daisy—or something flowery like that."

"Daisy. That's a nice name."

"Yeah. It's pretty." Janie glanced behind her and whispered, "Uh-oh. We've been caught chatting. Quick—look busy!" She rolled her eyes, and I stifled a giggle as Todd's mom, Mrs. Hughes, suddenly appeared behind us. Her resemblance to Todd struck me again. He'd obviously inherited his mother's dark hair and eyes, and her tall, slim stature.

"Girls, there's no time for chitchat this morning. The dining room is full." Mrs. Hughes gestured toward the kitchen and the pass-through where plates of food were awaiting delivery to the customers. "There are orders up. You two can talk later, all right?"

"Yes sir, Sergeant Auntie Trudy!" Janie saluted her aunt, and I swallowed a laugh.

Mrs. Hughes shook her head. "You're just as sassy as your mother."

"That's funny, because that's exactly what Mom says about you." Janie placed three plates of food onto her tray. "Duty calls. See you later, Chels."

I smiled at Mrs. Hughes. "Janie feels right at home here."

"Yes, she does," Mrs. Hughes said. "I was surprised she wanted to work here during her summer break, but the customers love her. You're leaving soon, right?"

"Yes. I need to go home and change before I head to the playhouse." I glanced down at my notepad. "I've taken orders for tables eighteen, sixteen, and twelve. They're all in the system."

"Nancy will be here any minute. Why don't you head out now? We can handle your orders for you."

"Okay, great. Thank you." I untied my apron. "I just want to say good-bye to Todd."

"You can pop into the kitchen before you go, but don't distract him for too long. We're busy, you know."

"Yes, ma'am. See you tomorrow, Mrs. Hughes." I slipped into the hot kitchen, inhaling the aroma of bacon and fresh biscuits. Since breakfast items were the most popular food on the menu, eggs and bacon sizzled on the long griddle while steam wafted up into the fans humming overhead.

Todd was standing at the griddle, cracking and frying eggs with great speed. I bit my lower lip as I admired his lanky body in the white chef uniform. It suited him, even though he'd told me earlier that he didn't enjoy wearing it. The uniform somehow made his eyes a deeper shade of brown.

"Hey." I poked him in the arm, and he jumped.

"Oh hey. I didn't hear you come in." He adjusted his chef's hat and glanced at the clock on the wall. "Are you heading out?"

"Yeah." I waved to Todd's father who was checking food orders on the kitchen computer screen. "Your mom told me I could go since Nancy will be coming in soon."

"I'll see you later, then. Let me know who gets the parts of Sandy and Danny." He turned and flipped the eggs before facing me again. "I think it will be Britney and Jimmy. They really look the part, and they can sing."

"Yeah, I think you're right. I actually saw Mr. Muller smile during their auditions, which is rare." I pulled my phone from my pocket. "I'll take a picture of the cast list and send it to you. I wish you could come to the playhouse with me."

"Yeah, I know." He touched my cheek. "I'll see you tomorrow morning, though. We'll always have work, right?"

"Todd!" Mr. Hughes's voice boomed from the other end of the kitchen. "Check those eggs."

"I'd better let you get back to work," I said. "Text me later, okay?"

"You know I will." He gave me a quick kiss on the cheek and then turned back toward the griddle.

"See you tomorrow, Mr. Hughes!" I waved at Todd's father

on my way to the exit. He just grunted as he headed toward the walk-in freezer.

I knew his father wasn't all bad. However, besides the day when Mr. and Mrs. Hughes interviewed me for the server's job, I could recall only a handful of times when Mr. Hughes had actually spoken to me.

When I complained to Todd about it, he always defended his dad, insisting he was a hard worker and a great cook. I knew Mr. Hughes was great at his job, but sometimes it would be nice to receive at least a one-word answer from him instead of the usual dismissive grunt.

After I clocked out, I waved to Janie and Mrs. Hughes as I hurried to my car. I couldn't wait to change and head over to the playhouse. After the cast was announced, the fun would begin. My fingers were itching to get started on the costumes. The summer production was officially under way!

♫

Later that afternoon, I was standing outside the dressing rooms in the playhouse with the cast list in my hand. I snapped a picture of the list with my phone and wrote a quick text to Todd to go with it.

"I love your skirt."

I looked up from my phone and saw a petite brunette with a pixie haircut standing next to me. I glanced down at my green-and-black, pleated plaid miniskirt and said, "Thanks. I made it myself."

"It's awesome. Very retro." She extended her right hand toward me. "I'm Kylie Buchanan. I'm going to be your assistant. Your costumes are, like, legendary."

"Thank you again." I shook her hand. "It's nice to meet you, but I doubt I'm legendary."

"Oh, you totally are. My drama teacher last year said you

made the most epic genie costume for *Aladdin*. She's really good friends with the drama teacher from CHS, and he totally brags about you all the time."

I returned the cast list to its spot on the playhouse bulletin board.

Kylie craned her neck to read it over my shoulder. "I see that hot college guy got the part of Kenickie."

"Which hot college guy?" I scanned the names on the list.

"Dylan McCormick." Kylie waggled her eyebrows at me. "He has amazing light blue eyes."

"Oh, him," I said with a shrug, even though I knew exactly who she was talking about. Dylan had blown me away with his confident rendition of "Greased Lightning" during auditions. "I think he's perfect for that part."

"Yeah, I do too. He's the hottest guy in the cast by far. And someone told me he can really sing."

I shrugged again.

Kylie straightened and said, "So, what do we do first? Get people's measurements?"

"Yes." I pulled my notes from my messenger bag. "I made a list of what costumes we'll need. Have you taken measurements before?"

"Oh yes. My aunt is a seamstress. I used to help in her shop."

"Cool. My nana was a seamstress too. Let's divide up the names." I gave her a copy of the list, and we set out to measure the actors who'd gathered at the playhouse for the first official cast meeting.

Kylie began taking measurements for the extras and the members of the chorus, while I worked with the main cast. I was finishing up with Jimmy, the actor who'd been chosen to play Danny Zuko, when Dylan approached.

"It's Chelsea, right?" Dylan said. "I hear you're the head costumer."

"Yep, that's me." I held up my tape measure to prove it. "And I hear you're Kenickie."

"That's what they tell me." He dropped his script on a chair and stepped up on the riser so I could measure him. "I was hoping to get the part of Danny, but at least I get to sing 'Greased Lightning.' "

"That's cool." I quickly decided not to say anything about listening to him sing during the auditions.

I began by measuring his waist and doing my best to ignore how handsome he was. I felt guilty for silently agreeing with Kylie that he was the best-looking guy in the cast. I pushed those thoughts away and tried to concentrate on the job at hand. I was working on the production to get a recommendation for my portfolio, not to meet guys. After all, I had the sweetest boyfriend around. No one could compete with Todd—not even this college guy.

"Are you a senior?" Dylan's question broke through my thoughts as I measured his sleeve length.

"No, I just graduated from CHS. I'm going to U in the fall. I want to get into the performing arts school and study costume design."

"No kidding. I'm going to the performing arts school there. I'll be a sophomore this year."

"That's great." I wrote down the measurements for his waist and his sleeves in my notebook.

"Maybe I'll see you around campus next year."

"Yeah, sure." I blew off the comment, figuring he was just being nice. Why would a drama major want to hang out with a costumer? Even though we all worked toward the same goal—a great production—our groups didn't normally mix and mingle.

"So how long have you been doing costumes?" he asked.

"I've been sewing since I was about five."

"Five?" Dylan's blond eyebrows shot up. "Really? That young?"

"My nana was a seamstress, and I used to spend summers with her. She taught me just about everything I know." I wondered why he was bothering to make small talk with me while I measured his shoulder width.

"That's very cool. Have you ever acted in a production?" he said with a sly smile. "You're awfully pretty to be stuck backstage."

I studied him for a moment. Was he flirting with me? I was silent.

"I guess you hear that all the time, huh?" he asked.

"No, I can't say that I have." I wrote down the last of his measurements. "Okay. You're all set."

"Listen, a group of us are going out for pizza after practice tonight. Would you like to go with us?" His ice-blue eyes were hopeful, and his crooked smile was mesmerizing.

"I can't," I said, even though my mind was screaming *Yes!* "I have to get home once I'm finished here. But thanks for the invitation."

"All right." He stepped down and fetched his script from the chair. "Maybe next time."

"Sure. Maybe next time." I watched him walk away. I knew Mom would have let me go if I'd asked her, but I had work to do. The schedule for the production was tight, and I had several poodle skirts to make from scratch. Still, the unexpected invitation lingered in my mind. I'd never spoken to a college boy before, other than greeting one at church or talking to my older sister Christina's friends. And they'd always treated me as a kid, not a member of their crowd.

"Are you Chelsea?" The tall college girl who'd been cast as Patty Simcox interrupted my daydreaming.

"Yes." I held up my notebook and pushed away any thoughts of Dylan. "Please step up onto the riser."

♫

"It smells kind of musty in here." Kylie scrunched her nose as we stepped inside Lonnie's Closet, the only thrift store in downtown Cameronville.

"I know it does. But believe it or not, I've found some great clothes and accessories here that I've used in productions at CHS." I scanned the clothing racks.

"So what exactly are we looking for?" Kylie perused a rack of faded T-shirts that looked like they'd seen better days.

"I have a whole list here. I called the store earlier, and Lonnie said she would—"

"Chelsea! It's so good to see you!" Lonnie, a tall, curvy woman who looked to be in her midthirties, hurried over to us. Her short, bleached-blonde hair stuck straight up, reminding me of a platoon of soldiers standing at attention. She was dressed in a loud ensemble that included a magenta top covered in sequins, a brown floor-length skirt, a teal cardigan that hung open, and bright red high-heeled pumps. All of it clashed with her bright purple horn-rimmed glasses, but the look worked for her. I often wondered if she picked through the store's donations before pricing them and placing them out on the floor.

"I'm so glad you called." She pulled me into her arms and hugged me so tight against her ample chest that I couldn't breathe for a moment.

"Who's your little friend?" Lonnie was now examining Kylie.

"This is Kylie Buchanan. She's going to assist me with costumes."

"It's so nice to meet you, Kylie." Lonnie pulled Kylie into a tight squeeze, and Kylie gasped for air.

"Thanks," Kylie said, taking a few deep breaths after Lonnie released her. "You too."

"So, you girls are working on *Grease*, huh?" Lonnie pushed her glasses up on her nose.

"That's right." I tapped my notebook containing the list of costumes. "Did you find anything we can use?"

"Did I ever!" Lonnie motioned for us to follow her. "I found quite a bit. I think some of our older neighbors have been cleaning out their closets."

I smiled at Kylie who still looked unconvinced.

"Did she get dressed in the dark?" Kylie whispered in my ear as we followed Lonnie to the back of the store, past colorful racks of clothes and shelves overflowing with books and trinkets.

I shot her a scowl and whispered back, "She's really awesome once you get to know her. She's helped me find amazing clothes that I could alter for other productions and saved me a lot of time."

"I'll take your word for it," Kylie muttered.

We stepped into the large back room, and I felt as if I'd been transported to the set of a hoarders reality show. Leaning towers of boxes lined the walls and clogged the center of the room. Random pieces of clothing, knickknacks, and furniture filled in the gaps between boxes.

"Excuse the mess." Lonnie gingerly stepped between the piles of donations as if she were crossing a field with land mines. "I haven't had time to sort through the latest donations. A Girl Scout troop brought in everything that didn't sell at their yard sale last weekend."

I looked at Kylie, and she raised her eyebrows.

"Here you go!" Lonnie returned with a medium-size cardboard box. "I think this will help you get started."

I examined the contents of the box and gasped when I found two pairs of penny loafers, three button-down plaid shirts, two retro formal dresses, four pairs of faded jeans, and several plain white T-shirts. "Lonnie! This is amazing!"

"The shoes need to be polished, but they'll work." She handed Kylie a tote bag. "I also found these skirts. They're just plain. I thought you might be able to sew poodles on them." She snapped her fingers. "That reminds me! A lady gave me her grandmother's button collection. I thought you might want to pick out the really shiny buttons and use them for the collars on the poodles." She dug through a few more boxes.

Kylie pulled a white swing skirt from the bag, and her eyes lit up. "Lonnie, these skirts are perfect." She grinned at me. "This is awesome!"

"I know." I held up a loafer that had seen better days. "We can definitely polish these."

"Here they are." Lonnie retrieved a blue cookie tin from a box near the bottom of the pile she'd been searching. "Look at these fabulous buttons." She opened the lid and pulled out two rhinestone buttons. "Wouldn't these make fantastic collars for poodle skirts? They'll sparkle under the stage lights."

Kylie and I gasped in unison.

"Absolutely!" Kylie took the tin and slipped it into the bag with the skirts.

"What do we owe you?" I asked, pulling my wallet from my messenger bag.

Lonnie waved off the question. "Oh, don't worry about it. Consider it my donation to the theater."

"We have to pay you something," I insisted. "I do have a budget."

"Could you comp me a couple of tickets for the show?" Lonnie asked.

"I'm sure we could." I grinned. "You said a couple of tickets. Do you have a new boyfriend?"

"Oh, maybe I do ..." Lonnie motioned for us to lead the way out of the back room and then closed the door behind us.

"I can't wait to meet him." I followed Lonnie toward the front door of the shop.

"We'll leave your tickets at will call," Kylie said as we stepped outside.

"Thanks again, Lonnie," I said.

"You're welcome, girls. I'll call you if I come across anything else." Lonnie waved as we headed to the parking lot.

"This is a great start." Kylie placed the tote bag in the back of my car.

I set the box beside the bag and slammed the rear door shut. "And here you didn't think she'd have anything worthwhile," I said, climbing into the front seat.

"Okay, I was definitely wrong," Kylie said, as she got into the passenger seat and buckled her seat belt.

"No, you just misjudged Lonnie. She's a little eccentric, but she runs a great store with lots of personality." I started the car and steered it through the parking lot before merging onto Main Street. "Now we can go back to my house and look through all that we have so far. I need to see if I have to pick up any fabric for the skirts."

"I think Dylan likes you."

I slowed to a stop at a red light and turned to face Kylie. "What did you say?"

"I said I think Dylan likes you." Kylie folded her arms over her pink T-shirt. "He was watching you yesterday while you were getting measurements from the other members of the cast. I think he's interested in you."

"Please, Kylie." I laughed. "He's a sophomore in college. Why would he be interested in someone like me?"

"You'll be a freshman in the fall," she said. "Did you know he lives in Castleton?"

"I have a friend who lives over there—Whitney Richards. She's really nice. And my best friend's boyfriend, Zander Stewart, lives next door to Whitney."

"Dylan's parents are super rich. They're always jetting off to Europe like it's nothing."

The light changed and I accelerated through the intersection. "Wow," I said, wondering what it would be like to travel Europe. I'd always dreamed of attending the runway shows during Paris Fashion Week.

"I think Dylan likes you," Kylie repeated. "Really, I do."

"I don't think so. Although, he did ask me to go out for pizza last night."

"He did?"

"Yeah. But a whole group of kids were going."

"I wasn't invited." Kylie sounded disappointed. "That means he really likes you. He didn't invite everyone."

"It doesn't matter. I have a boyfriend." I turned onto Rock Lake Loop, the entrance to my neighborhood, Rock Creek.

"You do?"

"Yeah." I smiled. "His name is Todd. His parents own Fork & Knife."

"Oh, I love that place! They serve the best bacon." Kylie shifted in her seat. "So, back to Dylan. He seems really cool. And I *love* his yellow Camaro. I can't imagine getting a brand-new sports car for high school graduation. I'll be lucky if my parents even let me drive their car. They already told me I'm not getting my own car anytime soon. It's so unfair."

As I turned onto my street, I wondered what it would be like to date someone who seemed so different from Todd. Instead of being shy and standoffish, Dylan seemed confident and sure of himself. He came from a wealthy family and had traveled to Europe. What it would be like to have a life like that?

I pulled into the driveway of the brick ranch where I'd lived since we'd moved to Cameronville in the middle of my seventh grade year. My stepfather's job had transferred him here.

"Did you go out for pizza with Dylan?" Kylie asked.

"No!" I hit the brake a little too hard, shifted into park, and yanked the key from the ignition.

"Why not?" Kylie stared at me as if I were crazy.

"Because I have a *boyfriend*," I said. I undid my seat belt and turned to get out of the car.

I met Kylie at the back of the car to retrieve our thrift store finds.

"If you didn't have a boyfriend, would you have gone with him?" she asked.

"No." I shook my head.

"Why not?"

"Because I have costumes to make."

"You have to stop and have a little fun sometimes, Chelsea," Kylie said as she picked up the tote bag. "You're only young once. And it's your last summer break before college. You should be living it up."

Kylie's words stuck in my mind as we walked into the house.

# chapter three

On Sunday, I sat next to Todd in our usual spot at Faith Covenant Church. I'd started sitting with him and his parents after we began dating in April.

I spotted my mother, stepfather, and brothers sitting across the aisle. J.J. was coloring in a car-themed coloring book, while Justin squirmed in his seat and ignored my mother's warning glances. I considered inviting Justin to sit with me, but I didn't want to interrupt the service and distract the people sitting around me.

I stood close to Todd and shared his hymnal while we sang the opening hymn. Once the song was finished, my stepfather made his way to the front of the church to read the Scripture lessons. I followed along in the bulletin as he read the first reading. When he read a portion of Psalm 119, I found myself focusing on verse 76: "May your unfailing love be my comfort, according to your promise to your servant." I stared at the verse, wondering why it spoke to me. What did it mean?

Todd rested his arm on the back of the pew behind me and rubbed my shoulder with his fingertips. I smiled up at him as my stepfather finished reading the second lesson.

Then Pastor Kevin stepped behind the pulpit and gave the Gospel reading before he gave his sermon. In his message he discussed God's loyalty to us and how we should mirror Jesus's life through our loyalty to each other and good works. The words floated through my mind, and I suddenly felt guilty for wondering what it would be like to date someone like Dylan. How could I possibly entertain the idea of dating someone else when I had such a strong and solid boyfriend like Todd? I felt terrible for even considering Dylan's invitation to go out for pizza.

Todd leaned over to me. "Are you okay?" he whispered in my ear.

"Yeah. Why?" I tried my best to act casual.

"You look like you're really concentrating on something. Is it the costumes?"

I nodded and hoped I looked convincing.

"I thought so." He patted my shoulder. "You'll do great. You always do. *Aladdin* was awesome."

"Thanks." I smiled up at him and felt even more wretched. I was blessed to have Todd as my boyfriend, and I vowed never to do anything to jeopardize our relationship.

Once the service ended, Todd held my hand as we followed the congregation outside for Fellowship on the Walkway, a summertime potluck tradition where church families shared snacks on the sidewalk after the service. I filled up a paper plate with a variety of fruit, while Todd piled his plate high with sausage balls, crackers, a bagel, and a giant slice of watermelon.

"You must've missed breakfast this morning," I quipped as we sat on a bench together.

"How could you tell?" He held up part of his bagel. "Would you like half?"

"No, thanks." I stuck my fork into a strawberry. "I have my fruit."

"Todd! Todd!" My brothers scrambled through the crowd toward us.

"Are you coming over to play today?" J.J. asked.

"You promised to finish the video game marathon with us!" Justin insisted.

They both started begging.

"Boys, boys." I motioned for them to lower their voices. "You don't have to yell. Just ask nicely."

"Pleeeeeeeaase?" they sang in unison.

Todd held up his hands in surrender. "Okay, okay. I'll come over."

"Yay!" The twins clapped their hands.

"As long as it's okay with your sister," Todd added with a grin.

The boys turned their begging on me, and their pleading voices soon drowned out the surrounding conversations.

Mom approached us with a plate full of fruit in hand. "What's all the racket about?"

"We want Todd to come over and play video games with us today," J.J. explained.

"And Todd says Chelsea has to say it's okay." Justin's arms flew around widely as he spoke. "So we're trying to convince Chelsea to let Todd come play with us."

"Yeah." J.J. nodded.

"I see." Mom looked at me and then Todd. "I think it's up to Todd if he wants to come over or not. He might have something else to do today. It's not nice to pressure people to do what you want. I've told you boys that before."

"It's fine, Mrs. Klein. I'd love to come over," Todd turned toward me, "as long as it's okay with Chelsea. She might have something else to do today."

I rolled my eyes. "The only thing I have to do is spend time with my sewing machine."

"Yay!" The boys cheered. "Let's go play!"

After finishing our snacks at church, Todd and I drove to my house, and then he followed my brothers into the playroom to start the video game competition. Instead of watching them play, I made my way to my room to continue working on the poodle skirts I'd started yesterday. And I tuned out the chorus of loud voices from the playroom.

Two hours later, I was sitting at my sewing table cutting out poodles that I'd traced onto pieces of colorful fabric using an image I'd printed off the Internet. When I heard footsteps coming up the stairs, I kept my eyes on my work since I wasn't sure I had enough of this material for a redo.

"How's it going?" Todd asked, taking a seat on my bed. "Hey, Buttons."

"Fine." I glanced back to where he was sitting on the edge of my bed with Buttons on his lap. "Did you win the video game marathon?"

"Not really." He smiled while rubbing the cat's head. Buttons purred loudly.

"You let my brothers win, didn't you?"

"I didn't say that." I could tell by his expression that he wasn't telling the truth. Todd was an only child, and he'd once shared with me that he'd always wanted siblings. I was certain J.J. and Justin were like Todd's surrogate little brothers. "Need any help?"

"You want to cut out poodles?"

"Why not?" He slipped off the bed and sat down on the floor beside my sewing table, folding his long legs underneath him. "It can't be any more difficult than painting the Agrabah skyline for *Aladdin*."

I handed him one of my poodle sketches, a pincushion filled with pins, a pencil, the material, and a pair of scissors. "Here's the pattern for the poodle. Just pin it to the back side of the material, trace it, and then cut it out."

"Did you draw this?" Todd looked impressed.

"Yeah. I found the design online and created a stencil."

"That's really good, Chels."

"Thanks." I turned back toward the desk. "Do you want to get a chair from downstairs so you don't have to sit on the floor?"

"No, it's okay. I'm fine here."

I looked down as he began tracing his first poodle. Obviously feeling left out now, Buttons was rubbing his whole body against Todd's arm. "Did you ever think you'd be helping me make poodle skirts?" I asked.

"I don't mind doing it as long as it gives me more time with you."

"You're sweet." The guilt I'd experienced earlier in the day crept back into my stomach. "So tell me more about the video game competition."

Todd gave me a blow-by-blow description of the marathon, chuckling now and then as he shared some funny comments my brothers had made.

Soon we had six poodles cut out, and I was out of material.

"Want to help me pick out buttons for the poodles' collars?" I asked, placing the pile of poodles next to the sewing machine.

"Sure. Why not?" His expression didn't quite match the enthusiasm in his words.

"Something tells me you had other plans in mind."

"I was sort of hoping we could watch a movie." He stretched out his long legs and crossed his ankles.

"Which movie?"

"I don't know. We can see what's available on iTunes." He pointed toward my laptop. "You pick."

"Really?" I crossed the room and picked up my laptop. "I can pick any movie I want?"

"Yes. Even a romantic comedy."

"Awesome." I sat on the floor next to Todd, opened iTunes on my laptop, and clicked "See All" in the New & Noteworthy movie category.

"How about this one?" Todd pointed at a new action movie.

"So, we can watch whatever movie *I* want, huh?" I laughed, and he gave me a sheepish look. "I'm teasing you. It's fine." I clicked "Rent Movie" and stood. "I'll go make the popcorn while you hook up the laptop to the TV, okay?"

"Sounds good."

While I headed downstairs to the kitchen, I thought about Pastor Kevin's sermon again. I knew I was blessed to have such an amazing boyfriend, and I'd be foolish to ever think of dating someone else—even a handsome, exciting college student like Dylan.

♫

The following afternoon, I stood in the dressing room and pointed toward the stack of plastic laundry baskets while members of the cast watched me.

"These baskets are for your costumes," I began. "Each of you needs to pick a basket and put your name on it." I held up a black Sharpie marker and two colors of sticky notes in one hand and a tape dispenser in the other. "Write your name on here—blue notes for the boys, hot pink notes for the girls—and *tape* the note to your basket. The basket can be stowed under your mirror. And I want to see all of your costumes back in your baskets after every dress rehearsal and show." I eyed the younger members of the cast. "That means I'd better not find any of your shoes, socks, or other costume pieces lying around the dressing room or any other part of the playhouse. Understood?"

A chorus of grunts and mumbles sounded.

"Great. I'll hand out bobby socks today, and the shoes, belts, and shirts later on this week. I want you to put those items into your labeled baskets for safekeeping. We'll hang up the other costumes, such as dresses and skirts and jackets, on the metal clothing racks over there to prevent wrinkling." I distributed markers and sticky notes to most of the cast members, and then set up baskets for the leads who were running lines onstage with Mr. Muller upstairs.

A medium-height girl with curly brown hair and chestnut eyes approached me to get a marker and sticky note. "You're a real professional. The costumer at my high school wasn't quite as organized as you are."

"Thanks." I'd seen the girl around the playhouse before but hadn't measured her for a costume on Friday. "Are you an extra?"

"Yeah, I am." She wrote *Marni Stern* on a hot pink note and taped it to a basket. "I'm just happy to be part of the chorus. I don't have any real aspirations to act, but I love to sing and dance."

"It's nice to meet you. Where do you go to high school?" I asked.

"Ridgewood, but my parents moved to Cameronville in May. I'm going to U next year."

"Cool." I opened my mouth to tell her about my own plans at U, but Kylie interrupted us.

"All of these skirts are good. We won't need to alter any of them." Kylie handed me a pile of swing skirts. "So we can add the poodles to them now."

"Great." I pointed toward the baskets. "I have most of the baskets set up for the cast. Would you mind finishing the job and then put the bobby socks into the girls' baskets? I'll go home and start sewing on the poodles."

"Sounds like a plan." Kylie gave me a mock salute. "I'll see you tomorrow?"

"Yes, you will." I turned to Marni. "I'll see you tomorrow too."

I carried the pile of skirts through the dressing room and upstairs to the stage area where Dylan was running lines with the other principal cast members. He nodded as I passed by, and without meaning to I quickened my steps as I headed outside to my car.

After loading the skirts into the back of my wagon, I climbed into the driver's seat, pushed the key into the ignition, and turned the key. Nothing happened.

"Oh no," I groaned. I rolled down the window to get some air moving inside the car and tried starting it again. Nothing. "No, no, no! Please start. Come on!" I tried encouraging my old car. "You can do it. Come on now." I turned the key again and heard nothing—not even a click.

I pulled my cell phone from my messenger bag and dialed my stepfather's cell number.

"Hello?" Jason's voice rang through the phone. "Chelsea?"

"Hey." My voice was tight. "My car won't start."

"Where are you?"

"I'm at the playhouse." I looked into the rearview mirror and spotted Dylan watching me from the back steps, which made me feel even more self-conscious about my old car. "I don't know what to do. I tried to start it and nothing happened."

"I bet it's the alternator again." I heard voices in the background. "I'm at an off-site meeting today, and I can't leave. I'll call a tow truck and have it towed to the Nissan dealership. Can you find a friend to take you home?"

"Sure." I swallowed, thinking how embarrassing it would be to ask for help. "I'll see if Emily can come get me."

"Great. I'll call the dealership now. Just wait there for the tow truck and call me back when they arrive, all right?"

"Okay. Thanks." I tried to start the car once more, but nothing happened. I dialed Emily's number.

"Hey, Chels!" Emily said. "What's going on?" Loud voices and the sounds of machines blared in the background.

"I'm sort of stranded." My voice cracked, and I hoped I wouldn't start crying. How silly was it to cry over a broken-down car? I felt like a moron. "My car won't start."

"Oh no!" Emily's voice became clearer, and I imagined her moving off the shop floor and into the office at the auto body shop where she worked. "What's the car doing? Does it click when you turn the key?"

"No. It doesn't make any sound at all. It's totally dead."

"Yikes. Sounds like the alternator."

"That's what Jason said when I called him." I leaned my head against the headrest and ran my hand over my face. Emily never ceased to amaze me with her car knowledge.

"Where are you?"

"At the playhouse." I explained that my stepfather was sending a tow truck. "I just need someone to give me a ride home."

"Oh wow. I wish I could help you, but my dad and his boss are at a meeting. So I'm running the office right now, and it's crazy busy. If you hang on a second, I'll see if Zander can run over there and get you. Just give me a minute." I heard muffled voices as she covered the mouthpiece of the phone.

A tap on my open window caused me to jump with a start. I turned and found Dylan looking at me.

"Hey." He tilted his head. "Are you okay?"

"Yeah. My car won't start." I hoped my voice sounded confident and casual, even though I was fighting back tears.

"Do you need a ride?" Dylan offered.

"Chelsea?" Emily's voice sounded through the phone. "Zander said he can come get you."

"Oh." I looked up at Dylan. "Well, my friend Dylan just said he can help me."

"It's no problem," Dylan said. "Let me go tell Mr. Muller what's going on."

"Thank you," I said.

I was watching in the rearview mirror as Dylan walked toward the playhouse, when Emily asked, "Who's Dylan?"

"He's one of the leads in *Grease*. He's a sophomore at U." I fiddled nervously with my keys. I knew if Emily were here with me, she'd know exactly what I was thinking right now.

"Interesting," Emily said slowly. "Can't Todd give you a ride home?"

"He's working full time at the diner now. The regular cook is out on maternity leave," I said, hoping I sounded matter-of-fact and not defensive.

I heard a phone ringing in the background.

"I'd better go. This place is nonstop." Emily sighed. "I need to ask my dad for a raise. Call me later, okay? We need to get together."

"Yes, we do. Please tell Zander thanks for offering to help me."

"I will. Bye!"

I disconnected the call and then climbed out of the car. After retrieving the swing skirts from the back of my car, I set them on top of my messenger bag on a patch of grass between the parking lot and the sidewalk, and hoped they wouldn't get too dirty. Then I sat on the curb to wait for the tow truck.

Thirty minutes later, I was playing a game on my phone when the tow truck driver finally pulled into the parking lot. I handed him the keys and called Jason back to tell him the tow truck had arrived and I'd found a ride home. While fighting back tears, I watched the driver hook the tow truck cable to the underside of my car.

"You all right, Chelsea?" Dylan returned and sat on the curb next to me.

"Yeah." My voice broke and a tear trickled down my cheek. I thought I might pass out from embarrassment. "I'm sorry. I guess it's stupid to cry over my dead car."

"It'll be fine." Dylan set his script on the sidewalk next to him. "I'm sorry I took so long. Mr. Muller wanted to meet with me and a few other cast members real quick and ... well, he's never real quick."

I wiped away another stray tear. "That's true."

The tow truck driver told me he was ready to go. I stood and picked up the pile of skirts and my messenger bag.

"Do you need help with those?" Dylan offered.

"Oh, no thanks. I got it." We crossed the parking lot to his shiny yellow Camaro. I couldn't imagine what he thought of my old car when he had a brand-new cool car to drive every day. "Your car is amazing."

"Thanks." He unlocked the doors with the push of a button on the key fob, and I envied the convenient luxury. My car didn't even have power locks or windows. He opened the passenger door for me. "You hop in, and I'll put the skirts in the trunk."

"Thanks." I settled into the black seat, and the sweet smell of leather filled my nose. The dashboard was filled with an impressive arrangement of gauges and buttons.

The trunk lid slammed shut, and then Dylan slipped into the driver's seat. He put the key into the ignition, and the car roared to life.

"My best friend Emily would love your car," I said.

"Oh yeah?" Dylan flipped on the air conditioner as he backed out of the parking space, and cool air blasted through the vents. It felt great after spending forty-five minutes out in the hot sun.

"Yeah, she's a car nut. Her father is the assistant manager at Cameronville Auto and Body out on Highway 29. Emily and her boyfriend, Zander, work there too." I pushed an errant lock of hair behind my ear.

"Zander Stewart?" He gave me a sideways glance. "Dumb question, right? How many Zanders could there be?"

I laughed. "Yes, it's Zander Stewart."

"We were good friends in high school. He lives a few blocks away from me."

"Oh really?" I pretended I didn't already know that Dylan lived in Castleton. "Emily's cousin Whitney lives next door to Zander."

"Wow. Small world, huh?" He slowed to a stop at a red light and faced me. "So now I know where Whitney and Zander live, but I still have one problem."

"What's that?"

"I don't know where *you* live." He grinned, and I was afraid I might swoon.

I hesitated a moment, embarrassed to admit that I didn't live in a high-class neighborhood like Castleton. For the first time in my life, I was embarrassed by my ordinary neighborhood.

"Do you remember where you live? Or do we need to pull out our phones and Google your address?" he teased.

"I live in Rock Creek," I said.

"Then let's go to Rock Creek." He slapped on the turn signal.

# chapter four

"What does your father do?" Dylan asked as he turned the Camaro onto Main Street.

"My stepdad is in sales." I smoothed my hands over my tan skirt. "My father is an engineer. He lives in Statesville. How about you?"

"My dad is a lawyer. He and my uncle are partners in a big firm in the city."

"Does your mom work?"

"No." Dylan shook his head while keeping his eyes on the road. "She mostly volunteers at the hospital. Your mom?"

"My mom works for a pediatrician."

"Oh. Is she a nurse?" He glanced over at me.

"No, she runs the front desk. She makes appointments, answers the phones, things like that." I felt embarrassed admitting my mother had an administrative job after hearing his mom spent her days being charitable. I frowned. Why should I be embarrassed?

"Cool." He merged onto Rock Lake Loop, and my stomach tightened as I gave him directions to my street.

Why did I feel so inferior next to Dylan? I knew I should be thankful for all that I had—a safe home and a family that loved me. But I was embarrassed for this rich kid to see the little brick ranch that I called home. My mother would be disappointed to hear that I was embarrassed by all we had. I was acting as if I didn't appreciate all of the wonderful blessings in my life. I had so much to be thankful for, yet I was worried what this boy, a son of a big-time lawyer, would think of my modest home. I longed to erase these feelings of inadequacy from my mind, but they haunted me as he pulled up to my house.

"This is it." I retrieved my messenger bag from the floor. "Thank you for the ride."

"You're welcome." I met Dylan at the trunk, and he gathered up the skirts. "Here you go."

"Thanks." I took the skirts and then hesitated, wondering if I should invite him in. He seemed to expect the invitation. "Would you like to come in for a soda or something?"

"Sure." He slammed the trunk shut and followed me up the concrete path to the front door.

I led him into the small foyer where Buttons greeted us with a loud meow and a leg rub. "Hey, Buttons."

Dylan leaned down and rubbed the cat's head. "Hi there. He's a big guy, huh?"

"Yeah, he is." I stepped into the kitchen and set the pile of skirts on a kitchen chair. "Would you like a soda?" I opened the refrigerator.

"Yeah, that's fine."

I grabbed two cans and handed him one.

"Who are the kids?" He popped open the can and pointed to a snapshot on the refrigerator of the twins, my older sister, and me grinning at the camera during our trip to the beach last summer.

"Those are my younger brothers, J.J. and Justin. And that's my older sister, Christina. She's in law school."

He nodded as he studied the photo, and I wished I could read his mind. "Where do you do your sewing?"

"Upstairs. Do you want to see what I'm working on?" I gathered the skirts in my arms.

"Sure."

Dylan followed me upstairs, and I dropped the pile of skirts on the bed before walking over to my sewing table.

I lifted a completed poodle skirt to show him. "This will be for one of the chorus members. I just need to sew on the buttons for the collar."

"That's cool." He touched the poodle. "I like that design. Did you draw that?"

"I copied the pattern from a skirt I found online."

"That's great." His eyes scanned the table and then settled on the sewing machine. "That looks like an ancient machine. Does it even work? It looks like an antique."

"Yes, it works." I felt a little defensive. "It was my nana's." I touched the old Singer, and the cool metal conjured up memories of the summers I'd spent at my grandmother's house. I missed those days. "She taught me how to sew on it."

He sipped his can of soda. "Do you and Kylie both work up here?"

"Yes, we do. When she was here on Saturday afternoon, we took turns sewing on the machine and by hand. It worked pretty well. She's doing a good job so far." Buttons jumped onto the sewing table, and I rubbed his chin.

"Cool." He walked over to my dresser and picked up a framed photo of Todd and me at the prom. "That's your boyfriend, right?"

"Yeah. Todd Hughes."

"He was sitting with you at auditions." Dylan replaced the photo on the dresser and looked at me. "Why isn't he working on the production?"

"He's working full time at his parents' restaurant this summer, so he's only doing the lights for *Grease*."

"Which restaurant?"

"Fork & Knife over on Lynnhaven Parkway."

"I've eaten there. It's kind of a greasy spoon."

"Not really," I said. "It's actually delicious. I work there as a server in the mornings. We have quite a few regulars who eat breakfast there almost every day."

"I guess some of the food is good." He turned back toward the photo. "How long have you and Todd been dating?"

"Since April." I smiled as I thought about the time we first met. "He was nervous about talking to me at first. But then we worked on *Aladdin* together last year at CHS. He finally got up the nerve to ask me out, and then we went to prom together." My eyes moved to the calendar on the wall above my sewing machine. "In fact, tomorrow's our three-month anniversary." I made a mental note to run to the mall to get him a gift certificate to the video game store. I absently wondered if he'd even have time to get together to celebrate. Maybe he could get off work early so we could have a date night.

"He's one of those quiet guys who's easily intimidated by girls, huh?" Dylan's question interrupted my thoughts.

Now I felt protective of Todd. Why did this guy make me feel defensive and inferior all at once? "I think it's cute actually." I tried to think of a way to change the subject. "So are you excited about the summer production?"

For the next thirty minutes, we talked about the cast and crew as Buttons rubbed against us in search of attention. Dylan finally glanced at his watch and then jammed his thumb toward the front door. "I'd better get going."

I took his empty soda can from him and headed down to the kitchen. "Thanks again for the ride."

"You're welcome."

I followed him out to the driveway.

"Hey, listen," he began as we stopped next to his car. "Do you like to swim?"

"Oh yeah. I love to swim. Why?"

"Well, I'm— " Dylan started to speak and then paused as he looked over my shoulder toward the street. "I think your boyfriend just pulled up."

"Todd?" I turned to look just as a red Focus stopped next to Dylan's car. Surprise filled me. Todd normally worked until well past seven o'clock each evening. What was he doing off work so early on a Monday?

Todd climbed out of the car and stalked toward Dylan and me with a scowl on his face.

"Hey, Todd! Why are you here? I didn't expect to see you this afternoon," I said, hoping my tone was light.

"That's exactly what I was going to say to him." Todd pointed at Dylan. "What are *you* doing here?"

Anger filled me as I stared at my boyfriend's scowl. *He has a lot of nerve showing up at my house with an attitude like that when Dylan was only trying to help me!*

"Dylan gave me a ride home," I said, struggling to keep my voice even.

"Why?" Todd aimed his frown at me and then turned toward the driveway. "Where's your car?"

"It wouldn't start. I was stranded at the playhouse." I explained how Jason had it towed to the dealership. "Dylan offered to help me since Jason and Emily couldn't leave work. Like I said, he gave me a ride home."

Todd turned back to Dylan. "Thanks," he spat out the word. It was obvious his appreciation wasn't sincere. I wondered why he was being so rude. My displeasure grew close to the boiling point.

"It wasn't a big deal." Dylan smiled as Todd's frown

deepened. Dylan clearly wasn't worried about having Todd's approval. I wondered what it would feel like to be so sure of myself and confident.

"So, as I was saying, do you two like to swim?" Dylan asked, cutting his eyes between us.

"Yeah, I do." I nodded with enthusiasm.

"Great. I'm having a get-together at my house tonight," Dylan explained, fishing his car keys from his pocket. "I guess you'd call it a swim party. Would you two like to come? A lot of the cast will be there."

Excitement filled me at the thought of attending a cast party. I'd never been invited to one before! I looked at Todd hopefully, but my excitement deflated when I saw he was still upset. I was tempted to accept Dylan's invitation, but I knew it would only cause problems between Todd and me.

I turned back to Dylan. "I can't tonight. Maybe next time?"

"Sure." Dylan shrugged. "Well, I'll see you tomorrow, Chels." He nodded at Todd before climbing into his car. The Camaro's engine roared to life before he eased it out of the driveway.

"So he's calling you 'Chels' now? You don't even know the guy. And why did *he* bring you home?" Todd's tone was accusatory, and I stiffened with irritation.

"I had no choice," I snapped. "My car wouldn't start. I already told you I called Jason, but he couldn't leave work. Then I called Emily, but she was busy at work too. She said Zander could come and help me. But then Dylan saw me in my car, and he offered to— "

"What about me?" Todd interrupted. "Did it ever occur to you to call me? The last time I checked, I'm still your boyfriend, Chels."

"Why would I call you?" I asked, and he winced as if I'd hit him.

"What's that supposed to mean?" He gestured widely. "Haven't I helped you out in the past? What about when your car broke down at the mall in May? You called me, and I came to get you, didn't I?"

I opened my mouth to stand up for myself, but he kept on going.

"Did I even enter your mind or did you jump at the chance to get a ride in that guy's Camaro?"

"Of course I thought of you, but you're always working!" The words burst from my mouth before I could stop them.

Todd paused, his expression transforming from resentment to regret. He said quietly, "I would've left work for you, Chelsea."

"Really?" I walked over to the porch and lowered myself onto the top step. He sat beside me. "Your dad rarely lets you take a break to go to the restroom. What makes you think he would've let you leave the restaurant to come rescue me?" I swept a few blades of grass off the porch with my hand. "I didn't want to get you in trouble by calling you at work. We hardly see each other as it is. The last thing I need is for your dad to say you can't see me this summer. I had to improvise. It was embarrassing enough that my car broke down. I didn't want to make a big issue out of finding someone to help me."

"I don't understand why you let him drive you home. You don't even know the guy. Why didn't you wait for Zander?"

I studied Todd as he kicked a rock off the bottom step. "What do you have against Dylan?"

"Are you kidding me?" Todd kicked another rock as if for emphasis then sat down next to me. "He's a player. He'll use you in a second and then forget your name the next day."

"I think you should take the time to get to know him. He seems pretty nice to me. And it's not right to judge someone without getting to know him."

"Sometimes you have to go with your intuition."

I bumped my shoulder against his in an attempt to lighten the mood. "You never answered my first question."

"Which question was that?" He shifted his weight and leaned his shoulder against mine.

"Why are you here?" I angled my body toward his. "How did you manage to get off work so early?"

He tilted his head and studied me. "You really don't know why?"

"No." I shook my head. "Am I missing something?"

"What's today?"

"Monday?"

"No, Chels. What's the date?" He finally smiled, and relief flooded me.

I gasped. "Oh no!"

"You forgot, didn't you?" He pulled a small box from the pocket of his jeans. "Happy anniversary."

"I thought our anniversary was tomorrow."

"It's not. I kissed you in the parking lot of the Dairy Barn at eleven thirty on April ninth." He jiggled the box. "Are you going to open your present?"

I grimaced. "I feel so stupid. How could I forget the date of our anniversary?"

He turned my hand over and placed the little box on my palm. "Open it, Chels."

I opened the box, and my eyes widened when I saw the silver necklace with a heart-shaped stone sparkling in the afternoon sun. I tilted the box, and the stone changed from purple to green to blue and then back to purple. "Todd." I looked up into his smiling face. "This is beautiful."

"It's alexandrite. It reminded me of you when I saw it. It's beautiful, creative, and always changing." He took the box from my hand and pulled the necklace off the cardboard. "Let me put it on you."

"This had to be expensive." I held my hair up, and he leaned over, his fingers tickling the back of my neck as he fastened the necklace. "How did you ever afford something like this?"

"I've been working a lot of hours at the restaurant, remember?"

I touched the necklace as it hung near my collarbone. "I feel like such a heel."

"Don't be silly. You can make it up to me." He poked my arm. "How about we go to the movies tonight?"

"Okay. I haven't had a chance to buy you a gift yet, so I'll pay for the tickets and the popcorn. When do you want to go?"

"We can go any time. I'm off for the rest of the day."

"Great. Let me call my mom and make sure it's okay if we head out."

"Sounds like a plan." He stood up, took my hands in his, and pulled me to my feet. "You don't really think I'd let you pay, do you?"

"It's only fair," I said as we walked up the steps and into the house.

"I don't think so. I'll pay."

After a quick phone call to get permission to go on my anniversary date, I found Todd sitting on the sofa in the family room, petting Buttons. The cat had claimed Todd's lap as his temporary bed.

"Let me change clothes, and I'll be ready," I said.

He glanced up. "You look fine to me."

"It's our anniversary. I want to wear something special." I started for the stairs.

"Wait."

I spun and faced him. "What?"

"Did you really want to go to Dylan's pool party?" His expression was hesitant, as if he dreaded hearing my honest answer.

I stepped into the family room and sat on the wing chair across from the sofa. "I'd be lying if I told you I didn't want to go to the party. Yes, I wanted to go. And I was hoping you would too."

Todd paused and his mouth formed a thin line. "Why would you want to hang out with him?"

"Why are you jealous of him?" I blurted. His expression darkened, and I held up my hands. "Wait. I didn't mean that the way it came out. You just seem so quick to judge him, and you don't know him. He was really nice to me when he brought me home. And think about it, Todd, how many cast parties have we been invited to?"

"We went to the all-cast party after the last performance of *Aladdin* in May."

"That's not what I mean. I'm talking about the private parties that only the actors go to."

"Fine." Todd held up his hands in surrender. "If it means that much to you, we can go."

"No, it's okay." I stood. "It's our anniversary. I'd rather spend it with you. I'll be right back."

As I made my way up the stairs toward my room, I wondered if I'd be invited to more cast parties. I hoped so.

# chapter five

Thanks for driving," I said, sitting in the passenger seat of Kylie's mom's sedan the following afternoon.

"You're welcome." Kylie steered the car into the parking lot of the local fabric store. "It just worked out that my mom didn't need to go out today. She did her grocery shopping yesterday."

"I'm supposed to have my car back by Thursday afternoon." I pulled the list of fabrics we needed out of my bag. "I'm just glad it wasn't anything major."

Kylie parked under a shade tree near the back of the lot, and we climbed out of the car. "You missed an awesome party last night," she said, as we started walking toward the store. "It was so fun!"

"That's nice." I smiled at her. "I sort of had big plans."

"Oooh?" Kylie rubbed her hands together. "Do tell, Chelsea!"

"It was Todd and my three-month anniversary yesterday. We went to dinner and a movie."

"Oh, how fun! Was the movie good?"

"Yes, it was." I fingered my necklace. "And he gave me this."

Kylie gasped as she examined the necklace. "Oh, Chelsea. That's gorgeous."

"Thanks. I need to get him something. For some reason I

thought our anniversary was today. Can we stop by the mall on the way home so I can get him a gift certificate?"

"Sure!"

"Thanks." I followed her through the automatic doors into the large store. The smell of new fabric filled my nose, and I felt like I was home. Sadness nipped at me as I recalled memories of visiting fabric stores with my nana. I pushed the thoughts aside and glanced at my list. "Let's check out the clearance area first and see if we can find some cheap fabrics we can use for a few more skirts."

"Sounds great." Kylie fell into step with me as we walked toward the back of the store. "So, Dylan's house is *amazing*. It's this huge brick colonial. I bet you could fit the house I grew up in inside his detached four-car garage. The pool is huge. I bet it's Olympic size. And his mom is so nice. She made these little appetizers, and they were so good. I just love those little hot dogs and egg rolls."

We approached a display of discounted fabric, and I began rifling through it, looking for anything that might work for the musical. "So who all was there?"

"Most of the cast." Kylie dramatically fanned herself. "Jimmy was there."

"You mean Jimmy French—the guy who's playing Danny?"

"What other Jimmy is there?" She frowned.

"You like him?" I put down a bolt of fabric and studied her.

"Yeah, but it doesn't matter. He doesn't even know I'm alive. He just talked to Britney all night. It's like they're the real-life Sandy and Danny even when they're offstage."

"I don't think they like each other that way. They were both in the musical at my school last semester, and I think they may have dated for a while. But according to what little I've heard from the rumor mill, they're only friends now. She's dating some guy who's a sophomore at U."

"Really?" Kylie's expression brightened. "So, you know Jimmy? That means you can introduce us."

"Why do I need to introduce you to him? You can talk to him. He's just a guy." I went back to sorting through the material. "Just pretend you're talking to anyone—like you're talking to me right now. It's no big deal."

"No, it's not like that. He's super gorgeous. I would stutter and feel like a fool." She held up a bolt of pink material. "What do you think about this for Frenchy's skirt? Can you use it?"

"Oh yeah." I ran my hand over the smooth material. "I love it."

"Great." Kylie found an empty cart and tossed the fabric into it. "So we swam, listened to music, and ate until nearly one in the morning. I'm so tired, but it was a blast. I know it was your anniversary and all, but you really need to come next time. Bring Todd. It'll be so fun."

"Maybe I will." As I turned my attention to a bin full of discounted buttons, I wondered if I'd be able to convince Todd to go with me if Dylan invited me to another party.

♫

"Did Todd like the gift card?" Kylie asked, as we worked on costumes in my room on Thursday afternoon.

"He did," I said around a mouthful of pins. I was pinning up the hem on a pair of trousers while we talked. After taking the pins out of my mouth, I continued, "He said he's been eyeing a new video game, so now he can go buy it. Of course, that's only if he has time to run out to the mall when it's still open."

"He works a lot, doesn't he?" Kylie sipped a can of soda and continued hand-sewing rhinestone buttons onto one of the poodle skirts.

"Yeah, he does. His father is a slave driver sometimes. I'm surprised he was allowed to leave work early on Monday. I'm sure he had to campaign hard to get his dad to agree to that. But that just makes our anniversary even more special because he took time off work to see me." I poked myself hard with the pin and sucked in my breath before shaking my finger. "Ouch!"

"You okay?" Kylie asked.

"Yeah. Stupid pin." I grabbed a tissue from the box on my dresser and wrapped it around my finger.

"You need to stop daydreaming about your boyfriend and pay attention to what you're doing," Kylie teased.

"You're right … Anyway, I'm thankful to have my car back again. My dad took me to pick it up during his lunch hour today. And I'm so glad it was just the alternator and not something more expensive to fix."

"Oh, I forgot to tell you." Kylie set the skirt on the bed next to her and leaned back against the headboard. "Guess who said hello to me when I got to the playhouse?"

"Jimmy?"

"Yes!"

"Really? Did he say, 'Hi, Kylie'?"

"Yes!" She clapped her hands.

"See? He *does* know your name. You didn't need my help. It happened naturally." I pointed a pin toward her for emphasis. "Before you know it, he may even ask you how you're doing, and then he'll graduate to 'How's your day going?' "

"You're just making fun of me!" Kylie tossed a stuffed cat at me. The toy bounced off my leg and landed on top of Buttons, waking him from his nap.

"I'm kidding. I'm glad he talked to you. Maybe you'll have a show-mance."

"A what?" Kylie scrunched her nose in confusion.

"You've never heard that term before?" I picked up the stuffed cat and placed it on the table next to the sewing machine. "A show-mance is a romance that lasts the length of the production."

"Do you think he likes me since he said hi to me?" Kylie's expression was eager. "And maybe he'll ask me out?"

"Maybe." I rubbed Buttons' head. "Talk to him some more. Get to know him."

"I think I will. I'll have to think of something to say to him."

"How about, 'Hi. How are you?' "

"Yeah, that's a good opener."

We worked in silence for a few minutes, and I continued to pin the trousers. I got lost in my thoughts about the production and the costumes.

"Was that the doorbell?" Kylie asked.

"I didn't hear anything." I stood and walked over to the window that overlooked the driveway. My eyes widened when I spotted a yellow Camaro parked behind my car. "Oh my goodness."

"What?" Kylie hopped up and joined me at the window. "Is that Dylan's car?"

"I think so." I stared at the car. "I don't know anyone else who has a yellow Camaro." Curiosity skittered through me as the doorbell sounded from downstairs. This time I clearly heard it.

"What are you waiting for?" Kylie grabbed my arm and pulled me toward the stairs. "Hurry up and answer the door before he leaves."

We raced to the front door. When I yanked it open, I was shocked to find Dylan standing on the porch with a large heavy box.

"Dylan?" Suddenly, feeling self-conscious, I pushed my hair behind my ears. "What are you doing here?"

"Hey." He nodded at Kylie and then me. "I didn't see you at

the playhouse today, so I thought I'd stop by on my way home from practice. I have something for you two ladies."

"Oooh!" Kylie clapped her hands. "I love surprises."

"Please come in." I made a sweeping gesture and moved away from the door.

Dylan moved through the hallway and into the kitchen then carefully placed the box on the table. "I thought you might be able to use this."

I peered into the box and found a new Singer sewing machine. I stared at the machine, speechless. It was the sewing machine I'd been dreaming about since I'd first spotted it at the fabric store last year. Although I adored the machine my grandmother had given to me, I'd longed to have a newer, digital machine with more options like adjustable sewing speed, push-button stitch selection, and an automatic needle threader.

"Wow!" Kylie ran her fingers over the machine. "This is brand-new, isn't it? I saw one like it at the store the other day, and I begged my mom to get it for me for my birthday."

"It's not brand-new," Dylan said. "My dad bought it for my mom last Christmas when she said she wanted to start sewing again. But she's so busy with her volunteering right now that she hasn't used it at all."

"So it's six months old and never been used, huh?" Kylie asked. "That's brand-new to me." She pulled the instruction manual out of the box and began flipping through it. "This thing is amazing! Listen to this, Chels: 'With the push-button stitch selection, select the desired stitch with just a simple push of a button. Optimum settings for length, width, and tension are set automatically. Buttonhole sewing is a one-step simple process with fully automatic, precisely balanced built-in buttonholes.' That is epic!"

While Kylie continued reading the instructions to me, I

searched Dylan's expression for some kind of an explanation for such a lavish gift. Was there an ulterior motive? Was Dylan just a player who broke girls' hearts, as Todd had suggested? *But Dylan knows I have a boyfriend, so why would he target me?*

"Dylan, why would you give us this machine?" I finally asked.

He crossed his arms in front of his chest and shrugged. "Why not? My mom's not using it. She said it was fine if I wanted to give it to you."

I longed to put the sewing machine on my table upstairs and figure out the digital components. But then my mother's voice echoed in my mind. I could hear her telling me it wasn't right for someone I barely know to give me something so expensive. If she saw the sewing machine, she'd insist that I return it, possibly even going so far as to drive me over to Dylan's house and assist me with the return. I couldn't imagine anything more humiliating than my mother marching me over to Dylan's house to tell his mother how inappropriate the gift was. As much as I wanted to use this fancy machine, I knew I had to thank him and then ask him to take it back.

"This is very generous, but I can't accept it," I said.

"Sure you can, Chels!" Kylie said with surprise. "This machine is amazing!"

"Why not?" Dylan's face fell, and disappointment filled his eyes.

"It's just too much. I'm sure your mother will miss it." I forced a smile. "Thank you, though. It's very generous of you."

"No, my mom suggested I give it to you when I told her about your old machine." He leaned back against the kitchen wall. "She said I should give you and Kylie the machine so you can both sew at the same time. It's her donation to the production this year. You two can finish the costumes faster if you have two machines, right?"

"That's right." Kylie tapped my shoulder. "Just say thank you. It will make things easier on us. You were saying earlier that you wished you had a more advanced machine. Well, here it is!" She tapped the box with a finger. "Would you carry it upstairs for us, Dylan?"

"Sure thing." He met my gaze, and his expression became hopeful. "So, what do you think, Chelsea? Can I take it upstairs?"

Kylie tapped my shoulder again, and I wanted to tell her to stop hitting me. Instead, I just nodded. "Sure. Thank you, Dylan."

"Awesome!" Kylie clapped her hands. "Let's get to work!"

Dylan carried the box up to my room. I cleared fabric off the top of my sewing table and shooed Buttons away from the desk chair. While Dylan hooked up the new sewing machine, Kylie talked nonstop about how amazing it was. Instead of contributing to the conversation, I kept staring at the new machine and silently marveled at the generous gift. He'd said it was for the production, but I still couldn't help feeling uncomfortable about it. Something felt off, yet I couldn't put my finger on what was bothering me.

Once the machine was set up, Kylie and I perused the instructions and tested out the different features on scrap pieces of material while Dylan watched.

"Oh wow," Kylie said, looking at her watch. "I'd better go. It's almost five thirty."

"Is it really that late?" Dylan stood. "I'd better head out too."

I followed them out to the driveway, and we stood by Dylan's car.

"Hey, I'm having some of the cast over to swim tonight," Dylan said. "It's sort of an impromptu party. Want to join us?"

Kylie nodded with emphasis. "That sounds great! What time?"

"Anytime really. My parents are really relaxed about my friends coming over. You can come anytime." He looked at me. "Do you think you can make it this time?"

"Oh, you have to, Chels!" Kylie whined while pulling on my arm again. "It will be so much fun."

"Okay." I nodded. "I'll check with my parents and see if I can come over."

"Great!" Dylan fished his phone from his pocket. "What's your number? I'll text you the address."

I rattled off my cell number, and he programmed it into his phone. I spotted Kylie's grin in my peripheral vision but chose to ignore her. "Please tell your mother we both thank her very much for the sewing machine. Kylie and I will put it to good use. And thanks for bringing it over and setting it up."

"You're welcome." Dylan slipped his phone back into his pocket and climbed into his car. He looked up at me from the driver's seat. "I hope to see you later. Text me and let me know if you're coming, okay?"

"I will."

Kylie and I stood in the driveway and watched him drive off.

"He totally likes you!" Kylie's voice squeaked as the Camaro disappeared from sight.

"What are you talking about?" I shook my head in disagreement. "I have a boyfriend, remember?"

"You may have a boyfriend, but Dylan is totally into you."

"Please." I blew off the suggestion but couldn't help but wonder if she was right. Even if she was right, what did it matter? I had Todd. "He's not into me," I insisted. "I'm not his type. And, like I said, I have a boyfriend, and I'm committed to him."

We walked over to her mother's sedan. "Dylan likes you!" She sang the words. "He was watching every move you made."

"When?" The curiosity was eating me alive. I had to know why she thought he liked me.

"He was watching you the whole time we were trying to figure out how to use the sewing machine." Kylie scowled. "It's so unfair. You have a boyfriend *and* Dylan likes you. I wish I could find a boyfriend."

"You will. Don't rush it."

"So are you really going to go to his house tonight?" Kylie pulled the car keys from her oversized purse. "Or were you just saying that to get him to drop it?"

"I'll ask if I can go tonight. Since his mother gave us this amazing sewing machine because of him, I feel like I should accept the invitation just as a way to thank him."

"I agree."

I looked at my watch. "My mom should be home soon. She arranged to get off work early today so she could pick up my brothers from day camp—just in case my car wasn't ready yet. If she doesn't need help with my brothers tonight, then I might be able to go."

"Cool." Kylie opened the driver's side door. "Text me and let me know if you're going to come. And don't forget to text Dylan." She grinned again, and I shook my head.

"You're terrible. I have a boyfriend, remember?"

"I do remember, but you're the one who keeps repeating it. Who are you trying to convince—me or you?" She winked as she climbed into the car. "See you later!"

As Kylie drove off, I made my way back into the house and headed for the kitchen. I opened the refrigerator and retrieved the container of meatballs I'd helped my mother make last night. Then I grabbed a double boiler from the cabinet and a jar of tomato sauce from the pantry. As I began pulling supper together, I wondered what it would be like to go to Dylan's house. I knew I had to tell Todd that I planned to go. I just hoped he would understand.

# chapter six

Those meatballs were delicious," Mom said as we cleared the table. "You're really a great cook."

"Thank you." I filled the sink with hot, soapy water, and it reminded me of Dylan's pool party. "I was wondering if I could go out tonight."

"I didn't realize you had plans." Mom placed a stack of dirty dishes on the counter next to me. "Did Todd call you?"

"No." I placed a tomato sauce-covered pot in the sink and began putting dirty dishes in the dishwasher. "My friend Dylan is having an impromptu swimming party at his house tonight."

"Dylan?" Mom looked confused. "I don't think I know him, do I?"

"No, you haven't met him yet. He lives in Castleton, not far from Emily's cousin Whitney. He got the part of Kenickie in *Grease*."

"Kenickie, huh?" Mom grabbed a dishrag and wet it under the running water. "He was my favorite T-Bird in the movie. He's so cool."

"Does that mean I can go?" I dropped the utensils into the dishwasher.

"Is Todd going?"

"I don't know yet. I have to call him." I needed to find a way to convince her to let me go since I assumed Todd wouldn't be going. "Kylie is going too. There will be other members of the cast and crew there, and Dylan's parents are going to be home. So there will be plenty of adult supervision."

Mom began wiping off the table. "What time will you be home? You have to work tomorrow morning. So you can't stay out late and then go to work exhausted. You know Mr. Hughes doesn't put up with any nonsense. And you need this job."

I swallowed a frustrated sigh. "Mom, I know I need the job." I wanted to add, *You don't have to keep reminding me!* But took a deep breath and said, "I haven't gone to work exhausted yet this summer, and I don't plan on starting now."

Mom kept silent as she pushed the chairs up to the table.

I tried a new approach. Folding my hands as if I were praying, I said, "Please, Mom? Please let me go. Let me prove to you that I'm responsible." I knew I had to tell her the truth—why this was so important to me. "Look, this is the first party a cast member has ever invited me to. I really want to go."

"This really means a lot to you?" Mom asked.

"Yes." I leaned against the counter. "It really does."

"Fine," Mom said. "You can go."

"Yay!" I jumped up and down.

"This is a test, Chelsea." Mom held up a finger as if to warn me. "Don't let me down."

"I won't!" I gave her a quick hug. "Do you want me to give the boys their baths before I go?"

"No." She waved off the question. "Go have fun."

I turned back to finish clearing the stack of dirty dishes off the counter.

"I told you to go. Get out of here," Mom said with a smile.

"Thank you!" I kissed her cheek before rushing upstairs to my room. I fished my bathing suit out of my dresser and stuffed it into a duffel bag with a beach towel, my cover-up, and a bag of toiletries. I wasn't certain I'd feel confident enough to wear a bathing suit in front of the actors, but I thought I should bring it along just in case I changed my mind.

My phone beeped, and I was surprised to find a text from a number I didn't recognize. I opened it and read: Hey Chelsea. R u coming to my party?

I knew the text was from Dylan. I gnawed my lower lip and debated answering him. I felt like I should talk to Todd first, but my mother had already given me permission to go. And I wanted to go no matter what Todd said. Yet a feeling of uneasiness crept over me. Why did I feel apprehensive about going to the party if Kylie was going to be there?

I texted him back: Yes, I'll be there soon.

Dylan immediately responded with: Great! C u soon!

I sat on my bed and dialed Todd's number. Buttons perched on my lap and rubbed his head against my arm. I absently rubbed the spot between his ears while I waited for Todd to answer.

"Hey," he said. He sounded tired. "How are you?"

"Fine. How was your day?" I said, sounding chipper.

"Long." He yawned. "I'm beat. The restaurant was so busy today that I never got a real break."

"Oh." I stopped rubbing the cat and fingered my necklace. "So I guess that means you don't feel like going out tonight."

"Not really." He yawned again. "What did you have in mind?"

"Well, Dylan invited us to another pool party. I'd really like to go." I held my breath while awaiting his response.

"But we both have to work tomorrow."

"I know." Buttons pushed against my arm, and I rubbed his head some more. "I can handle hanging out with some friends and then going to work the next day. So, will you go with me? Please?"

"I don't think so. I'm planning on taking a shower and going straight to bed."

Disappointment filled me. "You could just stop by."

"No. I'm really too exhausted. I'm actually trying to drum up the strength to go shower."

"Please, Todd?" I used my cutesy voice, hoping to inspire him.

"Chelsea, I'm serious when I say I'm tired. And, honestly, I'm not thrilled about you going to the party either."

"Why not?" I flopped onto my back, and Buttons curled up beside me. "It's just a little party."

"That guy rubs me the wrong way."

I rolled onto my stomach and stared at the sewing machine. I longed to tell Todd about it, but I knew it would only make him more suspicious of Dylan. *Am I lying to Todd by not telling him about the sewing machine? Is omitting the truth the same as telling a lie?* I decided not to tell him about the sewing machine—at least not yet.

"He's really a nice guy," I finally said. "You should get to know him. Maybe you can talk to him at the party, and you'll see he's okay."

"You're very quick to defend him." Todd's voice had an accusatory edge to it.

"What are you suggesting?" I asked, feeling aggravated all over again.

He paused. "Do you like Dylan?"

"I like him as a friend. I have lots of male friends, Todd. You know I like to talk to everyone." Apprehension coiled in my stomach. "Don't you trust me?"

Todd's voice softened a little, "Of course I trust you, Chelsea, but I don't trust Dylan."

My stomach settled slightly. "You have nothing to worry about, Todd. It's a party. I won't be hanging out with Dylan alone."

"Well, I just wish you wouldn't go."

"Todd, I understand you're tired, but I really want to go. This is our last summer before we head to college, and our lives are going to change completely after that. I don't want to spend all summer sitting at home." I sat up. "I really want to go, but I don't want this party to cause problems for us. I don't want you to be angry with me because I want to go. You need to trust me. You know me, Todd. You know I'd never do anything to jeopardize our relationship."

"Fine," he said. "I won't be angry if you go. Text me when you get home."

"I promise I will." Excitement filled me. "I'll see you tomorrow morning at work."

"Don't have too much fun without me."

"Don't worry. That's not possible. Get some rest so we can do something fun this weekend."

"I'll try. Bye, Chels."

I disconnected the call and checked my reflection in the mirror. I was pulling my hair back into a thick ponytail when I heard footsteps on the stairs.

"Is Todd going with you?" Mom said.

"No, he's too tired. Apparently the restaurant was totally crazy today." I freshened up my makeup while I spoke. "Other friends of mine will be there, though. Kylie said she was going. I'll text her and see if she needs a ride."

Mom crossed the room and stood in front of my sewing table. "Where did you get this machine?"

"Dylan brought it over today. His mother donated it for the production."

"Dylan's mother donated it?" Mom's eyes were wide. "That's a brand-new machine."

"Yeah." I reapplied my eyeliner. "Dylan's dad bought it for Dylan's mom for Christmas last year, but she's never used it. When he saw my old Singer machine, he thought Kylie and I might need something more up-to-date to make the costumes. And he said we can sew at the same time if we have two machines. Isn't that nice?"

"When was Dylan in your room?"

"Monday afternoon when he brought me home after my car died." I met her questioning gaze in the mirror. "He wanted to see the costumes, Mom. Why are you acting like I did something wrong? You trust Todd to come up to my room all the time."

"Yes, but I know Todd and his family. I've never met Dylan."

"Do you want me to invite Dylan over for dinner so you can meet him?" The words were laced with more indignation than I intended, and I immediately regretted my tone.

Mom pursed her lips and folded her arms over her chest. "There's no need for you to get defensive. I'm only worried about your safety. If you only just met this boy, then you don't need to be alone with him in your room when nobody's home." She turned back toward the sewing machine. "This is a very expensive gift, Chelsea. I'm not comfortable with you accepting it. What does he expect to receive in return for such a gift?"

"Nothing." I finished off my makeup with mascara. "He just wanted to donate the machine to the production. That's all. I don't think there's any hidden meaning or ulterior motive."

"If it's only for the production, then that means you'll return the machine after the costumes are done, right?"

I put the cap on the mascara and faced Mom. "Sure. I guess so."

"He didn't say that?" Mom picked up the instruction manual and examined it.

"No, he didn't."

"Wow." Mom flipped through the book. "Your nana would've loved this. It has a lot of features."

"I know." I craned my neck and read over her shoulder. "You'll have to give it a try this weekend."

"I'd like that." Mom closed the book and placed it back on the table. "I don't know how I feel about you keeping it though."

"It was a donation, Mom. That's all it was." I studied her, wondering why she was making such a big deal about this. "It's just a sewing machine. It's not like it's a new car."

"That's not the point. I just don't think it's right for you to keep this. I want you to return the machine after you're finished with the costumes."

I opened my mouth to protest but simply nodded. I didn't want to argue with her and risk losing my chance to attend the cast party. "I'll return it when I'm done with the costumes."

"Good." She glanced at the machine again. "If you really like it, then I'll look into getting you one for Christmas."

"Really?"

Mom smiled. "I'm sure that if you keep your grades up at college this fall, I'll be inspired to buy you something really nice for Christmas."

"Thank you! That would be amazing!"

My phone beeped, and I found a text from Kylie: At the party. Where r u? "It's Kylie asking me when I'm going to get there."

"Go have fun."

"I will. Thanks, Mom." I hugged her and grabbed my duffel bag. "I won't be out too late."

"Just be safe," Mom said. "Promise me."

"I will." I followed her downstairs. After hugging my brothers, I headed out to my car.

♫

Dylan's house was two blocks down from Whitney's. And while I'd always been impressed with Whitney's house, I was surprised to find that Dylan's was even larger. The sprawling red brick colonial had nearly a dozen windows in the front. A wraparound porch hugged the first floor, and an enclosed porch sat on the right side of the house. A circular driveway cut through the perfectly green front yard and led to the four-car garage Kylie had been telling me about. Dylan's car sat between two shiny European sedans parked in front of it.

Since the driveway was clogged with cars, I parked on the street and walked the length of the driveway toward the house. The aroma of chlorine filled my nose, and I heard the sound of music mixed with splashing, laughter, and loud voices. As I moved toward the noise, excitement and nervousness filled me. I couldn't believe I was going to attend my first cast party! For a brief moment, I longed for Todd's familiar company, but I pushed the thought away as I neared the back of the house.

I touched my ponytail to make sure it was straight and approached the gate of the wrought-iron fence that enclosed three sides of the Olympic-size, in-ground pool. Looking around, I saw a striped cabana, along with a few wrought-iron tables with colorful umbrellas and matching chairs, plus a couple rows of expensive-looking lounge chairs including white cushions with big green flowers on all sides of the pool.

I immediately recognized the cast members among the crowd. There were probably close to a hundred teenagers swimming, eating finger foods off disposable plates, and sitting on the edge of the pool with their legs dangling in the crystal blue water. Music boomed from invisible speakers in the pool area.

"Chelsea!" Kylie's voice rang out over the music and laughter.

"You made it!" She was clad in a hot pink, two-piece bathing suit that flattered her petite figure as she rushed over and opened the gate. "Isn't this place incredible?"

"Yeah," I agreed, scanning the backyard.

A large deck stretched from the back of the house to the concrete patio. As I took in the scenery, I was overwhelmed by Dylan's family's wealth. Just as Kylie had described it, I could imagine my little ranch house fitting inside that monstrous detached garage. I wondered what it felt like to live such a comfortable lifestyle, where receiving a brand-new car from my parents was the norm, if not expected. I was certain Dylan's college education wasn't ever a budget issue for his parents. In fact, I was even more certain that Dylan didn't have to work a minimum-wage job and apply for multiple scholarships, hoping he'd have enough money to cover the cost of his education.

Then it hit me—I was envious of all that Dylan had. I longed for a secure life where money was no object. I longed to not have to worry about my car breaking down or feel embarrassed when a new friend found out my mom worked as an administrative assistant or saw my little house. Then I remembered a recent youth group discussion about the seven deadly sins—wrath, greed, sloth, pride, lust, envy, and gluttony—and I was disappointed in myself. I knew I should be thankful for all I had. Yet at the same time, I longed for a newer, more reliable car.

"Guess who I've been talking to?" Kylie asked, as I followed her through the gate.

"Jimmy?"

"Yeah!" Kylie gushed. "He's so nice." She moved to the edge of the pool. "The water is perfect—not too warm but not too cold. Did you bring your suit?" She pointed toward my bag.

My eyes moved to the slim girls parading around the pool

in their skimpy two-piece suits. Although I was by no means overweight, I felt self-conscious at the notion of slipping into my one-piece bathing suit and swimming among them. "I brought it, but I'm not ready to get changed just yet. I think I'll sit and observe for a few minutes."

"Okay. Well, I'm going to swim." Kylie dove into the deep end with the grace of an Olympic diver and swam over to where Jimmy was talking with other members of the cast. He grinned at Kylie and said something that made her laugh.

I scanned the crowd and didn't spot Dylan anywhere. Looking behind me, I saw Marni Stern sitting at one of the patio tables. She waved, and I went to join her.

"Hey, Chels." She patted the chair next to her. "Have a seat."

"Thanks."

"Would you like something to drink?" She pointed toward a cooler near our table. Marni lifted her can of diet cola. "That's the nonalcoholic cooler. The alcoholic drinks are in coolers out on the deck."

"Alcoholic drinks?" My eyes widened. "You mean this is a drinking party?"

"Yes. Apparently this cast likes to drink."

I glanced around the crowd of partiers and then looked back at Marni. "I don't think anyone here is twenty-one, are they?"

"No, they aren't legal drinking age, but the cooler is up on the deck. I guess that's so Dylan's parents can say they're supervising us."

"Are you serious?"

"No." She shook her head. "I was being sarcastic."

"Oh." I spotted several members of the cast sipping cans of beer. "My parents would never allow drinking at our house. In fact, my parents don't drink."

"Mine don't either." Marni took a long sip of her soda. "Just give me a diet soda, and I'm happy."

I fetched a can of diet cola from the cooler and sank back into the chair. "Are you very religious?" I opened the can, which popped and fizzed.

"We go to temple, but my parents aren't orthodox."

"You're Jewish."

"Yes, I am." She held up her soda can. "Let's make a toast with our delicious diet colas."

I held up my can as well. "That's a great idea."

"To our nonalcoholic beverages," Marni said.

"Hear, hear!" I said, as we tapped our cans together.

A splash followed by loud hooting and hollering drew my attention back toward the pool. Water sprayed near the table. Dylan's head broke the surface of the water, and the group of nearby swimmers splashed him. The splashing war continued for several minutes while spectators around the pool cheered them on.

I leaned over to Marni. "Do you like to swim?" I asked, raising my voice to be heard above the splashing and the cheers and the rock music.

"I do, but I'm a little more modest than some of these girls." She pointed toward the bikini-clad girls in the pool.

I raised my soda can again. "I hear you, Marni." We tapped our cans together again, and I smiled. I was glad I'd met her.

I heard a rush of water and turned my head in time to see Dylan climb out of the pool. He grabbed a towel off the back of a lounge chair and walked toward our table as he dried himself off. I tried in vain not to stare at his tanned, muscular body.

"Well, it's the costumer extraordinaire. Glad you made it, Chelsea." He grabbed an open can of beer from a nearby table, wrapped the towel around his waist, and sat across from us. "Are you two having fun?"

"Absolutely." Marni sipped her soda. "It's nice to relax after rehearsing all day. I'm surprised I still have a voice."

"Yeah, it's nice to take a break. Kylie and I did a lot of sewing and shopping today. The costumes are coming together, though."

"Cool," Marni said. "I like to sew. How did you learn?"

"My nana taught me everything I know."

Dylan finished the last of his beer and tossed the empty can into a plastic container labeled with the recycling symbol. "You two don't have to drink diet soda. There's plenty of beer. We even have light beer, if you're counting your calories."

"No, thanks." Marni tapped her can. "I'm perfectly happy with my diet soda."

Dylan looked at me. "What about you? Do you want a beer?"

"No, thanks." I shook my head. "I'm fine."

"I'll be right back." Dylan stood and sauntered toward the deck, stopping to hug a girl and high-five a friend. I recognized both of them as members of the cast.

"So you moved to Cameronville two months ago?" I asked Marni.

"Yeah, my dad got a job transfer and wanted to move closer to the city. We're in Rock Creek."

"No kidding. That's where I live! What street do you live on?" I asked.

"Rock Lake Loop." Marni explained the location of her house in relation to the neighborhood's entrance.

"I'm only one block over. My house is just around the corner from yours."

"So you guys are neighbors?" Dylan had returned and chose to sit in the chair right next to me this time instead of across from me.

"Apparently so." Marni nodded.

"Let me know if you ever need a ride to the playhouse. I can pick you up," I said.

Dylan popped open a new can of beer and held it out to me. I shook my head as the bitter smell assaulted me.

Dylan studied me. "Have you ever tried beer?"

I paused, wondering if I should tell him the truth. Would he call me a prude or a loser if I admitted I never had? I'd always been strong in my convictions, but I suddenly found myself feeling worried about what this gorgeous college boy would think of me.

He smiled, and I was struck by his lopsided grin. "You haven't ever had a beer, have you?" he asked.

I shook my head, too mortified to admit it out loud.

"It's okay." He raked his fingers through his wet blond hair. "There's a first time for everything. Are you sure you don't want one?"

"I'm fine, really." I tried to think of a way to change the subject, but I felt tongue-tied while sitting so close to him.

"You really need to loosen up," he said.

"We don't have to drink, Dylan," Marni cut into the conversation. "We're having fun without alcohol, right, Chels?"

"Exactly," I said, finding my courage again.

"That's cool," he said.

"I don't understand why your parents allow underage drinking at your house," I said. "Don't they realize they can get in trouble for that?"

"My parents don't see it that way." He leaned forward, and my eyes were drawn to his tanned, wide chest. "My folks know parties are going to happen and alcohol will be served." He tapped the table for emphasis. "This way they're providing a safe environment for my friends and me. They'd prefer I have some beer with my friends where I'm safe, rather than taking a risk at some random place."

I gripped my soda can while I considered his words. "My parents wouldn't let me have a party with alcohol."

"You're going to run into alcohol eventually. You're going to U in the fall, right?" he asked.

I nodded. "Yes, I am."

"There is plenty of it at college. In fact, you can't go to a party without seeing it and smelling it." He pointed toward the house. "My parents know there are parties at college, but they don't even ask me about it. They allow me to have my friends here, and they check on us periodically." He turned toward the deck. "There's my mom now." He waved to an attractive blonde woman standing on the deck and talking with a few of his friends. She met his gaze and waved back. She was clad in white shorts with a pale lavender collared shirt with crisp white sneakers. She dressed similarly to my friend Whitney's mother, causing me to wonder if she'd recently returned from the country club. Her hair was in a no-nonsense french twist, and her makeup was perfect.

"I guess everyone's parents are different." Marni sipped her can of soda. "Mine would ground me if I asked for a beer. They'd go crazy if I wanted to have friends over to drink."

"Yeah, mine would too." My thoughts turned to Todd. "Todd's parents wouldn't allow it either."

"So where is your boyfriend tonight?" Dylan asked between sips of beer.

"He's home." I ran a finger through the condensation on the soda can. "He had a long day at work. He's filling in for the regular cook who's out on maternity leave. Apparently, the restaurant was super busy today."

"Which restaurant does he work at?" Marni asked.

"His parents own the Fork & Knife," I said.

"I love that place!" Marni's expression brightened. "The food is so good there."

"I know. I work as a server during the morning shift."

"Todd doesn't know how to have fun either, huh?" Dylan grinned. "This is your last summer before you become a college student, and I'm going to make you a promise, Chelsea Morris. I promise that I will teach you how to have fun before the summer is over. That way you'll be ready for college in the fall."

"Hey, Dylan!" Jimmy yelled. He was standing by the pool with his arm around Kylie. "Come over here!"

"I'll be right back, ladies." Dylan stood and headed toward his friend.

Marni leaned over to me and said, "You don't have to drink to be his friend or fit in at college. My older sister is a senior at U, and she never got into partying."

I watched Dylan talking with Jimmy and Kylie and wondered what it would be like to be so free and confident. What did it feel like to be cool like him?

A familiar song began blaring through the speakers, and Marni tapped my arm. "I love this song!" she yelled. "Want to dance?"

I shook my head. "I'm not the best dancer."

"Come on!" She stood and motioned for me to follow her toward a makeshift dance floor near the deck. "I'll teach you."

As I caught up with Marni, I smiled. Not only was I attending my first cast party, but now I was going to dance with one of the cool girls. This was going to be the best summer ever!

# chapter seven

The following morning, my clock radio alarm buzzed at six o'clock, yanking me from a fog of dreams involving music and swimming pools. I rolled over, looked at the clock, and moaned.

I dragged myself out of bed, through the shower, and down the stairs to where my mother was making breakfast for my brothers.

"Good morning," I managed to say through a yawn.

"Good morning." Mom peered at me while filling two bowls with cereal. "I didn't hear you come in last night. What time did you get home?"

"It was late." I grabbed a banana.

"How late?" She placed the bowls of cereal on the table. "Boys!" she called toward the family room. "It's time for breakfast. Turn off the television and get out here."

"After one." I braced myself for the lecture.

"Chelsea." She placed a hand on her hip. "You know better than that."

"I know, but I had a lot of fun and made some new friends. It was a blast." I glanced at the clock. "I'd better go now or I'm going to be late."

My brothers hopped into their chairs at the table, and

I kissed the tops of their heads. "Have a good day, guys." I started for the door, then turned to wave at my mother. "Love you."

"Have a good day, Chelsea," Mom called after me. "Love you too!"

I rushed off to work and managed to arrive on time without breaking the speed limit. I parked in my usual spot at the back of the lot next to Todd's car.

Once inside the restaurant, I quickly clocked in and received my table assignments from Mrs. Hughes. I was entering my first orders when I felt a hand on my shoulder. I turned and found Todd studying me, his brown eyes full of concern.

"Hey," he said. "I was worried about you."

I finished entering the orders into the system and faced him. "Why are you worried about me?" I cupped my hand over my mouth to cover a big yawn.

"You never texted me last night. I woke up around midnight and checked my phone. I was worried."

"Oh." I grimaced. "I'm so sorry. I got home really late and just fell into bed. I had so much fun, Todd. You missed a good party."

He crossed his arms in front of his chest. "Really?"

"It was a blast! Nearly the whole cast was there. Dylan's house is amazing. It's even bigger than Whitney's house. And it's so pretty." I gestured wildly with my hands, but he continued to look uninterested. "And the pool is huge, like Olympic size. We danced and ate until after midnight. I hung out with Marni Stern; she's a member of the chorus. She's really cool and so nice. She just moved to Cameronville from Ridgewood, and she lives less than a block away from me ..." I yawned again and then smiled. "... Excuse me."

"What time did you get home?"

"After one." I waved off the scolding comment before he could even make it. "It's no big deal."

"Apparently, it is. You look wiped out."

"It was worth it." I touched his arm. "You should come next time. It was so fun, Todd. You'd have a great time, and you could meet the rest of the cast." *Except you wouldn't approve of the alcohol, which is why I'm not telling you about that part.* "Will you come next time? Please? For me?"

"Chels, I don't know. I'm under a lot of pressure here." He braced a hand on the counter beside him. "I'd rather spend what little time off I have with you instead of a bunch of cast members I don't really know."

"But you can get to know them if you come to the parties."

The kitchen door swung open, and Mr. Hughes stuck his head out. "Todd. We have orders to fill."

"I'll be right there, Dad."

"Good morning, Mr. Hughes." I tried to sound chipper despite my overwhelming exhaustion.

Mr. Hughes grunted something that sounded like hello and then disappeared through the door.

"He's in a mood," I muttered to Todd.

"You have no idea. I'd better go." He kissed my cheek, and I smiled. "See you later," he said before heading into the kitchen.

I managed to get through the morning, taking orders, entering them, and delivering food—all while fighting the constant urge to yawn.

"Chelsea," Mrs. Hughes approached me after I'd delivered a meal to an elderly couple, two of our regulars. "Are you doing okay today?"

"I'm doing fine. How are you?"

"You seem a little off." She motioned for me to follow her back to the order counter. "Are you feeling all right?"

"Yes, ma'am." Another yawn gripped me, and I couldn't hold back. I cupped my hand to my mouth. "Excuse me."

"If you're not feeling well, then please let me know."

"I'm just tired, that's all." I glanced toward the tables she'd recently wiped down. "Would you like me to reset those tables?"

"That would be wonderful. They all need coffee mugs." She pointed toward a serving tray full of mugs. "Those just came out of the dishwasher. You can take them."

The phone began ringing, and Mrs. Hughes rushed toward the office to answer it.

I picked up the heavy tray of mugs and started toward the dining room. But as I took another step, the mugs shifted on the tray, and before I could readjust my hold, the tray went flying out of my hands and crashed to the floor.

I stared down at the shattered porcelain confetti and wondered how I was going to clean it all up.

Janie rushed over from the dining room. "Are you all right?"

"I'm fine." I bent down and began picking up the large pieces littered among the tiny shards and dropped them onto the tray.

"Wait. You're going to cut yourself." Janie squeezed my shoulder. "I'll get the dustpan and broom. Don't move." She rushed off toward the supply closet.

The whoosh of the kitchen door sounded behind me, and I glanced back to see Mr. Hughes staring at me from the doorway.

"What happened?" Mr. Hughes's expression hardened.

"I'm so sorry." My voice was hoarse. "I stepped wrong, I guess."

Todd rushed out behind him. "Chelsea!" He bent over beside me. "Are you okay?"

"Yeah." The tips of my ears burned with humiliation.

Janie arrived with the dustpan and broom. "Move away from the mess, and I'll clean it up for you."

"No, you need to go help the customers, Janie." Mr. Hughes pointed toward the front of the restaurant. "Chelsea will clean it up."

Janie gave him a mock salute and handed me the dustpan and broom. "It's okay," she whispered to me.

"Let me help you," Todd insisted as he picked up the large broken pieces and placed them on the tray. "You sweep, and I'll pick up what I can."

"Todd, you need to get back in the kitchen," Mr. Hughes barked. "Chelsea can clean up her own mess."

My shoulders hunched forward, and I kept my eyes on the floor as I swept.

"No, I'm going to help her." Todd emphasized each word. "It will go faster if I help."

"What a mess," Mr. Hughes said. "Do you have any idea how much those mugs cost?"

"She made a mistake, Dad." Todd's forceful tone surprised me. "We'll have it cleaned up in a minute."

The whoosh of the kitchen door alerted me that Mr. Hughes was gone again.

"Thank you for helping me," I said, my voice ragged with embarrassment.

"You're welcome." Todd placed the last large piece on the tray. "My dad is so unreasonable and cold sometimes. All he cares about is the restaurant and how much things cost. It makes me crazy."

I swept up more debris and dumped it into a nearby trash can. "I think I got it all."

Todd looked at me with a serious expression on his face. "I know it was a mistake, but you have to be more careful. In the past my dad has fired employees for breaking things. He's really stressed right now because money is tight. He could decide we don't need a part-time person."

"I know." I cleared my throat. "Thank you for defending me."

"You're welcome. I'd better get back in the kitchen before the warden comes to get me." He kissed my cheek and started toward the kitchen.

I watched him walk away and suddenly felt overwhelmed with guilt for going to the party without him. He had defended me to his father when he could've just walked away and left me to clean up the mess by myself.

As I put the broom and dustpan back in the supply closet, I remembered the Scripture verse my stepfather had read during church last Sunday: "May your unfailing love be my comfort, according to your promise to your servant." Maybe Todd was an example of Jesus's unfailing love, like Psalm 119:76 said. One thing was certain: Todd was a wonderful blessing in my life, and I shouldn't take him for granted.

♫

On Sunday, I sat in my usual spot beside Todd in church. His leg brushed against mine as a member of the congregation read the Scripture lessons. The man read the second lesson from the second chapter of Ephesians, and verse ten caused me to sit up straight. While he continued reading, I repeated verse ten over and over: "For we are God's handiwork, created in Christ Jesus to do good works, which God prepared in advance for us to do."

Pastor Kevin motioned for us to stand as he read from the Gospels. After the children's sermon ended, he began giving the main sermon. But my mind was still stuck on that verse in Ephesians. Pastor Kevin talked about good works and how we should live our lives as an example of Christ's love. As he spoke, I felt even guiltier about going to the party without Todd. Not only had I omitted important details about the party when I told my mom and Todd about it, but I'd also stayed at the party while other people were drinking.

*Does that make me bad? Am I still being like Jesus?*

The questions spun through my mind. I thought about how Marni had refused the alcohol and insisted I could do the same without consequence. She seemed so confident. I longed to be more like Marni—confident and secure in my convictions.

I tried my best to concentrate during the rest of the service, but the questions and doubt continued to assault my mind.

After the closing hymn, Todd and I held hands as we made our way outside to get snacks at the Fellowship on the Walkway.

"Are you okay?" Todd said in a low voice as he leaned his head closer to mine. "You seem to be a million miles away."

"I'm fine." I smiled up at him. "Just tired."

He studied me with one eyebrow raised. "Still recovering from that party on Thursday night?"

"No, not really. I've been up late working on the costumes." It wasn't a lie. I *had* been working on the costumes late into the night on Friday and Saturday, but that wasn't what was bothering me. I wanted to be honest with him, but my fear of losing him kept the truth bottled up inside.

Todd and I were eating snacks and talking with a few friends when my brothers rushed over yelling Todd's name.

"Come over and play with us today!" Justin said, his lips covered in chocolate.

I wiped a napkin across his mouth. "Did you get into the chocolate chip cookies?"

"Yeah." Justin grinned. "They were really good."

"He took mine." J.J. frowned. "He always eats my cookies."

Todd laughed. "I guess that means you need to eat faster."

"And you need to eat your own cookies, Justin." I finished wiping his mouth. "You're all clean now."

"Todd, are you coming over to play with us?" Justin asked, his brown eyes hopeful.

"You need to come over," J.J. chimed in.

Todd turned toward me. "I think that's up to your sister."

"Pleeease, Chels!" J.J. whined.

"You have to let him come over, Chels!" Justin sang.

I frowned at Todd. "Why are you putting this on me again? You're the one who's so busy working all the time."

"You know as well as I do that the restaurant is closed on Sundays." Todd grinned at my brothers. "Want to go to the park?"

"Yeah!" My brothers clapped.

"Hi, Todd." My mom approached us. "What are you four up to?"

"Todd's suggesting we take the boys to the park," I explained.

"Would that be okay, Mrs. Klein?" Todd asked before he finished the last cookie on his plate.

"Sure, but you listen to Chelsea and Todd," Mom continued her instructions. "They are in charge." She retrieved her wallet from her purse and handed me a twenty-dollar bill. "Pick up some lunch on your way."

Todd and I thanked her, and then we led my brothers out to his car and loaded them into the backseat. After we picked up some lunch at the Burger World drive-through, we enjoyed our burgers, fries, and sodas while sitting at a picnic table near the duck pond in the park. As soon as the boys finished eating, they ran off to the playground. Todd and I stayed at the table and watched them.

"How are the costumes coming?" Todd asked.

"Slowly." I moved the fries around on my napkin. "It's a lot of work, but it's a labor of love. I'm hoping to get a letter of recommendation for school."

"I'm sure you will. You're the best." He looped his arm around my shoulders and nudged me closer to him. "You'll be designing costumes for Broadway shows after you graduate."

"Wouldn't that be nice?" My thoughts turned to the restaurant. "So is your dad still upset with me?"

"No. I talked to him later, and he was fine. My mom was concerned that you'd been so tired all morning. You may not want to stay out so late again. I know you had fun, but my dad doesn't put up with much from his employees. He once fired a server for texting too much on the job. He's really strict." He rolled his eyes. "I've often prayed he would loosen up, but it's just his personality."

"I know. I honestly just missed my footing. I'm sure he's tripped before."

"He'd never admit it if he had."

"Todd!" J.J. yelled from the swing set. "Would you push me?"

"Sure, buddy!" Todd hopped up. "Duty calls."

"You're a good surrogate big brother."

Todd trotted over to the swings and began pushing J.J. Soon Justin ran over from the slide and hopped onto the swing beside his twin so Todd could push him too. My brothers hooted and hollered while Todd pushed them higher and higher. I smiled, silently marveling at how nice my boyfriend was. How many eighteen-year-old guys would choose to spend an afternoon at the park with five-year-old twins? Would Dylan do that?

The question surprised me. Why was I comparing Todd to Dylan? Why did I even care about Dylan?

I pulled my notepad out of my messenger bag and began making a list of the costumes I still needed to work on. I was fully engrossed in my list when my phone buzzed inside one of the pockets in my bag. I pulled it out, expecting to see a text from Emily or Kylie. Instead, I was surprised to find a text from Dylan.

I opened it and read: Hey Chels. Swim tonight? U can bring Todd if he's not 2 tired.

I stared at the text, not sure how to answer it. Questions raced through my mind. What would Todd say if he knew Dylan had texted me? Dylan was just a friend. I had nothing to hide. But at the same time, I knew Todd didn't like Dylan. I felt caught between the two of them since I wanted to be Dylan's friend but didn't want to lose Todd.

"Who texted you?" Todd asked, as he returned to the picnic table.

"Oh hey." I placed my phone on the bench next to me. "Are the boys done swinging?" I forced a smile despite my inner turmoil.

"Yeah, they're on the jungle gym now. Justin sure likes to climb." He grabbed a few fries and looked over toward the playground.

"You're sweet to push them so high for so long. My arms hurt when I push them like that on our swings at home. They never seem to get enough."

"I don't mind." He sank onto the bench beside me. "I guess since I'm an only child, I appreciate how cool it would've been to have younger brothers."

"Yeah, it's cool sometimes." I sipped my soda.

"So, who texted you?" He bumped his knee against mine.

I looked at my phone and then back at Todd who was now watching me intently. "Would you like to go swimming tonight?"

"Swimming?" He grabbed another fry. "Where would we swim?"

"At Dylan's."

"Why?" Todd's tone was accusatory. "Is he texting you now?"

"He texted a bunch of people, not just me." The lie flowed from my lips, surprising me. Why was lying coming so easily to me now? Who was I becoming?

Todd shook his head. "No, I really don't want to go."

"But then you could meet the cast, Todd. We could just drop by for a little while and then head home before it gets too late."

"No, thanks. I really don't want to go." He frowned as he turned back to watch my brothers.

I picked up my phone and texted back: Sorry but I can't make it tonight. Thanks.

My phone chirped as Dylan almost immediately responded: Why?

"Who's that?" Todd asked.

"It's Dylan." I kept my eyes trained on my phone. "He wants to know why we can't make it."

"Tell him it's none of his business." Todd stood. "I'm going to go climb on the jungle gym. Want to join me?"

I looked down at my rayon and polyester, blue dip-dyed, gauze maxi skirt. "I don't think so."

"Oh well. Your loss." Todd ambled over to my brothers. "Who wants to climb?" he asked.

The twins jumped up and down and cheered as Todd climbed to the top of the jungle gym. I smiled at the sight.

I picked up my phone and typed: Have plans with my brothers tonight.

Dylan quickly responded: Will miss u. See u next time.

I stared at his response. *He'll miss me?* I couldn't help but wonder if there was a hidden meaning there, but I doubted it. After all, he was so popular and handsome. Why would he like a girl like me? The question haunted me for the rest of the day.

Later that night as I climbed into bed and snuggled under the sheet, I wondered if Dylan and his friends were swimming in the pool. Was Kylie there? Were they all drinking?

Dylan's words about Todd echoed through my mind as Buttons snuggled up next to me. Was Dylan right—did Todd and I need to loosen up?

"What do you think, Buttons?" I asked as he pushed his nose under my hand, demanding that I pet him. "Should I have gone to the party so I could enjoy my summer with my new friends? Would you have gone or would you have stayed home?"

I continued to rub his head. Then I opened up my heart and prayed:

*Dear Lord,*

*Thank you for blessing me with a beautiful day at the park with my brothers and Todd. I'm thankful for everything you've blessed me with—my family, my home, and my friends. Please forgive me for not leaving the party when the other kids started drinking alcohol. I just wanted to be included. I've never been one of the cool kids, and it was fun to be a part of the group. Lord, please help me figure out my confusion about Todd and Dylan. Todd has been such a wonderful friend to my family and me, but sometimes I wonder if he's right for me. I don't know where I fit in sometimes. Should I be with someone like Todd, or should I spend more time with Dylan and his friends? I feel caught between them. Please guide me, Lord. Amen.*

I closed my eyes and soon fell asleep.

# chapter eight

Late Monday afternoon, Kylie and I carried two large, heavy bags full of blouses and skirts into the playhouse after spending more than two hours shopping at area thrift stores. We entered the girls' dressing room, and I found jeans, socks, and shoes littered around the room. Annoyance surged through me. "I guess they don't know why we make them baskets for their costumes."

"Uh, no," Kylie muttered. "They don't follow instructions very well, do they?"

"No, they don't." I deposited my bag of skirts and blouses on a counter and marched upstairs to the auditorium. Mr. Muller was talking to Dylan and Britney on the stage.

"Hi, Chelsea," Mr. Muller said. "How are the costumes coming along?"

"Pretty well." I pointed toward the stairs to the dressing rooms. "I have an issue with the way the chorus members are caring for their costumes. I'd like to have a meeting with them. Would that be possible?"

Mr. Muller nodded. "All right." He told the cast members to take a seat in the auditorium.

Dylan stepped over to me and said, "You look like you need to get something off your chest."

"You better believe I do," I muttered. "I'm tired of picking up after everyone."

"You sound like my mom," he said with a grin.

I rushed downstairs to the offending dressing room and grabbed Marni's basket before returning to the auditorium.

"Chelsea wants to make an announcement about your costumes," Mr. Muller said. "Please give her your full attention." He climbed down the steps to the stage, as I climbed up them.

"Hi, everyone." My resentment fizzled, and I suddenly felt self-conscious while standing in front of the entire cast. "Kylie and I brought more costumes in this afternoon, and I'm concerned about them getting mixed up in the dressing rooms. That's what I want to talk about today. Remember how I told you that your costumes belong in your baskets?" I held up Marni's basket, which included her white sneakers, bobby socks, heels, and cutoff jeans that I'd given her to wear during the production. "You can see here that Marni has followed my instructions, and all of the pieces of her costumes are currently in her basket."

Marni, who was sitting in the front row, sat up taller with mock pride.

"Teacher's pet!" someone at the back yelled. Everyone chuckled.

"Let's show Chelsea some respect," Mr. Muller said.

"I was only kidding," the heckler responded.

"As I was saying, your basket is supposed to hold all of your costume pieces that aren't hanging on the clothes racks. I've learned from experience that there can be confusion—especially during the chaos of opening night—if we're not organized from the beginning." I placed the basket on the floor next to me. "That means you keep your shoes, socks, pants, ribbons, and anything else that has to do with your costumes in your basket, or else they'll wind up lost. Kylie and I have a lot of costumes left to finish, so we don't have time to sort through the mess in the dressing room and figure out whose socks are whose. I hope this makes sense."

A few mutters and grumbles rippled through the group.

"All right." I picked up the basket again. "I need to meet with the female members of the chorus in their dressing room." I found Kylie in the sea of faces and motioned for her to follow me.

Kylie and I spent the next half hour distributing blouses and skirts to the members of the chorus. We had the girls model the outfits for us and pinned any pieces that needed to be tailored. We instructed the girls who didn't need their costumes altered to put them on their personalized hangers and hang them on the rack in the dressing room until dress rehearsals began.

After Kylie and I finished checking the last girl's costume, I gathered up the skirts and blouses that needed adjustments. "I'll start making these changes tonight."

"Do you want me to take any of them?" Kylie held out her arms. "I can use my mom's sewing machine to work on them. You know you don't have to do all of the tailoring yourself, right?"

"That would be awesome." I handed her four skirts and two blouses. "How's this?"

"I can handle that. I'll see how many I can get finished before you get off work tomorrow." Kylie folded the skirts and blouses over her arm, and we headed out to the auditorium.

Jimmy appeared next to Kylie and said, "Looks like you have some work to do."

"Yeah, you may have to watch me work on them tonight." Kylie grinned up at him, and I wondered if they were dating. Had they made things official, and she hadn't shared the news with me?

"I'll see you tomorrow, Kylie," I said, starting for the main door.

Dylan opened the door as I reached it and held it open. "Let me get that for you."

"Thanks." I slipped through the door, and he followed me up the stairs to the parking lot.

"You sounded like a natural-born mom," he said.

"Oh yeah?" I laughed. "Thanks ... I think. I guess I inherited that gene from my mom, or maybe it's because I'm sort of like a second mother to my brothers."

"Do you like having little brothers?"

"I adore them," I said. We crossed the parking lot to my car. "I can't imagine life without them. As my mom says, it would be too quiet."

"Huh." Dylan looked as if he were contemplating my words. "I always wondered what it would be like to have a little brother or sister."

"Are you an only child?"

He nodded. "Yeah, it's just me in the house."

I struggled to balance the pile of garments in my arms while I fished my car keys out of my messenger bag.

"Let me help you." He took the skirts and blouses off my arm and slung them over his shoulder.

"Thanks." I found my car keys and opened the rear door, revealing a sea of bags containing material, thread, and dresses in the back of my station wagon. "You can just toss them in there."

"Wow. You've been shopping."

"Yeah, Kylie and I hit a few thrift stores earlier. I need to go through everything. I have a few dresses for the dance scene, but I have to see if I can modify them to make them look more 50s and less modern. I have some ideas."

"You really love doing this, don't you?"

"Absolutely. It's my passion." I slammed the rear door shut and leaned against it. "Costume design is where my heart lies."

"I can see that. Do you like working at the diner?"

"I guess. It's a good summer job, but not something I'd want to do forever." I thought about how mortified I'd felt when I dropped the tray of mugs on Friday, but I wasn't going to share that story with Dylan. I could never admit to him that I'd made a fool of myself at work. I didn't want him to think I was a loser. I wanted to seem cool, like him. I couldn't imagine him dropping a tray full of mugs. I doubted he ever lost his balance.

"So how do you like working for Todd's parents?" he asked.

I paused for a moment, wondering why he asked that. "I like it. Why?"

"I was just wondering. Do you ever get tired of seeing Todd since you see him every day at work?"

"No. He's my boyfriend, so we *like* seeing each other every day."

"Right." Dylan crossed his arms in front of his chest. "How's the coffee at the Fork & Knife?"

I rubbed my chin and pretended to consider the question. "I guess it's good. I'm normally too busy to drink it when I'm at work. The restaurant's really hectic in the mornings, so I stay busy from seven until I leave at eleven."

"Maybe I should try their breakfast some morning. Then I'll give you my assessment of the coffee."

"If you come in, then you have to let me choose your breakfast for you. I know what's good. We have regulars who get the same breakfast every morning."

"I can't imagine eating the same thing every day." Dylan glanced across the parking lot to where Jimmy and Kylie were standing by Jimmy's car. "I guess they're ready to go." He looked back at me. "We're heading to the coffee shop. Want to join us? It'll be my treat."

"No, thanks. I need to get home. I promised my mom I'd cook supper tonight." He looked disappointed, so I added, "I'll take a rain check though."

"Maybe I'll see you tomorrow."

"Sounds good." I climbed into my car and watched as he trotted over to meet Jimmy and Kylie. I wondered why he was showing me so much attention. Why did he want to take me out for coffee? And yesterday he said he'd miss me because I didn't go to his house to swim. I couldn't understand why Dylan would be interested in spending time with me. He knew I was Todd's girlfriend. I didn't think I was giving him the wrong impression, but Dylan still seemed to be pursuing me.

I started my car and backed out of the parking spot. I was putting the car in gear when I saw Kylie approach. I rolled down the window.

She leaned in and said, "Hey, do you want to grab some coffee with us?"

"Thanks, but I can't. Dylan already asked me to join you guys, but I have to get home and start supper." I studied her smiling face and said, "So when were you going to tell me that you and Jimmy are dating?"

Kylie's smile got even bigger and brighter. "It was sort of unexpected."

"Why didn't you tell me while we were shopping today?"

"Because he only just asked me. Remember when you went to talk to Mr. Muller?"

I nodded.

"Well, Jimmy said he wanted to talk to me alone. We went out into the hallway, and he asked me to be his girlfriend. And then kissed me," she squealed, and then she let out a loud, dramatic sigh. "It was amazing, Chels. I'm so happy." She looked across the parking lot to where Dylan and Jimmy were talking. "Maybe we can double-date sometime, huh? Dylan said he wanted you to come to the coffee shop with us. Can't you blow off dinner and join us? Maybe your mom can cook tonight."

"No." I shook my head. "First off, I can't double-date with you and Jimmy unless Todd, not Dylan, comes with us. And, second, I'm not going to break a promise to my mom. I promised her I'd cook tonight."

"I know you're dating Todd, but Dylan really likes you."

I looked over toward Dylan and saw he was watching us. I couldn't deny that Kylie was right, but I didn't want to even consider the possibility. I was going to be loyal to Todd. Not only because it was the right thing to do, but also because I really cared about Todd. I was pretty sure I even loved him, but I hadn't said it out loud. I didn't want to mess up what I had with Todd just because Dylan was exciting and intriguing.

"I really have to go," I finally said. "Call me later and let me know if you need any help altering those costumes, okay?"

"I'm sure I'll be fine." Kylie stood up straight. "See you tomorrow."

"Have fun at the coffee shop."

"See ya." Kylie stepped away from the car.

I steered through the parking lot, waving at Dylan and Jimmy as I drove past them and made my way out to Main Street. As I drove home, I considered Kylie's words. *I have a boyfriend.* So why would Dylan even think about me like that? I found it all so confusing.

As I drove toward the center of town, I sent a silent prayer up to God, asking him to help me find the right path for me.

If Todd was the right boy for me, then why did I feel so drawn to Dylan?

*Please God, show me the right way.*

♫

Back at work at the Fork & Knife on Friday morning, I delivered an order and headed toward the front of the restaurant.

Janie walked up behind me and touched my arm. "Hey, Chels. Some cute guy just came in and asked to be seated in your section. He's over there at table twelve."

"What?" I glanced toward the front of the restaurant and gasped when I saw Dylan sitting there reading the menu. "Dylan?"

I couldn't think of anything more awkward than Dylan actually showing up at the Hughes's restaurant. But why should I feel awkward about seeing Dylan? I hadn't done anything wrong. Yet I knew it was more complicated than that. I hadn't done anything wrong, but the attention Dylan kept showing me made me feel awkward and self-conscious. I hadn't asked for the attention, but I hadn't rebuffed him either.

"Who's Dylan?" Janie grinned.

"He's playing Kenickie in *Grease*. He's a sophomore at U."

"Really?" Janie studied him. "Is he single?"

"Yeah, he is." An idea struck. "Do you want to be his server?"

"He asked for you." Janie's smile was back. "But you could introduce us."

"I'd be glad to."

"Great." She nudged me forward. "Go on. Take his order. Maybe I'll be the one to deliver it for you."

"That's a great idea." I pulled my notepad and pen from my apron pocket and approached his table. "Good morning."

Dylan peered up at me. "Why, good morning. I hear the coffee is good here."

I wielded my pen around like a sword. "I told you I couldn't guarantee that."

"I'm going to have faith that it's good."

"Would you like to start off with coffee, sir?"

"Please." He looked down at the menu. "What do you recommend for breakfast?"

"I would suggest the special." I rattled off the list of foods it included. "How does that sound?"

"Perfect." He folded up the menu and handed it to me.

"Great. I'll be right back with your coffee. Regular or decaf?"

"Regular, please. Thanks." He winked at me, and my stomach fluttered. Was I becoming more attracted to Dylan? Worry gripped me. I briefly wondered if I should ask Janie to fill the order so I could busy myself with other customers and avoid him.

I glanced across the restaurant and spotted Janie taking an order at a table on the far side of the dining room. I wanted her to bring Dylan his coffee, but I didn't want to make a big deal out of it either. Janie was Todd's cousin, and I wouldn't want her to get the wrong impression about my friendship with Dylan.

I entered his order into the register, retrieved the coffeepot, and returned to his table.

"Thank you, ma'am." Dylan handed me his coffee mug, and I filled it to the brim. "How's your morning going?"

"Busy." I carefully placed the mug back on the table. "The regular crowd is here, along with some customers I don't know. It's a typical morning."

"How are the costumes coming along?" His eyes flickered to something behind me and then back to me.

"Pretty well." I rested the coffeepot on the table. "Kylie and I finished up all of the blouses and skirts we had to alter. We still need to finish up the dresses for the dance. We also need to find the boys' suits and ties for the dance." I suddenly felt overwhelmed by the list. "We have plenty to do. The Pink Ladies' jackets are my biggest problem though. I may have to make them at this point. I haven't found the perfect jackets anywhere, and it's too expensive to have regular jean jackets lightened then dyed the right shade of pink."

"Oh." Dylan seemed preoccupied by something behind me. I wondered if he was even listening to me. "I'm sure you'll figure it out," he said.

"Yeah, I guess so."

"So how are you liking the new sewing machine I gave you?"

"It's amazing. I can't get over how much it can do."

"Hi, Todd." Dylan grinned.

I spun around and found Todd studying the two of us with his arms folded in front of his chest. "Todd. Hey. I didn't know you were standing there."

Todd nodded at each of us, but his expression clearly said he wasn't happy to see Dylan. Or maybe he was just unhappy to see me talking to Dylan, because something that looked a whole lot like jealousy was shining in his deep brown eyes.

"How's your day going, Todd?" Dylan asked. He casually lifted his mug and took a sip.

"Fine," Todd's response was barely a whisper. "Yours?"

"Great." Dylan looked at me with a smug smile. "I'm so glad to hear you like that new sewing machine I gave you, Chels. I had a feeling you'd put it to good use."

"Yeah." Heat slowly crept up my neck and into my cheeks as Todd stared at me. I felt as if I'd done something wrong, even though all I'd done was take Dylan's order and fill his coffee mug. "Kylie and I really appreciate how your mom donated her sewing machine to the production." I hoped my explanation of the gift would clarify for Todd how harmless it really was.

"You're welcome." Dylan lifted his mug and said, "You were right. The coffee is delicious." He looked at Todd. "My compliments to the chef." He placed his mug back on the table and started a new conversation topic. "Listen, I'm glad you're both here. I'm having a party tonight, and I'd love it if you two came. My dad is always complaining about how the pool costs too much to maintain, so I'm determined to have friends over as often as possible this summer to show him how much I appreciate it." He grinned. "I just like having friends over. It's the perfect place for a party. So, will you come?"

"No, thanks." Todd shook his head.

"I'd love to," I said. I knew I should have refused the invitation, but frankly, I wanted to go.

Todd frowned at me. "Can I talk to you in private?"

"Sure." I turned toward Dylan. "Your breakfast will be out soon."

"Can't wait." Dylan sipped his coffee.

I followed Todd into the hallway leading out to the loading dock.

He stopped near the exit and faced me. "What's going on, Chelsea?"

"What do you mean?" I knew exactly what he was talking about, but I played dumb anyway. Who was I kidding?

"What is Dylan doing here?" Todd pointed toward the dining room.

"He came in for breakfast."

"And why are you flirting with him?"

"I'm not flirting with him." I could hear the defensiveness in my voice. "I was only taking his order. This isn't a private restaurant, Todd. We don't serve members only, like some country club. I can't control who comes here to eat."

Todd raked his hands through his hair. "You looked really comfortable with him, Chels."

"He's my friend." I tried to keep my tone even, despite my growing anxiety. "I see him every time I go to the playhouse. You haven't been there this summer, or else you'd know that it's not so cliquey like it was during the high school productions. We're all equals there. It's a totally different atmosphere. I'm actually friends with the cast members."

Todd's eyes narrowed. "He bought you a sewing machine?"

My throat grew dry. "Not exactly."

"Really?" Todd folded his arms over his chest. "When I walked over to the table, I heard him ask you if you liked the new sewing machine he gave you, and you said it was amazing. I heard it. You can't deny it."

"I'm not denying it." His expression made me even more self-conscious and nervous, and I struggled to find the right words. "Dylan's mom donated her sewing machine to the production so Kylie and I could use it. Dylan thought I'd like to use something a little more modern than the one Nana gave me."

Todd's eyes widened. "He was in your room and saw your nana's sewing machine?"

"He saw it the day he brought me home after my car broke down. It was no big deal." I shook my head, and my voice became thick with emotion. "We're having the same conversation we had the other day, aren't we? Why don't you just admit it, Todd? You don't trust me."

Todd studied me, and his look of suspicion transformed to hurt. "Why haven't you been honest with me?"

"I've been honest with you."

"No, you haven't. You didn't tell me about the sewing

machine. How could you accept an expensive gift from a guy like that? He's flirting with you."

"He wasn't flirting with me. He only ordered breakfast. And my mom told me to give the sewing machine back to him when the production is over. It's actually helpful to have two machines in my room. That way, Kylie and I can sew at the same time. We can discuss the costumes and work on them at my house instead of her watching me sew or her sewing things at home and not being able to show me what she's doing." I touched Todd's hand. "It's just a sewing machine, and it's from his mom, not from him. You're blowing this out of proportion."

Todd pulled his hand away, and I felt my heart break a little. Was I losing him? I prayed not.

"I'm not blowing this out of proportion." Todd took a step back. "You don't realize how he's manipulating you and trying to manipulate me."

I moved toward him, my hands shaking with anxiety. "He was just being nice. He asked how the coffee was here, and I told him all about our regular customers. I explained that the food is so good that we have regulars who come every day. You should be thanking me."

"No, that's not it." Todd's voice filled with irritation. "He deliberately came here to cause problems between us. That's why he deliberately mentioned the sewing machine in front of me. He probably figured you hadn't told me about it. And he was right. He's trying to break us up."

"You're paranoid."

"Am I?" Todd's smile was wry. "So why are you going to his party without me?"

"Why not?" I demanded.

"I don't want you to go." Todd's voice was softer now, as if he were pleading with me. "Don't go, Chelsea. He wants to take you away from me. He wants us to break up so he can say he stole you away from me. He's one of those players who likes the thrill of a little competition. He focuses on sweet girls with boyfriends and tries to change them. I've seen it before."

"You're wrong. It's not like that. He's just my friend." I took a deep breath. "Please, Todd. Just trust me on this. Go to the party with me, and let me show you how badly you're misjudging him. You'll like the rest of the cast, I promise."

"Please don't go, Chels. If I'm not too tired, we can rent a movie tonight. We can have a nice quiet evening."

"But you won't promise me that we'll see each other tonight. You only say you'll spend time with me if you're not too tired."

"I can't predict the future, Chelsea." He was annoyed again. "I have no idea how I'm going to feel later tonight."

"No." My body quaked as I said the word. I knew I was hurting him, but I couldn't stop myself. "Why should I sit at home alone while my friends go to the party without me? I'm certain Marni and Kylie will be there. I'm tired of sitting at home alone because you're too tired to go anywhere after work. I'm too young to be home alone."

"Well, I'm sorry I have to work." Todd's words were laced with sarcasm as he walked down the hallway and headed back to the kitchen. "Have fun at your party."

"Todd," I called after him as tears filled my eyes. "Are you breaking up with me?" I swiped a tear from my cheek with the back of my hand and willed myself not to fall apart in front of him.

Todd turned around to face me. His eyes were full of regret. "No, I'm not breaking up with you. We'll talk more later."

"Okay." My voice broke on the word, and I cleared my throat.

"I have to get back in the kitchen or my dad will come looking for me." He pushed the door open with his hand. "I'll text you later."

He disappeared through the door, and I slipped into the bathroom. I dabbed my eyes with a cold wet paper towel. I stared at my reflection and wondered how things had gotten so complicated. I'd been thrilled and honored when Mr. Muller had picked me to be head costumer for the summer production. It had been my dream come true. But now I was beginning to wonder if taking the position had been a big mistake since the new friendships I'd made were destroying my relationship with Todd.

As I stood in front of the mirror, I prayed:

*Lord, please help me figure out who I am. Am I the girl who stays home on Friday nights and waits for her quiet, gentle boyfriend? Or am I the girl who goes to parties? I used to be so secure in my close friendships. I was lost after Eileen moved to Philadelphia, but then I met Emily and everything fell into place. Once I met Todd, I felt secure about who I am. I didn't mind sitting at home and hoping he'd come over to watch movies. But now I don't know where I fit in. I don't want to hurt Todd because I really care about him, but I also don't want to spend my summer sitting at home sewing while I wait for him to not be too tired to hang out with me. Help me figure out who I am, Lord, and where I belong. In Jesus's name, Amen.*

The bathroom door swung open with a whoosh. Janie walked in with a confused expression on her face. "Are you okay?"

"Yeah." I forced a smile. "My stomach was just a little upset." I started for the door. "Is Mrs. Hughes looking for me?"

"Yeah. She was starting to freak out."

"Oh, I just needed a minute." I stepped through the doorway and out into the hall. "I guess I have a few orders waiting for me."

"I delivered a few of them for you." She touched my arm and stopped me. "Is everything okay with you and Todd?"

"Yeah." I hoped my expression was nonchalant. "Why do you ask?"

"I just saw him in the kitchen, and he looked upset. He told me you might be in the bathroom." She studied me. "Are you guys fighting or something?"

I wanted to tell her the truth. In fact, I wanted to tell her everything and ask her advice, but I had to deliver those orders or risk losing my job. How could I admit to her that I doubted Todd was the right guy for me? She'd most likely side with Todd since he was her cousin. Even worse, she could tell Todd everything I admitted to her, and I'd risk losing both her friendship and his. I didn't want to lose either one of them—or my job.

"No, we're fine." I pointed toward the kitchen. "I'd better pick up those orders before they get any colder."

"I'll help you." Janie followed me to the counter.

I delivered two meals to table ten and then picked up Dylan's food. When I brought his order to his table, he was texting on his phone. He looked up and smiled at me.

"Here you go." I set the plate in front of him.

"Thank you." He rubbed his hands together. "It smells fantastic."

"I hope you enjoy it." I felt the urge to flee, to get away from the person who had caused so much turmoil between Todd and me. "Can I get you anything else?"

He shook his head and then raised his eyebrows as he asked, "Is everything okay between you and Todd? He seemed upset earlier when he asked to talk to you."

"Oh that?" I shrugged and hoped I looked casual. "Everything is just fine. He had a question about an order."

Dylan didn't look convinced but let it go. "Well, I'm looking forward to tonight."

"Me too." I smiled and then hurried back toward the kitchen.

# chapter nine

Later that evening, I found Marni sitting at a patio table next to Dylan's pool.

"Hey," I said, sinking into a chair beside her.

"Hey, yourself," Marni said. "How are you doing?"

"Fine, thanks." I placed my yellow-and-green-striped purse on the table beside me. "It feels good to relax. It's been a rough day."

"I'm sorry to hear that." Marni passed me a diet soda from the cooler next to her. "What happened?"

I considered how much to share while I opened the cold can. "Everything I touched today turned out badly. I should've gone back to bed and started the day over. I argued with my boyfriend at work, and then I couldn't seem to sew anything without messing it up." I took a long drink, enjoying the feel of the cold carbonation in my throat.

"Yikes." Marni grimaced. "Sounds like a rotten day. I couldn't sing today. My voice wasn't at its best. I need to warm up more."

My eyes scanned the crowd of partiers, and I spotted Kylie and Jimmy sitting close together in a corner on the deck. When they started kissing, regret and envy coiled together in my stomach. I longed to spend time with Todd, and I couldn't stop worrying that I was going to lose him. I touched the necklace he'd given me, and then I glanced down at my phone hoping to find a text from him. It was nearly eight o'clock, and he hadn't kept his promise to text me.

"Chelsea?" Marni leaned close. "Are you okay?"

"Yeah." I spotted Dylan with a group of cast members splashing around in the pool. He looped his arm around the girl who was cast to play Rizzo, and I suddenly felt the impulse to swim. I looked at Marni. "Do you have your bathing suit on?"

Marni shook her head. "No. I was planning to just sit here and supervise."

"Supervise?" I asked.

Marni frowned. "It was a joke. I need to teach you how to understand sarcasm. It was practically offered as part of the curriculum at Ridgewood."

"Oh." I turned back toward the pool, where Dylan was laughing while he kept the actress close. "I want to swim."

"You can swim. I'm not stopping you."

"Chelsea!" Dylan shouted my name over the music. "Join us!"

"There's your cue." Marni tapped my arm. "Go on. I'll sit here and play lifeguard. I'll make sure you don't drown."

My stomach fluttered at the idea of revealing my figure in my plain black one-piece suit. I set any feelings of modesty aside and shucked my denim shorts, olive-green knit tank with a crochet front, and solid back tank top. Whistles and catcalls sounded from the pool. Despite my growing humiliation, I jumped into the water and swam over to Dylan and the rest of the group.

I had expected the water to be a little cold at first, but instead it was warm like bathwater. It was obvious the fancy pool with the pretty white, blue, green, and gold Spanish tile had an expensive heater, which made me envy Dylan even more. I sidled up to Britney who was clad in a yellow string bikini. She smiled at me.

"Glad you could make it, Chelsea. Come on over here." Dylan motioned for me to move closer to him. "We were just about to start running lines."

"Great." I pushed my wet hair back and began treading water while they started from the first scene.

We all laughed together when someone forgot or messed up a line. I felt like a part of the group, and it warmed my soul. I began to wonder if this was a sign from God that I was supposed to be a part of this group. I was meant to be at the party. Maybe God was showing me that I did fit in, and I didn't have to feel guilty for going to the party without Todd.

More tension left my body with every chuckle. Although I was disappointed Todd hadn't texted me, I was thankful I hadn't sat at home waiting to hear from him. I needed this party; it was the best medicine for my stressed soul.

After they'd run through nearly half the script, Dylan held up his hand. "I think it's time for a break. Who wants a beer?"

The crowd cheered, and I silently bobbed in the water.

"Follow me, everyone." Dylan climbed out of the pool and headed toward a nearby cooler. He wrapped a towel around his waist and began distributing icy cans of beer.

I swam toward the other side of the pool where Marni was still sitting at the table drinking her diet soda. "Would you toss me one of my towels?"

"Sure thing." Marni stood and fetched one from my duffel bag.

I climbed the ladder and grabbed for my towel as she held it out to me. "Thanks." I squeezed water from my hair and dried my legs before wrapping the towel around my midsection.

When I turned back toward the group by the cooler, I noticed Dylan was watching me.

"He seems to study every move you make." Marni handed me my can of soda. "I think he has a crush."

"Kylie said the same thing." I sipped the drink. "I don't know. He's way too cool to be interested in someone like me."

"Don't sell yourself short." Marni frowned. "But you may want to think about Todd."

"What do you mean?"

"You said you argued with him earlier. What did you argue about?"

I looked back toward Dylan, and he held up a can of beer as if to offer me one. I shook my head in response. His handsome face formed an exaggerated frown, and I couldn't help but laugh.

"Did the argument have anything to do with Dylan?" Marni's question cut through my laughter like a sharp knife.

"How did you know?" I turned toward her.

"Just a feeling I have. Something tells me Todd has a sixth sense."

"It's apparent that you do too." I studied her and then looked over at Dylan, who was still holding up the beer and watching me.

"He's pretty determined to get you to drink that beer."

"I don't think it's a good idea." Even as I said the words, I wondered what it would be like to try the alcohol.

"You don't have to drink to be a part of the crowd," Marni repeated what she'd told me during the last party.

"I know, but aren't you ever curious?"

"Not really." Marni shook her head. "I had a sip of my uncle's beer once, and it was gross. I prefer the taste of soda."

Dylan moved through the group of cast members gathered near the cooler and started heading in our direction.

"Here he comes," Marni sang the words as she moved back toward the table. "Be strong."

I knew, however, that I wasn't strong. The closer Dylan came, the more curious I was about the unopened beer in his hand.

He held out the can toward me. "Do you want to try one, Chels?"

Maybe it was the urge to unwind after a bad day, or maybe it was the urge to belong. Or maybe, just maybe, it was the temptation to win the approval of the handsome college sophomore with the alluring smile on his face standing in front of me. I don't know what possessed me to say it, but the words rolled off my lips as easily as if I were ordering a cheeseburger and fries at the drive-through.

"Yes." I pushed a lock of wet hair behind my ear. "I'd love to."

Dylan grinned. "Cool."

And there it was—the acceptance I'd longed for ever since I saw him nod at me in the parking lot on the day of auditions.

He popped the can open and handed it to me. I took a sip and immediately fought the urge to gag. The beer was bitter—so bitter that I thought I might spit it right back out. Instead, I forced myself to swallow it and then drank some more. And then more.

"Well?" Dylan's expression was full of anticipation.

"It's ..." I searched for the right word. I couldn't possibly tell him it was disgusting and that I wanted to just keep drinking diet soda with Marni. I had to come up with a response that would satisfy Dylan so he wouldn't banish me to the loser category. "It's ... interesting."

Dylan nodded. "Yeah, it takes some getting used to." He lifted his own beer can to toast me. "But you're doing great."

I took another long swig and turned to Marni. "It's not so bad."

Marni shook her head. "You've made your point. You can stop right now."

"Don't be such a killjoy, Stern. Let her live it up a little. It's her first beer. This is a special occasion." Dylan took my hand in his. "Let's go join the rest of the group." He looked at Marni. "Come with us, Stern."

Dylan held my hand as we walked over to where everyone else was drinking and dancing. Kylie caught my eye, and her grin was wide. Did she think we were a couple now? I knew I was still seeing Todd, but why was Dylan holding my hand? And why was I enjoying it so much?

I knew the answer—I *wanted* Dylan's attention. I wanted him to like me. Did that make me a bad person? I was drinking alcohol. I was holding a boy's hand, and that boy wasn't Todd. I *was* a terrible person, but I didn't seem to care. Instead, I took another long gulp of beer, and my body began swaying in time with the blaring music.

Dylan let my hand fall to my side, and we danced together, moving in time with the music as we faced each other. "Are you having fun?" he yelled over the music.

I nodded and nearly lost my balance.

Confusion settled in as my thoughts became fuzzy. I knew where I was, and I was perfectly aware that I'd drank nearly half the can of beer. I suddenly felt free. And everything was funny. One of the cast members tripped over the cooler, and it was the funniest sight I'd ever seen in my life. A loud, high-pitched laugh came from my throat. I sipped more beer, and the laugh overtook me again, causing beer to shoot out my nose. I wiped my nose and laughed some more. I couldn't control my laughter, but I didn't care.

I finished the beer and then accepted another can from Dylan's waiting hand.

A hand on my shoulder startled me. I turned and found Marni frowning at me. "You should have a beer," I said, my words slurred.

"And you should stop drinking and go home." Marni leveled her eyes with mine. "You need to stop drinking, or you're going to be sick."

"I'm fine." I waved off the comment. "I can handle it."

"I'm driving you home."

I started to protest and then stopped. "Okay."

I danced and drank until I couldn't see straight, and I felt as if I could curl up in a ball and sleep right there on the concrete next to the pool. I was lounging in a chair when Marni stood in front of me and held out her hand.

"What?" I asked, resting my chin in the palm of my hand.

"Give me your keys now, or I will confiscate your cell phone and call your stepfather."

"Fine." I pointed toward my duffel bag, swaying momentarily before I righted myself. "Look in the side pocket."

Marni fished out the keys and held them in front of me. "Are you going to walk to the car or am I going to carry you?"

"I can walk." I stood and stumbled forward.

I heard laughter explode from somewhere nearby.

Marni took my arm and muttered something that sounded like "jerk." I was too busy trying to figure out how to walk to ask whom she was calling a jerk. She loaded me into the car, and I closed my eyes during the ride home.

I felt as if I were stuck in a revolving tunnel. We took a hard right turn, and my stomach roiled. I sucked in a breath and groaned.

"Are you all right?" Marni sounded as if she were standing

two rooms away when she spoke. "Are you going to throw up? I can pull over if you think you're going to be sick."

"I'm okay." I hugged my arms to my middle. "Just get me home."

The normally short journey from Castleton to Rock Creek felt like a lifetime while the car jostled me around and I hugged my waist. Finally, we came to a stop, and I opened my eyes. I stared at my dark house and groaned.

"Do you want me to help you get inside the house?" Marni stared at me from the driver's seat.

"No. I got it." I pushed open the passenger door and staggered around the front of the car. "See you Monday."

Marni handed me the car keys and started walking toward her block. "I'll text you tomorrow."

"Okay." I struggled up the front steps and tried to quietly enter the house. Instead, I tripped over the doormat and slammed my right knee into the wall. A fiery dart of pain shot through my knee, but I couldn't suppress the high-pitched giggles that escaped my lips. I leaned against the wall and bit my lower lip until the giggles subsided. I then started walking through the dark house toward the stairway. I felt something rub against my leg.

"Hey, Buttons." I leaned down and touched my soft cat. He hopped up and rubbed his head against my hand. I lost my footing and stumbled forward, bumping against a small table in the hallway.

I stood frozen in place, silently praying I didn't wake my parents. I couldn't let them see me like this. If they knew I'd been drinking, they would ground me for the rest of the summer and possibly take away my cell phone and car.

Buttons rubbed against my leg again, and I reached down and touched his back. "Let's go to bed, okay?"

I moved toward the stairs and gripped the banister as I made my way up the stairs to my room. I staggered on my way to the bed and was happy to find my pajamas in their usual spot—rolled up in a ball under my pillow.

I swayed as I pulled off my clothes and changed into the pajamas. I left my clothes in a pile on the floor and climbed into bed and snuggled under the covers. My bed had never felt so good.

Buttons leapt up beside me and purred as he curled up next to me. I felt as if my bed were spinning and wished the sensation would stop. I concentrated on one thing—sleep—and soon it overtook me.

♫

"Chelsea!" Mom's voice was loud, oh so very loud, as it sounded from the bottom of the stairs the next morning.

"Yeah?" My voice, on the other hand, sounded more like a frog with a bad case of laryngitis. My head pounded with the strength of a freight train. The light glaring through my window was too bright. I yanked my quilt over my head hoping to hide from the world.

"Chelsea? Are you awake?" Mom yelled louder.

*Why does she have to be so loud? Is she trying to wake the neighbors?*

"Yes." I answered from deep inside my cozy fort.

I heard the sound of shoes pounding up my stairs, and I groaned. Buttons appeared under the covers and rubbed his head on my knee, which set off a firestorm of pain. What had I done to my knee? Images of my struggle with the front door came to my mind, and I groaned again.

"Chelsea?" Mom's voice was closer and still too loud. "You're sleeping away this beautiful Saturday. It's almost eleven."

I peeked out from under the protection of my covers. "Is it?"

"Yes." Mom pointed at my clock radio, which read 10:44. "I'm going to take the boys to their swimming lesson. Are you getting up today?"

"I guess so." My voice was still hoarse.

"You look a little pale." She tilted her head with concern, and her red bob shifted to the left. "Are you okay?"

"Yeah." I tried to clear my throat, but the dryness remained. I suddenly understood why people complained about "cotton mouth" after a night of drinking.

"I have to go now or the twins will be late for their lessons. Do you need anything?"

"No, thanks." I lied. I needed a large glass of water along with a few pain relievers for my throbbing head and my sore knee.

"All right." Mom touched my shoulder. "You take it easy. You can't get sick now. You have costumes to finish."

I glanced over at pile of costumes awaiting my attention and suppressed another groan. All I wanted to do was sleep.

"I guess these are your dirty clothes." Mom picked up the pile from the floor next to my bed. "I'm going to throw in a dark load before I leave." She started toward the stairs. "Call me if you need anything. You're going to be home alone. Jason is running to the home improvement store to get weed killer and a few other things for the yard."

She disappeared back down the stairs, and I snuggled under the covers. Buttons moved up beside me and nuzzled my neck with his cool, wet pink nose.

"It's just you and me, Buttons." I said as I rubbed his velvety ear. "How about we go back to sleep?"

Buttons closed his eyes and purred.

"I'll take that as a yes." I closed my eyes and wondered if I could sleep off the headache. I assumed this was what a hang-over felt like. It was terrible, and I pondered why people chose to drink alcohol. It didn't seem worth the horrible aftereffects.

I felt myself drifting back to sleep when my cell phone pinged from somewhere across the room. "Can you get that?" I asked the cat.

Buttons continued to purr near my neck.

I rolled off the bed and stumbled across the room toward my duffel bag, hoping it was a text from Todd. Maybe he was texting to say he wanted to get together and work things out. I sank onto the carpet and pulled my phone from the side pocket.

I unlocked my phone and found a text from Emily: Hey Chels! R u busy? Whitney & I are heading to the Cameronville Diner for burgers. Want 2 join?

Buttons climbed into my lap and rubbed on my arm as I stared at the phone.

"Should I go?" I asked Buttons as he continued to walk in circles on my lap.

I searched my phone, hoping to find a missed call, voice mail, or text from Todd; but I found nothing. My heart sank as I rubbed Buttons' chin and considered what to do. I wondered if I should call Todd and push him to talk to me. My intuition told me to give him space. Suddenly, I longed to talk to Emily and pour my heart out to her. The lunch invitation would give me that opportunity.

I typed a text to Emily: Hi! Thanks 4 the invite. B there in about 30 mins.

Emily quickly responded: Awesome! C u soon!

"Let's get dressed, Buttons." As I gently nudged Buttons off my lap, I noticed a huge bruise on my aching right knee that was a colorful array of shades ranging from purple to red to blue. "Yikes."

I pulled on my favorite denim shorts, wincing when the fabric brushed against my knee, and I pulled the multicolored peasant blouse I'd designed during my junior year over my head. And then I brushed my long, red hair into a ponytail and tied a multicolored ribbon around it. I couldn't help but think my blouse and ribbon matched my knee.

After applying just a bit of makeup, I took two pain-killers to stop my head from pounding. I made sure Buttons had fresh water and food, and then I headed out to my car. The bright sunlight nearly blinded me when I stepped out the front door. I pulled my large sunglasses from my purse and slipped them on my face.

As I climbed into my car, I decided I'd better text Mom to let her know where I was going.

I quickly typed: Hi, Mom. I'm feeling better. Going to lunch with Emily. Be back soon.

I drove toward the neighborhood entrance and found my thoughts centered on Todd. Guilt rained down on me as I considered my behavior the night before. *What does God think of me?*

I tried to push the thought aside as I merged onto Main Street, but the guilt permeated me completely. I had gone against both my faith and Todd's wishes. If he knew how I'd behaved last night, he'd certainly break up with me. I flipped on the radio and, despite my headache, turned it up in an attempt to drown my thoughts. But they remained.

Fifteen minutes later, I steered into the parking lot at the Cameronville Diner and parked near the back of the lot. My phone chimed as I walked toward the entrance. A text message from my mom said: Glad you're feeling better. Have fun at lunch.

I entered the diner and found Emily and Whitney sitting at a booth near the windows facing Highway 29.

Emily's face lit up with a smile when she spotted me. She was dressed in shorts and a plain gray T-shirt. Her hair was a mass of brown curls falling to the middle of her back. Her mother's simple gold cross hung around her neck, and small gold hoops adorned her ears. She hopped out of her seat and pulled me into a crushing hug.

"I'm so glad you could make it." Emily sat on the bench and slid toward the window to make room for me.

"Thanks." I slipped into the booth beside her and faced Whitney.

"Hey, Chels. How are you?" Whitney wore a pretty blue blouse, and her long blonde hair was styled in a perfect single french braid. Her shiny blue earrings were the perfect shade to match her outfit.

"I'm fine. How are you doing?" I pushed my sunglasses to the top of my head and winced at the bright sunlight coming in through the windows. The brightness caused my head to throb even more. Why did the sun have to be so dazzling today?

"Doing fine. Just busy." Whitney nodded toward the menu. "Do you two know what you want?"

"The usual for me." Emily passed a menu to me. "I'm happy with a bacon cheeseburger, fries, and a cola. How about you Chelsea?"

The idea of food made my stomach churn, but I couldn't just sit there and watch them eat. "Sounds good to me."

"Great." Whitney gathered up the menus and placed them at the end of the table.

The server stopped by, took our order, and left with the menus.

"So Chels," Emily began, "how's the summer production going?"

"It's going well." I shared an update on the costumes, including what I'd finished and what was still on my list to complete. "It's fun, but it's a lot of work. I'll probably be up late tonight making vests for the boys to wear during the dance scene."

The server delivered our drinks and distributed straws before leaving again.

"That's so cool." Whitney swirled her straw in her soda. "I wish I had that kind of talent."

"You have plenty of talent." I unwrapped a straw and stuck it into my tall glass of soda. "How's cheerleading camp going?" I took a long drink, relishing the coolness on my parched throat.

"It's going well. I love teaching the kids. They are so fun."

"And how's Taylor?" I asked.

Whitney grinned. "He's wonderful. He's working full time at the bookstore at the mall and also mowing lawns. He's such a hard worker."

"I'm glad you two are still going strong," I said between long drinks. "He's a really great guy."

"And he's crazy about Whitney too," Emily chimed in.

"How about you, Emily?" I turned toward her. "You're staying busy at the body shop, aren't you?"

Emily nodded. "It's nonstop." She smiled. "And Zander is fine." She poked my arm. "We should all go on a triple date sometime soon. Maybe you can take a night off from sewing, and we can make our guys take us to a movie."

"Yeah." Whitney's eyes lit up. "That would be amazing."

I hesitated, wondering if Todd would consider going out on a date with two other couples. Would he even want to go on a date with me?

"What's wrong?" Emily's smile faded to a look of concern. "You look upset about something."

Whitney gasped. "Did you and Todd break up?"

"No." I shook my head as tears filled my eyes. "Not yet anyway."

Emily clicked her tongue. "Are you guys having problems?"

"Yeah, I guess so." I sipped my drink in an attempt to alleviate the lump in my throat. "We had a big fight yesterday. He's always working, and I've been invited to several cast parties this summer. I want to go to the parties, but he doesn't want me to go. I get tired of waiting at home for him, you know?"

Whitney and Emily shared a look of surprise.

"What?" I looked at each of them. "What are those looks supposed to mean?"

"You never used to go to cast parties," Emily chimed in. "You always said the crew didn't mix with the actors, and the actors partied too hard for you."

"This is our last summer before we leave for college." I glanced at each of them. "I've never been a party girl, but now I want to live it up a little. We're only young once, right?"

"That's right," Emily said, but she didn't look convinced. Her expression seemed to be an equal mix of surprise and worry.

The server arrived with our burgers, and my stomach twisted at the aroma. I didn't want to eat, but I had to at least pretend to. I picked at the fries while Emily and Whitney bit into the juicy burgers.

"I'm sorry Todd won't go with you to the cast parties. He's always seemed so supportive and easygoing." Emily placed her burger on the plate. "Maybe you should ask him to go to one party, and then he'll see why you like going so much."

"That's a good idea. Where are the parties?" Whitney asked, while smothering her fries in a lake of ketchup.

"One of the cast members lives in your neighborhood." I squirted ketchup onto my plate.

"Oh really?" Whitney asked. "Where?"

"Just a few blocks away." I swirled a fry in the ketchup. "His name is Dylan McCormick." I ate the fry, hoping it would settle my stomach. But my aversion to food remained.

"Dylan McCormick." Whitney rolled her eyes. "Yeah, I know where he lives."

"Who's Dylan McCormick?" Emily asked between bites.

"He's the guy who drives that yellow Camaro." Whitney pointed a fry as she spoke. "You and Zander have remarked about his car before. It has a big fancy engine or something."

"Oh right." Emily nodded. "He's over on Radcliff Road."

Whitney wiped her mouth with a paper napkin. "I'm not surprised he's an actor."

"What do you mean by that?" I asked.

"He's known for being a player," Whitney said.

"He's actually really nice." I could hear the defensiveness in my words.

"He acts that way at first, but he's known all over Cameronville for cheating on girls." Whitney emphasized her words with another fry. "He totally broke my friend Ellen's heart. She thought they were dating exclusively, but he was seeing someone else behind her back. She had no idea until she spotted them at a movie. Dylan had told Ellen he was sick with the flu, so she went to the movies with a few friends instead. She spotted him kissing another girl in the lobby. She was devastated."

My stomach tightened—and not because of the untouched food on my plate. Whitney's assessment of Dylan was nearly identical to what Todd had said. Yet I still didn't want to believe either one of them. Dylan was my friend, and I wanted him to be as genuine as I'd hoped he was.

Emily shook her head. "That's awful."

"He's a real partier too." Whitney continued to swing the fry. "I've heard his parties are wild. His parents even let him serve alcohol."

Emily turned toward me. "Is there alcohol at his cast parties?"

I swallowed, and my throat felt like sand. "Yeah."

"You don't drink, do you?" Emily asked, her green eyes probing mine.

"I did last night." My confession was a mere whisper.

Emily's mouth gaped with shock. "You never drink."

Whitney grimaced. "Tell me you didn't drive home."

"No, my friend Marni—who doesn't drink—drove me home. She lives about a block from me. She drove my car to my house and then walked to her house." I studied my uneaten burger. "That's why I'm not feeling so great today. I guess I have a hangover."

"Chels, your parents would be furious if they knew," Emily said.

"I know." I slumped back in the seat. "Todd would too."

"You need to be careful," Whitney said. "You'd be in a lot of trouble if one of Dylan's neighbors reports the party to the police."

"Besides that, it's just not safe to drink. It's not worth the risk if you get hurt or if someone tries to hurt you while you're drunk. If you're bored waiting for Todd, then call me and we'll get together instead."

"Right. Or the three of us can have some girl time."

"Exactly. Todd's right about those parties," Emily said. "I know I sound like your mom, but I'm worried about you. This isn't like you. You've always been so responsible."

"Maybe I'm tired of being responsible." My tone was sharper than I'd planned, and Emily winced. "Sorry," I muttered.

An awkward silence settled over us, and then Whitney changed the subject and began sharing a story about one of the girls she was teaching at the cheerleading camp. Whitney continued sharing stories, and I picked at my food during the rest of lunch.

Afterward, Whitney invited me to go shopping with them, but I told them I had to get home and work on the costumes.

I spent the rest of the afternoon working on the vests and waiting to hear from Todd. I stopped briefly to eat some dinner, and then I went straight back to the sewing machine.

When my phone chimed at 10:30 that evening, I excitedly read the screen. My hope deflated when I found a text from Marni instead of Todd.

She texted: Hi. Was wondering how u r feeling.

I responded: I'm fine. How r u?

She said: Fine. Been worried about u. Text if u need anything.

More guilt rained down on me. I'd been a lousy friend to Marni who had taken care of me last night. I hadn't even thanked her for driving me home. I considered calling her but decided to take the easy way out and just text her. I wrote: Thank u 4 being a good friend. Thanks 4 getting me home last night.

Marni responded with: U r welcome. C u tomorrow.

I said: Ok. G-night.

I went back to sewing. At one in the morning, I'd finally finished three of the four vests for the dance scene. As I crawled into bed, Whitney's warnings about Dylan and Emily's warnings about partying echoed in my head.

And as I drifted off to sleep, a prayer echoed from my heart:

*God, are you there? Are you listening? I hope you are. If so, then please forgive all of my sins, including the drinking, Lord. I know I let you down, and I'm sorry. I don't know what's happening to me. I'm so confused. I want to be friends with Dylan; but Todd, Whitney, and Emily are all warning me to steer clear of him. Aren't we supposed to follow our instincts about people? Isn't it a sin to judge others? Please help me sort through these confusing feelings. Please lead me down the right path. Amen.*

# chapter ten

I followed my parents and brothers into the church sanctuary the following morning and spotted Todd sitting in our usual spot. I hesitated, and my mother hung back too, standing near the back row of pews.

"Are you okay?" Mom asked, lowering her voice as people filed past us.

"Yeah, I'm fine." I swiped my sweaty hands over my blue-and-white polka-dotted sundress. "I'm just tired."

"You were up too late sewing again, weren't you?" Mom frowned. "You can't do that to yourself. You'll wind up sick if you push yourself too hard. You'll get those costumes done on time. I have faith in you." Mom patted my arm, and I wished I had as much faith in myself as she had in me.

My stepfather turned back with a questioning look as he stood next to the pew my family usually occupied.

"Are you going to sit with Todd's family?" Mom asked.

"Yeah." I glanced toward Todd who was studying his bulletin.

Mom's expression filled with concern. "Chelsea, do you need to talk about something?"

"No." I shook my head. "I'm fine."

"Okay." Mom nodded toward our family. "I'm going to go sit down."

"I am too." I followed her down the aisle and stopped next to Todd. "Hey."

He glanced up at me and then scooted over. "Hi." He looked handsome in his gray pants and navy button-down shirt.

I gripped my bulletin as I sank into the seat next to him. "How are you?"

"Fine. You?"

"I'm fine." I waited for him to say something more, but he simply studied me. I longed to read his thoughts. Did he still care about me? Did he even notice that he hadn't texted me like he'd promised?

"How was your weekend?" I finally asked.

"Busy." He rubbed his clean-shaven chin. "I worked all day at the restaurant yesterday, and it was crazy. I know you're normally off on Saturdays, but my dad was considering calling you in."

Relief flooded me. Maybe Todd hadn't texted because he was busy! I was thankful his dad hadn't asked me to work because I'd been in no shape to serve food to anyone yesterday. But at least Todd had thought about me.

"I wish I could get Saturdays off like you do," he said. "I'm wiped out today."

"Well, I may get Saturdays off, but you're making a lot more money than I am."

"True, but you have a social life."

I cringed at the comment.

His expression hardened slightly. "How was the party Friday night?"

I tried to look nonchalant. "It was okay. You didn't miss anything too exciting. Just a bunch of kids swimming and listening to music." The lie jumped from my lips as if I were an old pro at twisting the truth.

Todd's expression relaxed, and he draped his arm across the pew behind me. "That's good."

As I watched his demeanor transform from uptight to normal, I realized I had manipulated him. I had made him believe that nothing happened Friday night and that everything was okay between us. I was ashamed of myself, but I still didn't tell him the truth. *Who am I becoming? This isn't me.*

The organ began to play the prelude, and Todd and I turned our attention toward the pulpit. I stared at the stained-glass cross hanging from the ceiling, and I felt the urge to pray. Yet I couldn't form the words. How could I possibly ask for forgiveness again? God had to be really disappointed in me after all the bad things I'd done this week.

Although Todd had spoken to me before the service began, I felt a different vibe from him during the service. He seemed to deliberately scoot over a fraction of an inch so our legs didn't brush against each other and our arms didn't touch. We were just inches away from each other, but I felt as if we were worlds apart. Were we growing apart?

After the service, Todd and I walked outside to the Fellowship on the Walkway.

"What are your plans this afternoon?" I asked, as we stood with our plates full of cookies.

"I have a few things I need to do at home."

"Oh." I waited for him to elaborate, but he didn't. He remained mysterious, which wasn't like Todd. At least, he wasn't usually so vague with me.

"Todd!" J.J. rushed over to us. "Can you take us to the park today?"

Justin trailed behind him. "Are we going to the park again today?" he echoed.

Todd bent down till he was eye level with them and shook

his head. "I'm sorry, guys, but I can't today. Maybe another time, okay?" He mussed their hair, and they both frowned.

Todd and I made small talk about the weather and his work schedule until our plates were empty. Then he took my empty plate and piled it on top of his.

"Well, I'd better get going." He gave me a weak smile. "I'll see you at work."

"See ya." Confusion and regret flooded me as Todd walked over to speak to his parents. After a short conversation, Todd crossed the parking lot and left in his car.

"Is everything okay?" Mom sidled up to me.

"Yeah." I smiled weakly at her.

"Boys, go find your daddy." Mom pointed to where my stepfather stood talking to a couple of other men. After the boys had followed her instructions, Mom motioned for me to walk with her to the parking lot.

"It's apparent by the look on your face that everything isn't okay." Mom studied me. "Are you and Todd arguing?"

"I guess we are." Why couldn't I just admit the truth?

"Do you want to talk about it?" Mom stopped by the back bumper of our van.

"I don't know what to say. We're growing apart. We don't seem to have the same things in common anymore."

Mom draped her arm around my shoulders. "Don't give up on him too easily. God puts special people in our lives for a reason, and I believe Todd is very special."

"I do too, but I don't know what to say to him."

"God will give you the words. Just listen."

I nodded. "I'll try."

♫

Thursday afternoon, I exited the playhouse and made my way to my car. Kylie and I had spent the afternoon distributing more costumes to the cast members and making sure they fit properly. But all day long my thoughts had revolved around Todd.

Although we'd made small talk at work all week, I still felt the emotional distance between us. My mother's words lingered in the back of my mind, and I held out hope that I'd find the right words to say to Todd to make things better. I hoped God would grant me those words.

"Chelsea!" Kylie shouted my name and pulled me from my sad thoughts. "Hey, Chels!" She ran up to me. "Come to the coffee shop with us."

"Who's going?" I asked, as I unlocked my car.

"Jimmy, Dylan, and I are going." Kylie stuck out her bottom lip. "Please, Chels? You never go with us."

I looked at my watch and saw it was almost five o'clock. "I guess I could go for a little while."

"Great!" Kylie jammed her thumb toward the playhouse. "I'll go tell Jimmy and Dylan."

"Hey." I touched Kylie's arm to stop her from leaving. "Things are getting pretty serious between you and Jimmy, huh?"

Kylie seemed to glow. "He's amazing."

"That's great. I'm really happy for you."

Kylie grabbed my arm. "Chels, he is the *best* kisser." She fanned herself for emphasis. "Just incredible." She rushed back to the building. "See you in a minute!" she called over her shoulder.

I hoped Kylie's relationship with Jimmy would be more successful than mine and Todd's.

Twenty minutes later, I was sitting next to Dylan at the coffee shop. I sipped my large cup of Earl Grey tea while they enjoyed their icy coffee drinks.

Kylie and Jimmy sat across from us, and Jimmy's arm encircled her waist. They looked so content, and I couldn't help but feel a twinge of envy. I wasn't interested in Jimmy. Instead, I missed having that kind of closeness with Todd.

"You're awfully quiet," Dylan quipped, as he moved his straw up and down in his half-full drink. "Are you regretting ordering that tea instead of a cool iced latte?"

"No, it's not that. The tea is fine. I'm just tired." I looked at Kylie. "We were up late working on those dresses for the dance scene, weren't we?"

Kylie nodded with emphasis. "Yes, we finished them around midnight."

"They look good," Jimmy said. "You both did a great job."

"Thanks." Kylie smiled up at him, and he kissed her.

I sipped my tea and averted my eyes. I felt awkward watching them kiss.

"Did I ever tell you the story about that party at the frat house last semester?" Dylan asked. "The one when the police came?"

"No, man, you didn't." Jimmy grinned. "I need to hear that story."

Dylan launched into a story involving alcohol, loud music, stair diving, and togas. I sipped my tea and wondered what Todd was doing. Was the restaurant full of customers? Was he going to have to work late tonight? Was he thinking of me?

My phone began to ring from somewhere inside my messenger bag. As I reached for it, Dylan shook his head.

"Let it ring," he said. "You have to hear what my best friend said when the officers arrived at the house."

Jimmy laughed. "This story is hilarious!"

Kylie grinned.

I, however, was more interested in who was trying to call

me, but I continued listening to the story. My phone chirped, indicating the caller had left a message, and my curiosity piqued.

Almost immediately, my phone began to ring again.

Suddenly, I turned to Kylie. "It's Thursday, right?"

"Yeah." Kylie looked at me as if I were crazy. "All day long."

I looked at my watch—it was 6:15. "Oh no!" I stood and gathered up my bag as panic hit me. "I was supposed to pick up my brothers by six."

"Uh oh." Kylie grimaced. "You're late. I bet that's your mom calling."

"I gotta go." I didn't wait for my friends to respond. Instead, I pulled my phone out of my bag as I rushed to my car. My mother's phone number was displayed on the screen. "Hey, Mom."

"Chelsea Grace! Where are you?" my mother's voice boomed through the speaker. "You were supposed to pick up the boys fifteen minutes ago!"

"I know, I know." I fumbled with my keys and finally unlocked my car. "I'm so sorry. I'm on my way home now."

"Where are you?" she asked again, her voice more angry this time.

"I forgot, Mom, okay? I'm really sorry." I clicked my seat belt and started the car. "I'm on my way now."

"Do you realize they charge me seven dollars for every minute we're late picking up the boys?" Mom demanded. "Do you have any idea how much money that is?"

"I'll pay you back, Mom. I promise." I backed out of the parking space and drove toward the exit.

"That's not the point, Chelsea."

"You're right. I'm sorry." I blew out a sigh. "I'm on my way. Let me go now so I can concentrate on driving."

"Text me when you get the boys. We'll talk about this later." The phone line went dead.

Trepidation filled me as I navigated the rush hour traffic toward the church where my brothers attended day camp. I knew I was going to be in trouble when I got home. I had to do something to make it up to my mother. Ideas floated through my mind as I merged onto Main Street and headed toward Horseshoe Road.

I finally reached the parking lot of Morning Star Church at 6:45. I slammed the car into park and ran through the entrance to find Miss McClane, the day camp director, standing in the lobby with my brothers.

"I'm so sorry." I worked to catch my breath. "I lost track of time."

Miss McClane peered at me over her half glasses. "You're forty-five minutes late, Chelsea. I called your mother several times to let her know that I'll have to charge her."

"I realize that, and I sincerely apologize. It was completely my fault. It was my job to get my brothers today, and I messed up. It won't happen again."

"See that it doesn't." Miss McClane jammed a hand onto her wide hip.

"Have a good night." I glanced down at my brothers who looked bored standing there with their backpacks at their feet. "Let's go, guys."

"Bye, Miss McClane!" My brothers said in unison.

"Good-bye, boys." Her voice was sugary sweet when she responded. At least she was nice to my brothers.

"You're late," J.J. announced as we walked to my car.

"Yes, I'm aware of that." I tossed their backpacks into the back of my car. "Climb into your seats, guys." I sat in the driver's seat and quickly texted my mother to tell her I had picked up the twins. I then turned around to make sure they were safely strapped into the backseat.

"You were *really* late," J.J. said as he snapped his seat belt over his booster seat. "Miss McClane had to call Mom."

"I think it's cool." Justin strapped himself in. "We got to play longer."

"Well, we're not going to play when we get home." I started the car and drove out of the parking lot. "We have things to do."

Justin moaned. "I want to play."

"You both need baths," I explained. "And we also have to eat."

"Fine." Justin folded his arms over his middle. "But I won't smile."

"I'll take my bath first," J.J. said.

I smiled, silently amused at the difference between my brothers. They were mirror images but acted completely different. J.J. was happy to comply with any rule thrown at him, while Justin moaned and complained about everything.

By the time my mother arrived home, the boys were bathed and changed into their pajamas, and they were eating hot dogs with macaroni and cheese. A pan of roasted chicken was baking in the oven. I'd also made a salad, and a bowl of green beans was ready to throw into the microwave.

My mom entered the kitchen and kept her eyes focused on my little brothers. "Hello, hello."

"Mom!" J.J. sang, opening his arms for a hug.

Mom hugged J.J. and kissed the top of Justin's head. "That looks yummy."

"Chelsea made it." J.J. pointed at me. "It's delicious."

Justin rubbed his stomach in agreement. "My favorite."

Mom looked at me, and I pointed to the table set with three salads. "I have chicken in the oven, and I have green beans ready to warm up."

“I’m going to go shower, and Jason is working late tonight.” She dropped her bag by the doorway. “I’ll eat later.”

My heart sank when she rejected my supper. I knew I’d messed up, but I’d hoped I could make it right by lightening her load.

“That’s fine,” I said, suppressing my disappointment. “I’ll take care of the dishes.”

After the boys finished eating, I sent them off to the family room to play until bedtime. I cleaned up their dishes and then made myself a plate of baked chicken and green beans.

I was eating the chicken when Jason arrived home. I popped up from the chair and made him a plate of food. “I hope you’re in the mood for chicken.”

“Great.” He smiled. “Everything smells good.”

After washing up in the bathroom, he sat down at the table. I wondered if he was angry with me too.

“How was your day?” I asked, attempting to ease into a conversation.

“Long.” He dribbled ranch dressing onto his salad. “We have a big project due at the end of next week. I have to make a presentation to the regional director.”

“Oh.” I pushed the green beans around on my plate. I couldn’t take the guilt anymore. “I guess you already know I messed up today.”

“With the boys?” Jason stabbed at his salad.

“Yeah. What else?” I slumped in my seat.

“Your mom called me.” His expression was sympathetic. “It’ll be okay, Chelsea. We all make mistakes.”

My voice was thick with emotion. “I made supper and got the boys ready for bed hoping to ease the tension. She went straight upstairs to shower. I don’t know what to do.”

“She’ll get over it. You know how your mom gets. She has

to blow up first and then she's fine." He stuffed a fork full of salad into his mouth.

"Should I go talk to her? I can't stand the silent treatment."

Jason finished chewing and then wiped his mouth with a napkin. "No, she'll come to you. Just give her time to cool down. It will all blow over."

"I feel terrible. You know the twins mean the world to me. I would never deliberately forget them."

"Chelsea, we know you love your brothers. Everything will be fine. Your mom loves you. She's just stressed. She has a new office manager at work who is giving her a hard time about everything she does. I think everything went wrong at work today. Having the day camp call her was just the icing on the cake."

I heaved a deep breath, trying to calm my frayed nerves. "Okay. I'll give her time."

"So, tell me about your day. How are the costumes coming along?"

I gave Jason an update and then he talked about his day. After we'd finished eating, he went to see the boys, and I cleaned up the kitchen. I was loading the last of the utensils in the dishwasher when my mother walked in, clad in her favorite terry cloth robe with matching pink slippers. Her hair was wet, and her expression was sullen.

"We need to talk," Mom said as she stood by the counter.

"I know." I kept Jason's advice in the back of my mind. I needed to let her calm down. "I'm really sorry, Mom."

She folded her arms over her chest. "I know you're sorry, but I don't think you realize how much this is going to literally cost us. The fee for today is three hundred and fifteen dollars. You were forty-five minutes late."

"I'm sorry," I repeated with consternation. "I don't know what else to say. I'll pay you back after I get paid."

Mom ran her hands through her wet hair. "That's not the point, Chelsea. I need you to be responsible. I thought you were capable of doing this for me, which is why I didn't text you to remind you."

"Maybe you should've texted me. It slipped my mind. I'm only human." I poured the soap into the dishwasher, closed it, and hit the Start button.

"I know you're only human, but your family needs to come first."

"I realize that, Mom. My family *does* come first. It always has." My voice shook more as I grew angrier. She knew I loved my family. How could she accuse me of not caring about my brothers? "I messed up this one time. Don't act like I do it all the time. Besides, I'm only eighteen, and I have a lot going on this summer. I'm working part time, and I'm the head costumer for the theater."

Mom studied me. "Where were you when I called? What was so important that you forgot your little brothers?"

"I was out with my friends."

"Out where?"

"The coffee shop." I cleared my throat. "Look, Mom, I'll pay you back. I get paid next week." I motioned toward the stairs. "I can go write you a check right now if you want. I'll go get my checkbook."

"No." Mom touched my arm. "You need your money for school. I'm trying to make a point with you. You can't blow off your brothers to go hang out at the coffee shop with your buddies."

My body shook with my growing frustration. "Mom, I didn't blow them off. I made a mistake. Kylie was pressuring me to go out with her, Jimmy, and Dylan. I forgot it was Thursday. That's all that happened. I just wanted to have some fun. This is a special summer, and I want to make it memorable. I understand you want me to be responsible, and I am. You can count on me. Stop treating me like I mess up all the time because I don't."

"You're grounded for two weeks." Mom crossed her arms over her chest again. "That means no parties, no hanging out with friends, no coffee shop dates."

"Two weeks?" My voice rose nearly an octave as I contemplated the cast parties I was going to miss during that time and the possible dates with Todd—if there were going to be any more dates. "That's a bit harsh."

"I don't think it is." Mom shook her head. "Harsh is getting a phone call that your children are waiting for a ride and not being able to leave work to pick them up. You have two weeks to prove to me that this won't happen again. If there is a next time, then you *will* pay the fee to the day camp."

"Fine." I swallowed some angry words as I headed to my room. I flopped onto my bed and stared at the ceiling while I thought about my punishment. Buttons curled up next to me and purred while my frustrated thoughts flew through my mind. Not only would I miss all of the parties, but I would also miss out on seeing Todd if he decided he wanted to see me. My eyes moved toward the pile of costumes I needed to fix before I could get to my last big project—creating the Pink Ladies' jackets. I needed to stop wallowing in self-pity and sew.

Pushing aside my aggravation with my mother, I showered and then kissed my brothers good night before sitting down in front of the sewing machine. I was working on changes to the dress that the Miss Lynch character would wear to the dance, when my phone began ringing. I assumed it was Kylie checking to see if I was okay after rushing out of the coffee shop.

"Hello?" I answered without looking at the number on the display.

"Hi." It was Todd's voice.

"Todd?" I was so shocked that I nearly dropped the phone.

"You sound surprised to hear from me."

"Well, I am." I leaned back in my sewing chair. "What's going on?"

"I just thought I'd say hi. We haven't really talked in a while. How was your afternoon?"

"Awesome," I snorted sarcastically. "How was yours?"

"Busy. The restaurant has been slammed. I guess you had a bad day?"

"Yeah." I told him what had happened when I went to the coffee shop and how I'd forgotten to pick up the boys. "So now I'm grounded for two weeks."

"Yikes."

"I can't go out at all. This is totally going to ruin the rest of my summer."

"It's only two weeks, Chels. You'll be fine. It could've been worse. She could've taken away your car and your phone. At least you're not totally cut off from the world."

I paused, at a loss for words. I was shocked to hear Todd taking Mom's side. "Yeah, but I wanted to just pay the late fee and be done with it. Now she has to drag it out for two weeks. I told her I was sorry. I don't know what else I can do."

"I know, but I guess she feels like she has to do something to get your attention. Sometimes parents overreact because they think they'll get through to us that way."

"Believe me, she got through. She didn't have to prolong it."

"She just wants to make sure you know how upset she is. I think two weeks is reasonable. My dad would've gone totally overboard and taken my car, my phone, and maybe even made me pay the fee too. You're lucky your parents are so easy on you."

"Easy on me?" I sat up straight. "I don't think my parents are easy on me at all. They're pretty strict."

"Not really. You only have to work part time this summer while I'm working almost sixty hours a week. Emily is working full time too. I'd love to spend my afternoons at the playhouse. You've got a totally slack summer, Chels. You have no idea how lucky you are."

"What?" Exasperation boiled anew within me. "I don't think I have it easy at all. I'm busting my butt making all the costumes for a huge cast, plus I have to help take care of my brothers at home. Today I worked at the restaurant, sewed, delivered costumes, picked up my brothers, bathed my brothers, made dinner for them and my parents, and cleaned up after everyone. And now I'm sewing again. I don't think I've got it easy at all."

"Chelsea, I've already worked fifty-five hours this week, and I've spent most of it on my feet in a greasy kitchen. I really don't have much sympathy for you."

I bit my lower lip. "I have to go."

"Are you angry?" He sounded genuinely surprised. "I was only being honest."

"My mom is calling me," I lied. "I'll see you tomorrow." I hung up the phone and then stared at it. A feeling of dread coiled in my stomach as I wondered if Todd and I were going to break up.

Buttons crawled onto my lap and gazed up at me. I ran my fingers over his ginger-colored fur. "I'm confused, Buttons. I don't understand why things have suddenly taken a turn for the worse. Is it me? What's wrong with me?"

I looked back at the dress I'd been shortening. Suddenly,

I'd lost all of my ambition and decided to go to bed. The dress would be there tomorrow.

After turning off the sewing machine and the lights, I climbed into bed. Buttons curled up next to me and purred while I rubbed his chin in the dark. Closing my eyes, I sent a quick prayer to God:

*God, Mom told me you put special people in our lives. I assume that means these people turn into lifelong friends and maybe even more than that. If Todd is one of those special people, then why am I constantly fighting with him? Please help me figure out who my real friends are. And God, please soften my mother's heart toward me. I made an honest mistake today, but I feel like she's punishing me too harshly. I keep wondering if people are treating me differently because I'm changing. Is it me, God? If so, then why am I changing? Why is everything so complicated? I don't know who I am anymore. Please help me make sense of it all. Thank you, God. Amen.*

# chapter eleven

The following morning, I found Todd sitting on the edge of the loading deck out back, fiddling with his cell phone. His white chef uniform was riddled with stains, evidence that he'd been busy all morning. The exit door banged shut behind me, which announced my approach.

"Hi." Todd glanced over his shoulder at me before returning his full attention to his phone.

"Your mom told me you were out here." I stayed by the door.

"Yeah, this is my new place to escape to during breaks." He kept his eyes trained on his phone. "I like it out here because the air doesn't smell like grease, and I can get away from my dad's nagging."

"Makes sense." I folded my arms in front of my chest. "I guess you've been pretty busy. I haven't seen you all morning."

"Yup. Busy."

I watched him for a moment, wondering if he'd look at me again. We hadn't spoken since I'd arrived at work, and now my shift was over. My stomach had been in knots all morning while I worried about our relationship. I prayed God would give me the words to make things right between us, but nothing came to me.

"I guess I'll see you." I turned to go.

"Did you want something?"

His question caught me off guard. I turned back around and found him watching me with an unreadable expression.

"What?" I asked.

"I thought you might want something since you came out here."

"Yeah," I said exasperated. "I wanted to talk."

"So talk." Suddenly, I felt like I didn't even know him. His expression wasn't intimate or familiar. He looked like a stranger on the street, not the boyfriend I'd shared all my secrets and dreams with since April. "Well?" he asked impatiently. "What did you want to talk about?"

"I felt like things weren't settled between us last night."

"Really?" He raised his eyebrows. "Maybe that's because you hung up on me."

"I had no choice. You were putting me down."

He shook his head. "No, I wasn't, Chelsea. I was disagreeing with you. There's a difference. We've disagreed about things before, but you've never hung up on me. I guess that shows how little you think of me."

"No." I took a step toward him. "That's not it at all. I'd had a really bad day, but you just lectured me instead of listening to me."

"No, I didn't. I listened to you and offered my opinion. I do think you got off easy with a two-week grounding. My father's punishment would've been a whole lot harsher if I'd done something irresponsible like that." He paused as if to collect his thoughts. "You've changed."

"How?"

"When I first met you, I thought you were the coolest girl at CHS. You were so sweet, and you always had a smile for everyone—even the kids in the cast who were totally into themselves and treated the production crew like dirt." He paused. "You used to be happier."

"I'm still the same person, Todd. I just have a lot going on."

"No, that's not it. I feel like I don't know you anymore. The Chelsea I knew wouldn't have hung up on me last night. In fact, she probably would have agreed with me."

A lump formed in my throat. "I don't know what to say." I felt my throat constrict even further.

"Neither do I." His expression was pained.

"Are you breaking up with me?" I asked, my voice hoarse with emotion.

"I'm not breaking up with you. I'm just making an observation about our relationship. I guess we're going through a phase. It just feels to me like we're growing apart. Maybe it's all the stress over leaving for college." He glanced down at his phone and then stood. "I have to get back to work before the warden comes looking for me. I'll see you at church on Sunday."

He slipped past me and entered the kitchen. I felt as if a piece of my heart had disintegrated.

♫

Later that afternoon, I stood in the girls' dressing room at the playhouse, labeling hangers and hanging up dresses and skirts on a long metal rack. I knew I should be home working on the remaining costumes. But I'd found that mindless tasks like organizing kept me from focusing on my raw emotions and the questions that had been spinning around in my brain ever since my conversation with Todd. Were we growing apart? A feeling of dread began swelling inside of me.

I was hanging up the last prom dress when Dylan stopped at the door of the dressing room.

"Hey. Kylie said you were working in here."

"Hi." I forced a smile and continued organizing.

"What's up?" He leaned against the doorframe. "You seem stressed."

"I got in a lot of trouble yesterday." I told him about my arguments with Mom and then Todd.

"That's harsh," he said.

"That's what I thought." I hung up the dress I'd tailored for the actress who was playing Miss Lynch. "I apologized and offered to pay my mother back, but she decided to ground me instead."

"Don't let your parents bring you down," Dylan said. "This is your last summer before your life completely transforms. And Todd was holding you back anyway. If he wants to waste his summer at the restaurant, let him. You're not like him. You know how to have fun. Carpe diem, Chelsea! Seize the day! Seize the summer!"

I nodded slowly and wondered if his assessment was right. Should I forget my feelings for Todd and just seize the summer?

Dylan tilted his head. "You think I'm nuts."

"No, it's not that. I was just thinking ... Todd said I've changed and he doesn't know me anymore."

"That's because he doesn't know how to have fun." Dylan walked over to me. "You're cool, and he's not." He gently lifted my chin with his finger until I made eye contact with him, and then I got lost in his blue eyes for a moment. "Just forget about Todd. You and I will have some fun this summer."

"Okay." I stared up at him. "You're right. Seize the summer."

"You got it. See you later, Chels."

♫

"I hope these leather jackets fit," Kylie said as we carried a load of costumes inside the playhouse.

"They should," I said. But I felt a pit form in my stomach as we walked down the hallway toward the boys' dressing room. It was already Tuesday, and the dress rehearsals were coming up fast. I needed to get the rest of the costumes done quickly, or I might get in trouble with Mr. Muller. "We need to get all of the Burger Palace boys in the dressing room so we can check the jackets."

"I'm on it." Kylie dropped the load of costumes on the counter and headed out to the hallway. "Listen up!" she called. "I need Kenickie, Sonny, Doody, Roger, and Danny in the dressing room. Pronto!"

I grinned. Kylie certainly wasn't shy.

The actors filed into the dressing room, and we laid out their costumes. We had them try on the shirts and vests for the dance. I breathed a sigh of relief when they all fit the guys perfectly. Then we had them try on the black leather jackets we'd decorated with their names in rhinestones on the back. Again, all five of them fit perfectly.

"The Burger Palace boys are all set," Kylie said as she hung up a vest and shirt on a hanger marked for Doody.

"I'm so relieved we're almost done with the costumes." I slipped Roger's shirt and vest onto another hanger.

"Great job, ladies." Dylan shucked his leather jacket and handed it to me. The aroma of leather filled my nose. "You're the best costumer I've ever worked with, Chels, and I've been in a lot of musicals since I was a kid."

"Thanks." I looked up at him, wondering if his compliments were genuine. Was he just a player like Whitney and Todd said?

Kylie and Jimmy walked into the hallway, leaving Dylan and me alone in the dressing room.

"Do you need help?" Dylan glanced toward the rack.

"No, I think this is it." I hung up the last shirt and vest.

"What are you doing tonight?" He rested a foot on the bottom of the rack.

"Sewing. I have plenty of work left to do."

"That's a shame." Dylan's exaggerated mournful expression reminded me of my neighbor's basset hound. "I was hoping you'd be free."

"Why are you giving me that hound dog face?" I laughed.

"I'm having a few friends over." He trailed a finger up my bare arm, and the lingering warmth of his touch surprised me. "It won't be the same without you, that's all."

"You're having a party on a Tuesday night?"

"Why not? Every summer night is the perfect night for a party."

I hesitated, embarrassed to remind him that I was grounded. "That may be true, but I still can't go." I pointed toward the rack. "I have four pink jackets to make from scratch, not to mention Sandy's black velvet one-piece for the final number. I'm way behind. And frankly, I'm surprised Mr. Muller hasn't taken my head off yet. I should've been done with all of the costumes by now. Dress rehearsals are coming up quick."

"Why can't Kylie do some of that for you?"

"Kylie is fantastic, but I have more experience than she does. I have to give her guidance."

"So she's not much of an assistant then, huh?" Dylan frowned.

"No, it's not that. You can't learn costuming unless you practice. I'm helping her improve." I straightened the hangers as I spoke, making sure all of the costumes were organized alphabetically on the rack. "Mr. Muller says this summer production is all about learning and growing as theater professionals."

"Right." He snorted sarcastically. "It's supposed to be fun. So come out tonight and have fun with me."

I was tempted, but my conscience warned me to say no. "I'd better sit this one out."

"Oh, come on, Chelsea." Dylan touched my arm again. "Look, I really like you. I want you to come over tonight."

*Dylan likes me?* I'd suspected he did, but I couldn't believe he'd said the words out loud. Confusion twirled through my mind. I felt a strong desire to say yes to him and give in. How could I *not* go to his party after he admitted that he likes me? I opened my mouth to say yes, but suddenly remembered I was grounded.

"Look, Dylan, I really want to go, but I just can't."

"Why not?" he smirked. "Are you washing your hair tonight?"

"I wish it were that simple. Not only do I have a lot of sewing left to do, but I'm also grounded."

"Grounded? What are you, a middle school kid?" He looked incredulous. "You just graduated from high school—how can your parents still ground you?"

"Remember last week when I forgot to pick up my brothers from day camp and it cost my mom $315?"

"Oh right." He shook his head. "Well, just come over anyway."

"My stepfather will hear my car leave the driveway. I can't come."

"Sure you can. You deserve a break after working so hard on these awesome costumes." He smiled. "I'll pick you up. It's no big deal. Your parents will never know you're gone if you sneak out."

I gnawed my lower lip. "I can't disrespect my parents like that."

"All right." He started for the door and then turned to face me. "Let me know if you change your mind." He stepped into the hallway and looped his arms around two female members of the chorus who were passing by the dressing room. "What are you girls doing tonight? Want to come to another awesome pool party?"

The girls grinned up at him, and I gritted my teeth. *I thought he liked me.* The urge to go to the party grew stronger, but I knew I couldn't do it. Not only would I get in deeper trouble if I got caught, but I knew I could never live with myself if I defied my parents that way.

Still, the desire to go continued to haunt my thoughts.

♫

Later that night I stared at the ceiling while Buttons snuggled next to my head. The image of Dylan inviting those two girls to the party had remained in the back of my mind all evening. I wanted to be a part of his inner circle. I hated feeling left out. After all, I was supposed to seize the summer!

I glanced at the clock and saw that it was a quarter past midnight. I knew my parents were already asleep since they faithfully went to bed by ten thirty during the week. And I was pretty sure I could easily sneak out since their bedroom was on the other side of the house from the front door.

*But how will they feel when they find out I defied them?*

I turned toward Buttons' pink nose. "I want to go to the party, Buttons," I whispered. "What do you think?"

Buttons rubbed his cold, wet nose against mine.

"Aww." I smiled. "Thank you for the kiss." My eyes moved back to the clock. "If I sneak out now, I'll stay for just an hour. That would be okay, right, Buttons?"

Buttons closed his eyes and purred.

"I'll take that as a yes." I hopped out of bed and fetched my phone from the bottom of my purse. I unlocked it and texted

Dylan: Hi. Can u pick me up at the corner of Rock Lake Loop and Grey Slate?

My heart raced as I awaited his response. Until I started hanging out with Dylan two weeks ago, I'd never done anything blatantly disobedient in my life. And now I was going to sneak out of the house and go to a party while I was grounded. Oh, if my mother only knew.

My phone chimed, and I jumped with a start.

Dylan texted: Awesome! Be there in 10.

I changed into a pair of denim shorts and a blue T-shirt. I pulled my hair up into a ponytail and put my flip-flops in my purse before I tiptoed down the stairs. My heart was pounding in my chest and echoing in my ears as I moved through the hallway and toward the front door. A tiny voice in the back of my mind told me to turn right around and go back to bed, but I kept moving forward.

I slipped out the front door, pulled on my flip-flops, and rushed to the corner. I kept glancing back toward my house while I waited for my ride. Guilt washed over me, but I did a mental headshake. *I'll be home in an hour. Mom and Jason never have to know. And what they don't know can't hurt them.*

A few minutes later, Dylan's Camaro roared around the corner and stopped.

"I'm glad you changed your mind," he said, as I climbed into the passenger seat and buckled my seat belt.

"Me too," I said.

"The party is just getting interesting." He steered out of the neighborhood and turned onto Main Street. "You haven't missed much."

"Great." I tried to slow my racing heart as he talked some more about the party. I couldn't believe I'd just sneaked out!

When we arrived at his house, the usual group of friends was gathered around the pool. Loud rock music blared from the surround sound.

"Chelsea!" Kylie shouted from the pool. She and Jimmy were swimming with a few other cast members. "I'm so glad you made it!"

I waved to her as I made my way to a patio table. I sank into a seat beside Marni, who was clad in denim shorts and a bright yellow sleeveless top with embroidered detail and a round neckline. She wore a matching headband, holding back her brown corkscrew curls, and large yellow hoop earrings. I immediately thought of my yellow bangle bracelets that would match her outfit perfectly. "I see you're in your usual spot," I said.

"I told you I'm the adult supervision." Marni tilted her head in question. "I thought you were grounded for two weeks."

"I am." I smiled, and her mouth gaped.

"Did you climb out a window or something?"

"Actually, I used the front door. My window is too high off the ground since I'm in the bedroom over the garage."

"Chelsea!" Marni smacked my arm. "I didn't know you were a rebel."

"I honestly didn't know I was either."

Dylan approached the table with three cans of beer in his arms. He sat next to me and held one of the cans out as an offering. "Beer?"

"Sure. I've already broken one rule tonight. I might as well make it two." I popped open the can and took a long drink.

Dylan snickered and held out another can toward Marni, who shook her head. "You sure? I'll drive you home."

Counting on her fingers, she said, "First off, I am *not* going to get in a car with you after you've been drinking. And second, I'm not going to drink alcohol. I come here to see my friends and relax. I don't come to drink, make a fool of myself, or get sick."

"Suit yourself, but Chelsea and I are going to live it up, right?" Dylan held out his can for a toast, and I tapped mine against it.

"You got it." I took another drink and turned toward Marni who was sipping a diet cola. "Is it against your religion to drink?"

Marni shook her head. "No. I just don't want to. My parents aren't big drinkers either." She pointed toward the can of beer. "Can you honestly say you like drinking that more than soda?"

I paused. The truth was I thought it tasted horrible, but I wanted to be cool. I wanted Dylan to like me. "It's okay." I sipped some more to prove I really liked it.

"Yuck." Marni scrunched up her nose. "Give me a diet soda any day."

"So you *have* had alcohol before," Dylan chimed in. "You said you hadn't."

"That's not what I said." Marni wagged a finger at him. "I said I don't drink. I didn't say I'd never had a drink."

"What did you drink then?" Dylan said.

"I already explained to Chelsea that I had a sip of my uncle's beer once." She scrunched up her face again and stuck out her tongue. "Yuck."

I laughed at her look of disgust.

Dylan waved off the comment. "You must've had cheap beer."

"Whatever you say." She sipped her soda.

I considered her decision not to drink. "So it's not a religious issue for you?"

"No." Marni shook her head. "It's not against my Jewish beliefs to drink, but I like to live conservatively. My parents are very conservative too. They don't drink, and they live quiet lives."

"Mine too," I said.

"I'm a Christian, and I drink. It's not a big deal for me or my parents." Dylan took a long drink from his beer can.

"How do you justify that?" I asked.

"What do you mean?" he asked, popping open another can of beer.

"How can you call yourself a Christian and party like you do?" I gestured around the deck and pool area. "My parents would say the behavior at this party isn't 'emulating Christ.' "

"Jesus drank wine," Dylan said matter-of-factly. "Why wouldn't Jesus want us to have fun after working hard all day? We're not hurting anyone. We're including all of our friends, so we're not being exclusive. Right, Marni?"

Marni held up her hand. "I'm staying out of this one. You already know my feelings about drinking."

I contemplated Dylan's words. "I guess you're right." A familiar song started blaring through the speakers, and I looked at Marni. "Want to dance?"

"I'd love to!" Marni stood, and I followed her to join the others who were dancing on the deck.

The weight of my guilt soon evaporated as I lost myself in the buzz from the alcohol and the loud music.

# chapter twelve

Chelsea!" Mom's voice roused me from a deep sleep.

I rolled over and moaned. My head felt five times its normal size, and it pounded as though someone were hitting it repeatedly with a sledgehammer.

"Chelsea Grace!" Her voice was louder this time. She was getting closer, but I didn't care. I rolled back over and pulled my pillow over my face. *Maybe if I hide under the covers, she'll go away so I can sleep off this headache in peace.*

"Chelsea!" Her voice was muffled, but I could tell she was standing right over me. She grabbed my arm and shook it. "Chelsea, it's after seven! You overslept!"

"Oh no!" I sat up too fast, and my stomach lurched. "I'm going to be sick."

"Chelsea?" Mom asked.

I ran past her and flew down the stairs to the bathroom just in time.

Afterward, I washed my face and stared at my pale reflection. My complexion resembled one of my nana's antique porcelain dolls. And my hair looked redder than usual next to my skin. I tried to remember what happened last night. Most of the events were a blur, but I remembered dancing with Marni, drinking more beer, and then Marni drove me home again.

According to my clock radio, I'd climbed into bed around three this morning.

"Are you okay, Chelsea?" Mom asked through the bathroom door.

"Yeah, I think so." I leaned against the sink as my stomach roiled. How was I going to get through the day when I felt like this?

"You might have the stomach flu. We're getting a lot of cases at the doctor's office. Do you want me to call Mrs. Hughes and tell her you're too sick to work this morning?" Mom offered.

"No." I opened the door. "I'll go."

"Well, I'll call her and at least tell her you're going to be late. Go get dressed and see how you feel."

"Thanks, Mom. I'm sure it will pass." She studied me with worry and sympathy in her brown eyes, and a wave of guilt washed over me. How could I lie to her like this?

Thirty minutes later, I steered my car into the parking lot of the Fork & Knife. Mrs. Hughes was standing at the hostess station when I walked in.

"Good morning," I muttered.

"How are you feeling?" Mrs. Hughes's eyes were cold and her expression hard.

"I'm better now, thanks." I nodded toward the back. "I'll clock in and get to work."

"Please do," she said. "We're busy this morning."

Somehow I managed to go through the motions of taking and delivering orders with a phony smile pasted on my face. My stomach twisted and nearly rebelled at the aroma of bacon, eggs, and coffee.

"Here you go," I said, placing two plates piled high with breakfast foods on an elderly couple's table. "Enjoy your meal."

"Miss," the man snapped, pushing his plate toward me. "I ordered sausage, not bacon."

"Oh, I'm so sorry, sir." I tried to smile but wanted to cry because of the lack of empathy in his sharp tone. "I'll get you an order of sausage right now."

I hurried to the kitchen. Todd was standing in his usual spot behind the griddle while his father checked an order. The loud hum of the fans exacerbated my unrelenting headache.

"Hey." I did my best to sound friendly despite Todd's steely stare. "I need an order of sausage pronto. I have an angry elderly man at table four who wanted sausage instead of bacon."

"Sure thing." Todd grabbed a plate and filled it with links.

"Do you think that's too much?" I asked, taking the plate from his hand.

"It will make the customer happy. When the customer is happy, my dad is happy."

"Okay. Thanks." I lingered for a minute, longing for him to say something more to reassure me that we were still friends.

He studied me for a long moment but said nothing more, so I turned to go. Before I could push through the kitchen door, a strong hand stopped me.

"Wait." Todd held my arm. The intense look in his chocolate-brown eyes caused my heart to thump faster and faster until it matched the tempo of the thumping in my head. "I heard you were sick this morning."

I nodded.

"Did you go to one of Dylan's parties again last night?"

"No," I said quickly. "I'm grounded, remember?"

He released his grip and gave me a disbelieving look. "Chelsea, I can read you like a book. I know when you're lying. Not only that, but you were perfectly healthy yesterday, and now you look like you were run over by a train. Just because I don't party doesn't mean I don't know what my friends look like after they do." His expression softened. "What's going on with you? You know you can talk to me."

The concern in his face caused my eyes to fill with tears. I wanted to pour my heart out to him. I wanted to tell him how confused and miserable I was. But I couldn't speak. Instead, I stood there feeling lost and stupid.

Mrs. Hughes stepped into the kitchen. "You both need to get back to work."

Todd kept his eyes on me for a long moment before he returned to the griddle.

Mrs. Hughes then turned her full attention on me and gave me a hard look. "Mr. Hughes runs a tight ship, and he doesn't put up with tardiness." Then her expression softened slightly. "Chelsea, you've always been such a good worker, and you're usually very conscientious. I'd hate to see you lose your job because you made some bad decisions. You're a smart girl. Don't give in to peer pressure." She pointed toward the dining area. "Now go deliver that sausage before it gets cold."

"Yes, ma'am," I said.

♫

Later that afternoon, in the girls' dressing room at the playhouse, I held up two swatches of pink denim material for Kylie and Britney to judge. "So which one do you like better for the Pink Ladies' jackets?"

Britney pointed to the lighter color pink. "I think I like that one."

Kylie nodded. "I agree. It's pinker than that other pink, you know? It's like a little girl's room kind of pink."

"You're right. Okay, we'll go with that one. Now I need to take jacket measurements for all of the Pink Ladies. Would you round them up for me?" I asked Kylie.

"Sure." She turned to Britney and said, "Let's go find your pink posse."

While I waited for the actresses to appear, I fished my notebook and a pencil out of my bag.

Marni popped her head into the room and said, "How are you feeling today?"

"Okay." I frowned. "My head is still killing me though, and I overslept this morning."

"That's why I stick to diet soda," Marni said, stepping just inside the doorway.

"Thanks for driving me home again last night. I owe you."

"It's no problem," she said with a wave of her hand. Hearing some kind of commotion outside the room, she took a quick look down the hallway. "Mr. Muller is heading this way, and he looks like he's on a mission. I'll see you later." She scurried out into the hall and headed in the opposite direction.

"Miss Morris." Mr. Muller's voice echoed in the empty dressing room. "Britney tells me you're just now choosing material for the Pink Ladies' jackets."

"That's right," I said, removing one of Sandy's outfits from Rizzo's section of costumes on the rack.

"Why aren't those jackets finished by now?"

"I told you last week I couldn't find any jackets to buy that fit my budget. And the only theater in the area that's done *Grease* recently lost all of their costumes in a fire. So I have to make them."

He tapped his clipboard. "You do realize we're doing dress rehearsals for the scenes in act one at the end of next week, right?"

My stomach tightened. "I will get them done, Mr. Muller."

He wagged a large finger just millimeters from my nose. "Don't make me regret picking you as head costumer."

"I won't, sir." Tears threatened, but I took a deep breath to stop myself from crying in front of him. I was determined to remain professional.

"I want to see those jackets completed by a week from Friday. No excuses!" He stomped out of the dressing room.

I stared after him and wondered how I was going to make that deadline. My original plan had been to have the jackets done by opening night. After all, they were just jackets, not vital pieces of the scenery. Now I had no choice but to sew nonstop, which was impossible since I had a job and two little brothers to look after, and I also craved a social life.

I stared at the rack of costumes and wondered how this day could possibly get any worse.

"What was Muller flapping about?" Dylan appeared in the doorway, looking attractive in jean shorts and a blue polo shirt that accentuated his eyes.

Although he was gorgeous, I really wished Todd were here instead. The thought shocked me for a moment.

Dylan stepped into the room, and his expression filled with concern. "Are you all right?"

"Yeah." I shook off any thoughts of Todd and cleared my throat. "Mr. Muller just gave me a hard time because all the costumes aren't finished yet. I'm not one of his favorite people right now."

"What's the big deal?" He sat on a folding chair. "They'll be done before the first performance, right?"

"That's what I had planned. I'm going to stop and pick up the material on my way home today and start working on the Pink Ladies' jackets tonight. I have the pattern ready to go."

"Don't worry about him." Dylan leaned way back in the chair, balancing it on two legs. I cringed, hoping he wouldn't topple over. "So how are you feeling today?" he said with a knowing smile.

"Rough. I was late for work this morning." I grimaced. "Not a good day for me."

"You really were buzzed when you left my house."

"No, I think I was all-out drunk. I'm sure glad Marni drove me home."

"Did you get caught sneaking back in?"

"No, thank goodness. I was worried I would, though, since I tripped and ran into a wall." I rubbed my right shoulder where it was still sore.

"Do you want me to pick you up again tonight?" he offered. "Just the two of us can hang out and have a couple beers."

"No, thanks." I motioned toward the costume rack. "I'll be busy working on the jackets so I don't lose my glowing reference from Mr. Muller."

He stretched. "Just text me if you change your mind." He stood and disappeared into the hallway.

I finished organizing the last of the costumes, packed up my bag, and headed into the hall. When I spotted Todd leaning against the wall, my mouth gaped. He straightened, and I immediately wanted to retract my mental compliments for Dylan. Todd looked fabulous in his tight jeans and gray Henley shirt. His dark eyes reminded me of a lion's.

"Todd," I said. "What are you doing here?"

"Mr. Muller is ready for me to start working on the lighting plan for the show. My dad hired a part-time cook so I can be here in the afternoons." He jammed his hands into the front pockets of his jeans. "Did you forget I'm involved with the production? You've probably forgotten all about me since you've been so busy partying with Dylan."

"That's not true." My throat constricted. "I haven't forgotten about you." I took a step closer to him and lowered my voice. "In fact, I've missed you. I've missed *us*."

"Is that why you're whispering right now?" He nodded toward the end of the hallway where some cast members were laughing loudly at one of Dylan's stories. "I'm sure you don't want Dylan to know you still like me because then he'll think you aren't cool."

"Todd, no." I shook my head. "That's not it at all."

"Look, I overheard your conversation." He pointed toward the dressing room behind me. "I was starting to walk in to say hi to you, but then I heard Dylan's voice and stopped."

"How much did you hear?" My voice was thin.

"Let's talk somewhere in private." He pointed toward a storage room, and I followed him inside. After the door shut behind him, he said, "I know you lied to my parents."

"What?"

"You were late this morning because you were hungover, not because you were sick."

"Todd, I just— "

"Please don't try to talk your way out of it." He held up his hands to shush me. "I'm not going to tell my parents, but you should know they aren't very happy with your performance at work lately. You need to stop drinking and partying, or you're going to lose your job." His eyes narrowed. "I feel really stupid now, Chelsea, because I've defended you more than once to my dad. I defended you again today when he went off because you were late this morning. I'm not going to defend you anymore. I can't stand up for you when you refuse to tell me the truth. You're on your own."

"Todd, I'm so sorry." I couldn't stop a tear from trickling down my cheek. "I never meant to hurt you."

"You say you didn't mean to hurt me, but that just shows how little you've been thinking of me lately. I'm tired of being an afterthought."

"You're not an afterthought." Panic rose within me. *I can't lose him!* I reached for his arm, but he moved away. "I already told you I miss you. Why don't the two of us go out tonight? I can probably sneak out, and we could grab something to eat and catch a movie."

"No, it's too late." His expression was a mixture of anger and pain. "I'm done, Chelsea. It's over."

"What?" My heart thudded. "You can't be saying— "

He nodded. "Yes, I am. I really liked you, Chelsea, but you're not the person I thought you were."

"Yes, I am." I nodded emphatically to show I really meant it, and tears streamed freely down my cheeks. "Let me make it up to you."

"I don't think you can. I'm not sure I could ever trust you again. Chelsea, it's time we face the fact that we've grown apart and just end things. And then you'll be free to party with Dylan without having to worry about lying to me. Do whatever you want, but don't expect me to be waiting for you when it all falls apart." Todd stepped toward the door. "I'll see you at work."

"Hey, Todd!" P.J. Bishop, the stage manager, called from the top of the stairs at the end of the hall. "Let's go!"

"Coming!" Todd called back. "I gotta go. Take care, Chels." He stalked down the hallway toward the stage.

"Todd," I said, trailing after him into the hall. "Todd, I'm sorry!" I said louder this time. But he didn't bother turning around. I touched my necklace as I watched him disappear.

"Hey, don't worry about him." Dylan appeared behind me and patted my shoulder. "He's a total loser. You're better off without him." He grinned at me and continued on his way.

I couldn't move. I stood frozen in the middle of the hallway while the rest of the cast quietly filed past me on their way to the stage, shooting curious glances my way. I may have been surrounded by people, but I had never felt so alone. Guilt and regret flooded my heart and soul as the tears began to flow again.

"Chelsea." Marni grabbed my arm and propelled me through a small dressing room and into the attached bathroom. She locked the bathroom door and faced me. "Everything is going to be okay."

"No," I blubbered, wiping my hands over my cheeks. "Nothing will ever be okay again."

"Just try to calm down." Marni handed me a paper towel, and I wiped my eyes and face before blowing my nose. "Todd looked upset when he walked past me. What happened?"

"He broke up with me." Saying the words out loud somehow made it real, and my heart shattered into a million pieces. "It's over."

"Oh, Chelsea." Marni hugged me. "Tell me what happened."

Between sobs, I shared my story while Marni listened sympathetically. When I'd finished, I said, "Thank you for coming to my rescue out there. I'm sure the whole cast witnessed my humiliation."

"Don't worry about what anyone else thinks." She hopped up and sat on the bathroom counter.

"I can't believe he broke up with me." I wiped my eyes as more tears flooded them. "Oh, who am I kidding? I had a feeling this was coming. We've completely grown apart in just a few weeks' time. But he's such an amazing guy. We really connected when we first met, but now it's just over."

Marni shook her head. "I think he still cares about you."

"Really?" I felt a glimmer of hope spark inside me.

"I've seen the way he looks at you. He wouldn't have looked so upset if he didn't care about you at least a little bit."

My bottom lip quivered. "He said he's tired of being an afterthought."

"So show him you still care about him," Marni said matter-of-factly. "He's doing lights now, which means you'll see him at work and here. Well, that's after you get those denim jackets finished. You're going to be busy sewing for a while."

"Yeah, I am." I looked at my watch and gasped. "I'd better get going."

"Let me walk you out." Marni hopped down from the counter and walked beside me to the parking lot.

"Thank you." I hugged her when we reached my car. "You're a really good friend."

Marni smiled. "Now, go make the best Pink Ladies' jackets ever. Call me if you need help. I actually know how to sew a little."

"I'll keep that in mind." I opened the driver's door and climbed in.

After a quick stop at the fabric store to buy pink denim and thread for the jackets, I was almost halfway home when my phone chimed. While stopped at a red light, I glanced down at my phone and read a text from Emily: Hey! Can I stop by? I'm near your house.

I quickly responded: Yes! Be there soon!

Emily was sitting on my front porch when I pulled into the driveway. Her red Honda was parked on the street. She smiled and waved as I climbed out of my car, but her smile soon faded as I got closer.

"What's wrong?" she asked.

"Do you want to come in?" I asked, opening the front door. "Jason is bringing dinner, so I don't have to cook tonight."

"Sounds good." Emily stood.

When we stepped into the house, Buttons greeted us with a rub and a few loud meows. I filled his food bowl, grabbed two sodas from the refrigerator, and we moved into the family room.

"You've been on my mind all day," Emily said. "I had the strongest urge to call you, so I decided to stop by instead."

"It must be a God thing because I had the worst day ever." I flopped onto the sofa and opened my soda.

"What happened?" Emily sat across from me in my stepfather's favorite brown leather recliner.

I told her the whole story, starting with my mother grounding me and why, sneaking out to the party, waking up late and hungover, and ending with Todd's confrontation at the playhouse. Emily's eyes got bigger and bigger while I talked. When I finished, she stared at me in disbelief.

"I'm sorry you and Todd broke up," she said after a long pause. She looked as if she had more to say.

"What are you thinking?" I asked. "You're staring at me like I'm crazy."

"You're not crazy. But I feel like I don't know who you are anymore."

"What?"

"Chelsea, I've never seen you drink alcohol, and I've never known you to deliberately go against your parents. But last night you actually snuck out—even though you're grounded—got drunk, and then went to work with a hangover this morning?" She looked disgusted with me.

"Yes." I felt my whole body stiffen as I tried to think of what I could say to defend my actions. I'd expected to receive sympathy and compassion from Emily, not judgment.

"Wow. That's all you have to say?" Emily shook her head. "I can see why Todd is so upset."

"Why?"

"You've totally changed. You used to be so responsible." Emily pointed toward the coffee table where a framed photo of my brothers stood. "I can't believe you forgot to pick up the twins last week. That's not like you, Chels."

"Well, I can't believe you're sitting there and judging me like you're so perfect," I snapped. Anger surged through me. "You act so pious, but I remember how you acted when you first moved here. You were so mean to Zander when he was trying to be your friend."

"Whoa." Emily held up her hands in surrender. "I was being honest with you, Chelsea. That's what friends do. I don't want to argue with you about which one of us has acted the worst." She stood. "Maybe I should go."

"Wait." The anger and defensiveness drained out of me. I couldn't bear the thought of losing her too. "Please stay. I'm just so confused. You're right—I've changed. I don't know who I am anymore. I feel lost."

She returned to her spot in the recliner. "It sounds like you need God."

"Yeah." My voice was hoarse. "I think you're right."

"Remember how I was when my dad and I first moved here? I'd lost my mom, and I felt like I couldn't pray. It seemed pointless." Emily's voice wavered. "I felt so alone. But then I realized God was there beside me all along. Right now you may feel like you're alone, but you're not. You have me and your family and your friends at the playhouse. And most of all, you have God. You need to open your heart and listen to what God wants to say to you."

I nodded. I knew she was right.

"Maybe you should spend some time reading your Bible tonight." She smiled. "*Before* you start working on those jackets."

"I think I will."

Emily's expression became serious again. "I think you're headed down the wrong path with Dylan. You need to stop going to those parties—especially while you're still grounded. You're going to make things so much worse for yourself if you get caught."

"I'm just having fun. Dylan is a good friend."

"I'm not so sure. It sounds like he purposely pursued you even though he knew you were dating Todd. And he's encouraged you to drink and sneak out of the house in the middle of the night. What kind of friend does that? Plus, I talked to Whitney, and she's heard some bad stories about him from more than one girl who got burned." She folded her hands in her lap. "Please be careful, Chels. I don't want anything to happen to you."

I wondered why she was being so dramatic. "Nothing bad is going to happen, I promise."

"I don't like the idea of you staying out late and drinking alcohol." Emily grimaced. "Now I sound like my dad, but I'm worried about you. You're not acting like yourself. You've never taken such big risks before. I don't want you to get hurt—emotionally or physically."

"My friend Marni drove me home last night. She never drinks alcohol."

Emily glanced at her watch. "I'd better get home. Call me, okay?"

"I will." I walked her to the door. "Thanks for stopping by."

"You're welcome." She hugged me. "I mean it when I say I'm worried about you, Chels. Please do some praying tonight. Think about everything you're doing. You need to take a step back and look at yourself. You and Todd were so good together. Don't throw everything away for some cute college guy with a cool car and a big house with a pool. Todd is real and down to earth. And he's crazy about you."

I scowled. "I wouldn't be so sure about that. He just broke up with me because I'm not the girl I used to be."

"He's just protecting himself because you hurt him when you chose Dylan's party over him, and then you lied about it." Emily touched my arm. "Think about it. You know I'm right."

I leaned against the front door. "I don't know."

"Don't let Todd go so easily. You'll regret it if you do." As she walked down the porch steps and out to her car, she looked back and said, "Call me."

♫

Later that night, I took a break from cutting out the pieces for the first Pink Ladies' jacket and pulled out my Bible. I flipped through it until I came to the book of First John. My eyes stopped on verse seven of chapter one: "But if we walk in the light, as he is in the light, we have fellowship with one another, and the blood of Jesus, his Son, purifies us from all sin."

I reflected on what Emily had said to me earlier. Was I walking in the light? Was my behavior pleasing to God?

I knew the answer to both of those questions: No. My behavior wasn't pleasing to God or anyone else—not even myself. So why was I going through this whole transformation? What did it mean? Where did I belong—with friends like Todd and Emily or friends like Dylan and Kylie? And where did Marni fit in? She liked to go to parties, but she didn't drink. Instead, she took care of me. None of it made any sense.

As I fell into bed and snuggled with Buttons, I opened my heart to God like Emily had suggested and I prayed. After silently crying while reciting the verse from First John, I eventually fell asleep.

# chapter thirteen

On Sunday morning, I spotted Todd sitting with his parents in church. However, instead of sitting at the end of the pew next to the aisle, like he usually did, Todd was sitting in the center, leaving no room for me. I followed my parents and brothers to our spot across the aisle, and I sat on the end next to Mom. Studying my bulletin intently, I tried not to give in to the urge to look over at Todd.

Mom leaned toward me. "Are you okay?"

I shook my head and kept my eyes trained on the bulletin. "Can I go sit in the back?" I whispered.

"Why do you want to go sit by yourself?"

I looked up at my mother. "Is he looking at me?"

"Who, Todd?" She glanced over my shoulder at him, and I wanted to crawl under the pew to hide my humiliation. "No, he's talking to his father. What happened, Chelsea?"

"He broke up with me." It was painful to admit that out loud to her.

"Oh, sweetie." Mom rubbed my back, and I willed myself not to cry again.

I'd cried myself to sleep last night as I thought about seeing Todd in church this morning—the first time since our breakup—and the reality of the loss hit me all over again.

"Do you still want to move to the back of the church?" Mom asked.

I shrugged.

"Let me tell you something." Mom leaned closer to me and lowered her voice. "If you stay here and pretend like nothing happened, then he won't know how much it hurts. You'll appear strong."

"But I'm not strong."

"Yes, you are. You're a strong, intelligent, and beautiful young lady. I know how it feels, Chelsea. I still remember how much my first boyfriend hurt me." Mom brushed a strand of red hair off my face. "But you'll have more boyfriends. Someday you'll meet the man who will love you completely." She rubbed my back some more. "The hurt will fade. It *will* get better, I promise."

"Thanks, Mom." I leaned my head against her shoulder and felt like a little kid again. I was so thankful for my mom. I knew I could count on her to give me love and support just when I needed it most.

I spent the remainder of the service trying to concentrate on Pastor Kevin's words and to ignore the urge to look at Todd.

When the service ended, I followed my family out of the sanctuary. When we reached the door to the hallway, I touched Mom's arm. "I'm going to head home and get back to sewing."

"Okay." Mom hugged me. "Love you."

"Love you too."

When I left the church building, I saw Todd standing at the top of the stairs, leaning against the railing.

He met my gaze, and my heart turned over in my chest. His lips were turned down in a pout, and his eyes resembled molten chocolate. He was wearing charcoal khakis and a light grey button-down shirt. He gave me a quick nod, and I returned the gesture. I suddenly remembered the necklace he'd given to me for our third anniversary last month. I hadn't taken it off since he'd put it on me. And then it hit me: This coming Thursday would have been our four-month anniversary.

My fingers flew to my throat and touched the heart-shaped alexandrite stone. His eyes followed my hands.

We stared at each other, and my pulse raced. I wanted to tell him I was sorry. I wanted to beg him to give me another chance. But no words formed on my lips. Instead of speaking, I just stared into his gorgeous eyes and gripped the necklace until my knuckles turned white.

Mrs. Hughes, who'd been speaking to another church member a few feet away, moved over to us. "Hello, Chelsea. How are you?"

"I'm fine, thanks." My voice was strained.

She turned to Todd. "Are you ready to head out, Todd?"

"Yeah." Todd straightened and turned toward the parking lot. "See you at work tomorrow."

"Yeah," I muttered, as I watched him walk away.

When I got home, I dropped the necklace into my jewelry box and prayed that somehow I could repair the damage I'd done to my relationship with Todd. I spent the rest of the afternoon working on the first of the Pink Ladies' jackets.

♫

The next few days blurred together as I stayed up late sewing, dragged myself through my shift at work, and did more sewing in the afternoon and evening. My conversations with Todd were limited to short comments about food orders.

By Thursday evening, I'd completed the first Pink Ladies' jacket. I was finishing adding the words *Pink Ladies* in sequins across the back when my phone dinged. I dug out my phone from beneath a pile of pink material and found a text message from Dylan: Tired of sewing? Come swim for a bit!

I glanced at the clock and saw it was after eleven. My eyes moved toward the pile of material that was already cut for the next jacket. I longed for a break, but I knew it was wise to either keep working or get some sleep. I'd been up past midnight every night this week, and bags were forming under my eyes.

I texted back: Can't. Still behind on PL jackets.

Dylan quickly responded: PLEEEEASE? Just for an hour?

I stared at the phone. I could take a break for just an hour. That seemed perfectly acceptable since I'd been working hard all day.

Dylan texted again: Well . . . ? Should I come get u?

I continued to stare at the phone and weighed the pros and cons of sneaking out. Mom had taken pity on me after learning that Todd and I had broken up, and she commuted my sentence by a couple days. So I wasn't grounded anymore. But if I got caught sneaking out tonight, then she'd probably ground me again—and for longer this time.

At the same time, it didn't really matter that she'd canceled my grounding since I didn't have time to go out anyway.

My phone dinged with a longer text from Dylan: If u don't respond soon, I will drive to ur house and ring the doorbell until u come down and talk to me.

I texted back: U r relentless.

Dylan: U have no idea. So am I coming to get u?

I responded: Meet u on the corner in 10.

Dylan: Cool!

Twenty minutes later, I was sitting next to Marni with my legs dangling in the warm pool water. I sipped a beer while she drank a soda. Dylan and his friends were swimming, and he periodically glanced over at me and grinned.

"How are the jackets coming along?" Marni asked.

"I finished Rizzo's tonight. I was just adding the last of the sequins when Dylan texted me." I took another gulp of beer.

"So you've finished one already?" Marni asked, surprised.

"Yeah, just one. The others should go together more quickly now that I have one under my belt." I stared across the pool where Dylan swam with Kylie, Jimmy, and Britney. "I'm so behind, it's not even funny."

"Then why are you here now?" Marni asked.

"I guess I'm tired of working so hard. I've done nothing but deliver greasy breakfast food and sew since Monday morning. I'm running on a few hours of sleep every night, and I'm watching my summer evaporate."

"I guess I can't blame you for wanting a break. But isn't Kylie helping you with the jackets?"

I shook my head. "She's never cut or sewn denim material before. It's a little more difficult."

"I know."

I studied Marni. "You've sewn denim?"

"One time." Marni shrugged as if it weren't a big deal. "I helped my cousin make a jean skirt once. I mostly watched, but I paid attention. Do you want my help, Chelsea?"

"No." I waved off the offer with another sip of my beer. "I've got it."

"Mr. Muller said you had to have all four of the jackets done by tomorrow, right? What's going to happen when he finds out they're not finished?"

"I'm not going to go to the playhouse until they're done."

Marni looked unconvinced. "Doesn't he have your phone number?"

"I won't answer."

Marni grimaced. "Do you really think that plan is going to work?"

"No, but it sounds good."

"You're crazy." Marni's expression softened. "So how are things with Todd?"

"Nonexistent. He only talks to me when it's work related. This morning he asked if I needed more bacon for an order." I paused. "Today would've been our four-month anniversary."

Marni shook her head. "I'm sorry."

"Thanks." I looked toward Dylan. "It's my own fault. I messed up, and now I have to face the consequences."

Marni touched my arm. "I'm here if you need to talk."

"Thanks."

Dylan swam over. "Are you going to join us?"

"I don't have my suit on." I glanced down at my denim shorts and bright orange T-shirt.

"So?" Dylan grabbed my ankles.

"No!" Panic gripped me. "No, Dylan!"

A few claps and hoots erupted throughout the group.

"Dylan ..." I gritted my teeth. "Please don't."

"Is your phone in your pocket?" he asked.

"No, it's in my purse over there." I pointed toward the table behind us.

"Good." Before I could brace myself, he yanked me off the side of the pool and into the deep end.

I screeched just before I hit the water. When I surfaced, I gasped and pushed wet hair out of my face while treading water to stay afloat.

"How could you?" I demanded, furious that my clothes were now soaked. "I don't have any dry clothes with me!"

"Got you." He winked at me, and I splashed him in the face.

"You jerk!" I chased him across the pool, splashing him as best I could.

When I caught up to him, we both started laughing. It was the first time I'd really laughed since Todd had broken up with me. It felt good to release all of the stress that had been weighing on me for the past week.

"Want to get out and get a drink?" he offered.

"Yeah."

He climbed out of the pool ahead of me and brought me a large beach towel.

When I followed him up the pool ladder, my wet clothes clung to me. I felt self-conscious as he wrapped the towel around me.

He looked apologetic. "Do you want to throw your clothes in the dryer? You can borrow something of my mom's until they're dry."

"No, I'll be all right."

"Let's get a beer." He retrieved two cans from the cooler and motioned for me to follow him to an empty table.

I hugged the towel around my midsection and sat across from him. "I didn't think you'd actually pull me in." I opened the can and took a long drink. "I thought you were just teasing."

"You're a good sport." He held up his can to toast me. "Thanks for not drowning me."

"I considered it." I laughed.

"I'm glad you came over tonight. I've missed seeing you at the playhouse this week."

*He's missed me?* The comment surprised me. "I've been really busy. The costumes aren't going as planned."

"Really? I thought you were Super Seamstress." He raked his fingers through his wet hair.

"I did too, but this project has really humbled me. I've spent all of my free time this week sewing, and I have only one of the Pink Ladies' jackets completed."

"That's not good." He took another swig of beer. "I hope the rest of them come together quickly."

"Thanks." I glanced across the pool to where Kylie and Jimmy were kissing. "They've gotten pretty close, huh?"

"Yeah, Jimmy is totally into her. I warned him not to get too attached."

My eyes met his. "Why?"

"Jimmy is heading to State in the fall, and Kylie will only be a junior. That relationship is doomed to fail."

"Why are you such a pessimist?"

Dylan snorted. "Are you serious? Do you really think showmances are meant to last? Please tell me you aren't that naïve."

I studied him as Whitney's warning echoed through my mind. "So you don't believe in true love?"

"True love is entirely different. I'm talking about a summer romance during a theater production."

I turned back to where Kylie and Jimmy were standing together in the pool, talking and smiling as if they were the only two people on the planet. "I think summer romances can sometimes turn into something stronger. They do look happy."

"They'll be happy until Jimmy goes off to college and Kylie's back at Maywood High. Then she'll be brokenhearted, and some sorority girl will get Jimmy's attention." Dylan sipped his beer. "Why are you staring at me like I'm the world's biggest cynic? Aren't your parents divorced?"

My mouth gaped. "Why are you bringing my parents into this?"

He held up his hands in surrender. "I'm just trying to point out that sometimes it doesn't last. That's all I'm saying. I'm not criticizing your parents."

"Yes, my parents divorced when I was little. But my stepdad is a great guy. He and my mom have a really good marriage. I'm not soured on love because of my parents' divorce." My thoughts turned to Todd, and I frowned a little. I drank more beer, hoping to drown my disappointment and regret.

"You will be." Dylan tapped the table. "I hope you're not

still upset about Todd. He's obviously not the right guy for you. You deserve someone better than that loser."

"Todd isn't a loser."

Dylan grinned. "You still like him, huh?"

"I don't *dis*like him. Just because we broke up, that doesn't mean I hate him now. It's a little awkward when I see him. Church was super awkward on Sunday, but work was even worse." I wondered why I was pouring my heart out to Dylan. It must have been the alcohol.

"Why was church awkward?" Dylan asked.

"I used to sit with him and his family. So I sat with my parents and got out of there as soon as the service ended."

"Come to church with me this Sunday," Dylan said casually, as if it were the only logical solution.

"Really?" I asked.

"Sure. You can sit with my parents and me. That way you won't feel weird about going to church."

"That would be great. I'll ask my mom if it's okay."

"Why wouldn't it be okay? It's still church. I'll pick you up. We can work out the details later."

"Awesome." I finished my beer with a gulp.

♫

I awoke the following morning to the sensation of the bed shaking.

"Chelsea!" Jason's voice was urgent. "Chelsea! It's after seven. You're late for work!"

I sat up and gasped. "No!"

"Yes. Your mom woke you up before she left for work. She thought you were getting ready." He walked over to the closet and starting rifling through it. "What do you need?"

I leapt out of bed. "I have my work clothes right here."

"Do you want me to make you breakfast?" he offered as he walked to the stairs.

"I don't have time, but thanks."

"I'm sorry I didn't wake you up sooner. I thought you'd left already until I saw your car parked out front."

"It's my fault. Thanks, Jason."

"Do you want me to call the restaurant?" Jason called up from the bottom of the stairs. "I can explain that you overslept and are on your way."

"No, thanks. I'll handle it." I quickly got dressed and rushed out the door. A car accident two blocks from the restaurant delayed me nearly ten minutes. When I finally walked through the door at Fork & Knife, I was officially forty-five minutes late. Mrs. Hughes was standing at the hostess station frowning.

"Mrs. Hughes, I'm so sorry," I began. "I just— "

"Chelsea, stop." Mrs. Hughes held up her hand to shush me. "I need to talk to you in private. Let's go into my office."

An ominous feeling filled me as I followed her across the dining room. I walked past Janie, and she gave me a sympathetic frown. After we entered her small office off the kitchen, Mrs. Hughes closed the door.

"I'm really sorry," I said again in a rush. "I overslept, and I didn't call because I wanted to get here as fast as I could. And then there was a car accident two blocks from here on Lynnhaven, and I couldn't get around it. It won't happen again."

Mrs. Hughes's expression softened slightly. "Chelsea, I hope you know I like you. I do. I think you're a wonderful young lady. But I'm afraid I have to let you go."

"Please, no." Tears filled my eyes. "I'm really sorry."

"I know you are, but I need reliable employees." She gestured toward a row of framed photos of the Fork & Knife that hung on the wall behind her desk. "Steve and I have invested everything we have into this restaurant. It's our livelihood; our only source of income. We can't take any financial risks in this economy, and having you on staff is a risk right now."

I wiped an errant tear. "I know I've messed up, and I promise I'll do better. Please let me prove it to you."

"Sweetie, I can't give you any more chances." She touched my arm. "I've seen a big change in you since the summer began. I don't know what's going on with you, and you don't have to tell me. I do know that Todd has been really upset. Just be careful. Make sure that whatever it is you've gotten wrapped up in doesn't take you too far off the straight and narrow. You're a very intelligent young lady. Don't lose your head."

I cleared my throat and tried to hold back my tears. "Is there anything I can do to prove I can be a better employee?" She hesitated. "Mrs. Hughes, I really need this job. I'll do anything to make it right. Please give me one more chance?"

Mrs. Hughes shook her head. "I'm sorry, but I can't." She stood and opened the office door. "Good-bye, Chelsea. I'll see you at church on Sunday."

I rushed through the dining room and out the front door of the restaurant.

"Chelsea!" a voice yelled my name as I approached my car.

I spun and found Janie running after me. "Janie! What are you doing? You'd better get back in there. Before your aunt sees you talking with the enemy."

Janie shook her head. "She can wait. What happened?"

"She fired me." I sniffed. "I was late again, and she fired me. She says she needs reliable employees."

Janie hugged me. "I'm so sorry."

"It's my own fault. I overslept. I guess I did it one too many times this summer." I pulled my keys from my purse. "I'll miss you."

"Yeah, you're the only sane one in that place." She crossed her arms over her blue uniform shirt. "I heard you and Todd broke up. I'm sorry about that. I thought you two were a great couple."

"Thanks. It's just been a rotten summer."

"I think he misses you. He's been really mopey."

"Really?" My curiosity piqued.

"Yeah, he never smiles anymore. He's even more intense than usual. I told him to call you, but he said you're into that actor guy. Todd is super jealous." Janie studied me for a moment. "Do you still like Todd?"

I nodded. "Yes."

"You should tell him."

"No." I shook my head. "It's over. He said he's done with me."

"You're both so stubborn. He still cares about you." She glanced back toward the restaurant. "I'd better go back inside, but don't be a stranger. We need to keep in touch." She gave me a hug. "Call me, okay?"

"I will." I climbed into my car and stared at the steering wheel. It felt as if the world was crashing down around me. First I'd lost Todd and now my job. Could things get any worse? I jammed the key into the ignition and started the car.

While the engine hummed, I wondered how I would tell Mom I'd overslept again and gotten fired. She'd already know that I'd overslept because she and Jason talked about everything. But they wouldn't know I'd been fired unless I told them.

As I backed out of the parking space, I decided not to tell them just yet. I would go home and sew. And I'd figure out the best way to tell them the bad news later. Right now, I had to focus on one thing—getting those costumes done before I lost my job as the head costumer of the production.

♫

Later that afternoon, Kylie and I were sitting in my room while I worked on the second denim jacket.

"So, you mean to tell me you overslept this morning, and she just fired you?" Kylie looked incredulous. "That's ridiculous! You should sue her for wrongful termination. My best friend's dad is a lawyer. I think he handles a lot of cases like that. Do you want me to talk to him for you?"

I stared at Kylie in disbelief. "Mrs. Hughes can do whatever she wants. She owns the business. And I knew about their tardiness policy when they hired me. Besides, it's not like I'm in a servers' union or something."

"Huh." Kylie crossed her arms over her chest. "I guess you're right." She craned her neck to see what I was doing. "Now you're working on the hem?"

"Yes." I finished pinning it.

"Whose jacket is this one?"

"Frenchy's."

"What can I do?" Kylie asked.

I pointed toward the jacket pieces that were already cut out. "Do you want to try to do the hem on Marty's jacket? Just follow my lead. You pin, and I'll sew."

"Okay."

We worked in silence for a few minutes.

"What are you going to tell your mom about the job?" she asked, breaking the silence.

"I don't know yet." That very question had been nagging me since I left the restaurant this morning.

"You definitely need to wait until she's in a good mood. I wouldn't hit her with the news as soon as she comes in the door tonight."

"I wasn't planning on doing that." I considered her suggestion while I inserted another pin into the heavy material. "You're right, though. I should wait until she's in a good mood."

"Definitely." Kylie grinned. "You and Dylan were getting pretty friendly last night, huh?"

"Not really. We were just talking." I pushed the pinned material under the presser foot.

"You looked really good together. I guess it's a good thing you and Todd broke up since you've become so close with Dylan."

I felt my shoulders tighten at her comment.

"Jimmy is so amazing," Kylie continued with a dreamy pitch to her voice. "I've never been so sure about anyone before. He and I just fit together so well."

Kylie yammered on about her amazing relationship, and I tried to drown her out with the chatter of the sewing machine. I didn't want to be jealous of her, but I had to admit I was. She was glowing with happiness over her relationship with Jimmy, and I was wallowing in self-pity after losing Todd and my job. I felt sorry for myself, and I was miserable. I longed to pack up my things and head to college early to escape my problems and get a new start. But, deep down, I knew running away wouldn't solve anything.

Kylie and I spent the rest of the afternoon working on the jackets. She talked on and on about Jimmy while I wondered how I was going to admit to my parents that I'd lost my job.

At the end of the day, I hadn't found any solutions to my problems, and I also didn't have the confidence to tell my parents the truth. Instead, I hid in my room and kept sewing and praying a solution would fall from the sky.

# chapter fourteen

I was eating breakfast in the kitchen on Sunday morning when my phone chimed on the dining room table.

"Chelsea!" J.J. ran into the kitchen with my phone. "It's for you!"

"Thank you."

It was a text message from Dylan: Want to go to church with me? Leaving in 15.

I put my breakfast dishes in the dishwasher and went to find Mom. She was standing in front of her bedroom mirror applying makeup. She wore a simple short-sleeved dress with her pearl stud earrings and matching pearl necklace, making her look elegant and younger than her midforties. Her soft brown eyeliner made her deep chestnut eyes stand out.

"Hey, Mom," I said from the doorway. "My friend Dylan invited me to go his church today. Is it okay if I go?"

Mom stopped applying her mascara and met my gaze in the mirror. "Are you trying to avoid Todd?"

I gnawed my lower lip. "That's not the only reason I want to go. I think it would be fun to attend another service."

Mom studied me. "How have things been with him at work? You haven't mentioned it all week."

Here was the perfect opportunity to tell Mom the truth. All I had to say was, *Mrs. Hughes fired me on Friday.*

"It's been okay," I said, fiddling with the hem of my mint-green sheer yoke top. I absently enjoyed the feel of the soft jersey knit and sheer georgette yoke.

"We only talk when we have to. And it's usually about food." I'd chickened out and lied right to her face. What was I thinking?

"That's good." Mom walked over and hugged me. "I know it's hard. My first boyfriend was in almost all of my classes during my junior year in high school. After we broke up, I still had to see him every day. And he was even my lab partner in chemistry."

"That's the worst." Guilt filled me as she continued to comfort me.

"Going through this experience will make you stronger in the end. Ask God to comfort you. Give your burdens to him." She touched my hair. "If it would make you feel better to go to church with your friend today, then you should go. But don't stay out too late. You have to work on those jackets."

"I won't. Thanks, Mom." I hesitated in the doorway as my inner voice nagged me to tell her the truth about my job.

"Are you okay, Chelsea?" Mom asked.

"Yeah, I'm fine. I'll see you later."

♫

Dylan and I sat with his parents near the front of Calvary Church. The service was very similar to the ones I'd attended my whole life.

During the sermon, my mind grappled with questions that had nothing to do with the pastor's message. I contemplated how different Dylan's parents were from mine. Although he had grown up in the church, he didn't feel guilty about partying and drinking the alcohol his parents provided for his friends and him. I wondered how they justified their actions. Were my parents wrong to be more conservative and strict, and were his parents right? Or was it the other way around?

*Is everyone right and no one is wrong?*

The questions circled around and around in my head and then stopped on the one issue that had been burdening my thoughts since Friday—how do I tell Mom I got fired? I knew prolonging it would only make things worse. I was already lengthening my coming punishment by not telling her about it right when it happened. But my lips couldn't seem to form the words.

I felt so guilty for letting her down. I knew she'd lose all faith and trust in me if she found out I was fired for oversleeping after a night of drinking. Just like Todd and Emily, she'd tell me she didn't know me anymore. And then she'd probably compare me to my sister, Christina, who'd never given Mom a day of trouble in her life. I couldn't bear the thought of breaking my mother's heart or being compared to my sister, who'd always done everything right.

During the prayers I lowered my head, but I couldn't pray. I knew God was disappointed in my behavior too, and I didn't bother praying for guidance. I already knew I should do the right thing, and I knew what the right thing was—telling Mom the truth and facing the consequences. I just couldn't bring myself to do it.

After church, Dylan and I talked with his parents and a few members of the congregation before we walked out to his car.

"How about some lunch?" Dylan asked as he opened the passenger door for me. "My treat?"

"Sure." Anxiety filled me as I climbed into his car. *Is this a date?* I wasn't sure how I'd feel if he asked me out. I couldn't deny that I missed Todd. Dylan was cool, but I didn't have the same connection with him that I'd once shared with Todd.

"How about the diner?" he suggested, as the Camaro engine roared to life.

"Sounds great," I held onto the door handle as he steered the thundering sports car into traffic.

We chose to sit in a booth, and I sat across from Dylan. After the server took our order for cheeseburgers, fries, and shakes, I thought about the last time I'd eaten there with Whitney and Emily—just three weeks earlier. So much had changed since that day. *How did things get so messed up so quickly?*

"Is something on your mind?" Dylan asked, pulling me from my thoughts.

"Yeah." I fingered a paper napkin while I spoke. "I was late to work on Friday, and Mrs. Hughes wasn't too happy with me."

"What happened?"

"She fired me." I began to fray the napkin.

Dylan grimaced. "What did your folks say?"

"That's the problem. I haven't told them yet." I moved the ripped pieces of napkin around on the table, creating random patterns.

"So don't tell them." He shrugged as if it were the most logical solution.

"Are you saying I should lie to my parents?"

"No, I didn't say lie to them." Dylan spoke slowly to emphasize his point. "I said, 'Don't tell them.' That's not really lying, is it?"

The server delivered our drinks, and I took a long drink of my strawberry shake, savoring the sweet, cold flavor and wishing it would erase all of my problems. Dylan sipped his vanilla shake and wiped his mouth with a napkin.

"Omitting the truth isn't technically lying," he continued. "I'm just saying you can buy yourself some time by not telling them."

"They'll know the truth when I don't leave for work tomorrow."

"Pretend you're going to work and then come home and work on the jackets while your parents are at work. That way you'll finish the jackets, and Mr. Muller won't be angry with you." He swirled the straw in his shake. "You'll still get your glowing recommendation for college, and everything will be fine."

"Until my parents find out I lied to them."

"You're not lying. You're just not telling them what happened right away."

I considered his words, but they didn't sit right with me. I took a long drink of the shake. "I don't think that would be the best solution to my problem."

He raised an eyebrow. "Why not?"

"My parents value my honesty. My mom always tells my sister and me that we can come to her with our problems, and she'll listen without judgment as long as we tell her the truth. I'm going to break her heart when she finds out that I've been lying to her by not admitting to her that I was fired on Friday. I don't know if I can live with myself, knowing that I've broken her trust that way."

Dylan took a long drink of his shake. "Sometimes you have to tell little white lies to keep the peace at home."

I shook my head. "It's not keeping the peace if it's going to cause more arguments later. It's just delaying the arguments."

"Here's a perfect example of what I'm talking about." He set his shake back on the table. "My dad got a speeding ticket last year. Instead of upsetting my mom with it, he just paid the fine. Mom never found out, and everyone is happy at home."

"That's different." I picked up my milk shake. "He didn't lose his job and not tell her about it." I took a long drink.

"It's a summer job, Chelsea. You're not supporting a family."

"But the summer job is supposed to help pay for college. My parents are counting on that money to cover the cost of my textbooks and other incidentals."

The server brought our burgers and fries, and I doused my fries with ketchup. I passed the ketchup bottle to him, and he did the same to his fries. I changed the subject and asked how rehearsals were going since I hadn't been to the playhouse for more than a week. We discussed the production for the remainder of lunch.

After we finished eating, Dylan paid the check, and we headed toward the exit.

"Chelsea!" a familiar female voice yelled my name.

I turned and saw Emily and Zander sitting in a booth near the door. "Hi!" I waved to them and tapped Dylan's arm. "My best friend Emily is here. You know her boyfriend, Zander."

"Cool."

We walked over to their table.

"Hi, Emily. This is Dylan." I gestured between them. "Dylan, you already know Zander."

"Hi, Dylan." Zander shook Dylan's hand. "It's good to see you, man."

"It's been a long time," Dylan said. "How's that Challenger coming along? Have you gotten it running yet?"

Emily snickered and tossed a fry at Zander. He responded with a feigned warning glance. A tender look passed between them, and my heart ached for Todd. I missed knowing someone else's thoughts before he said the words. I missed reading his expressions.

"Did I hit a nerve?" Dylan asked with a grin.

"He still hasn't gotten it running right." Emily wiped her hands on a napkin. "We were going to work on it this summer, but we haven't had time."

"That's because she keeps finding other things for me to do." Zander pointed toward Emily.

Emily playfully stuck her tongue out at Zander

Zander grinned. "You know it's the truth, Chevy Girl."

"Chevy Girl? Do you work on cars too?" Dylan asked Emily.

Emily nodded. "Yes."

"She's a really great mechanic," I chimed in. "She's given my Nissan a tune-up before."

"How is your car doing?" Emily asked.

"It's running fine now that it has a new alternator," I said. "Did you two just come from church?"

"Yeah, how about you?" Emily moved over. "Do you want to sit down?"

"Oh, no thanks. We're on our way out. I went to church with Dylan this morning." I touched Dylan's arm.

Emily gave me a curious look.

"I'll see you around the neighborhood, man." Dylan nodded at Zander and then Emily. "Good seeing you."

"Enjoy your lunch," I said. As we walked away, Emily mouthed the words, "Call me."

Dylan talked about the production some more as he drove to my house, but my thoughts were back at the diner with Emily and Zander and their great relationship. If I had stayed on the straight and narrow, as Mrs. Hughes called it, would I have been eating lunch at the diner with Todd and the two of them right now? What could I do to make things right? Should I take Dylan's advice and *not* tell Mom and Jason that I'd been fired? Was lying ever the right solution?

"You're awfully quiet," Dylan said, stopping the car in front of my driveway.

"Yeah, I have a lot on my mind." I unbuckled my seat belt. "I had a nice time today."

"Did you?" He looked unconvinced.

"Yes, I really did. Thanks for taking me to your church and buying me lunch."

Dylan leaned over and touched my cheek. "I really like you, Chelsea."

"I like you too, Dylan." My hands quaked with anxiety. *Was he going to kiss me?*

He leaned closer, and I breathed in his spicy cologne. My eyes closed as his lips touched mine. I waited for the fireworks, but none came. My stomach didn't flip, and my pulse didn't dance. Instead, it seemed ordinary. It was nothing like when Todd kissed me.

Dylan smiled. "I'll text you later, okay?"

"Yeah." I forced a smile. "Thanks again."

I climbed out of the car and waved as his Camaro sped down the street. Staring after him, I was shocked by how uneventful his kiss had been. It was nothing like I'd imagined it would be. I wondered if he considered me his girlfriend now. Was that our first date? If so, then why wasn't I more excited about it? I wondered why I wasn't doing cartwheels on the front lawn. Instead, I was wondering what Todd was doing now. Did he miss me in church today? Did he even notice I wasn't there?

I stepped through the front door and heard my brothers arguing over a video game in the family room. I dropped my purse on the dining room table and found Mom folding a load of clothes in the laundry room.

"Hi." I came up behind her and started helping her fold.

"Hi there." She smiled at me. "How was church?"

"It was good." I nodded. "It was a little different than ours, but it was nice."

"Great. Did you get some lunch?"

"Yeah, he took me to the diner afterward, and he paid."

"Oh?" Mom raised her eyebrows. "Was it a date?"

I folded a pair of my jeans and considered the question. "I don't know. Maybe. He kissed me when he dropped me off just now."

"He kissed you?" She studied me. "You don't seem too excited about it. I remember how you were bouncing off the walls when Todd kissed you the first time. Why aren't you more excited about Dylan?"

My throat constricted. "I guess because he's not Todd."

"Oh, sweetie." Mom rubbed my arm. "Are you okay?"

I nodded as I folded a blue-and-white-striped lightweight knit blouse.

"Todd wasn't in church today. I saw his parents, and they said hello."

My stomach twisted. "They said hello to you?"

"Yes." She folded a pair of Justin's shorts. "Are you okay? You look upset."

I considered Dylan's idea about how omitting the truth wasn't the same thing as lying. I wanted to tell her the truth so badly, and the words were on the tip of my tongue. "Have you ever felt confused about something?"

"Of course, I have. Do you want to talk about it?"

"I'm not sure I'm ready. But there's something that's been difficult for me to figure out. What would you do if you needed to make a decision about something, but you were afraid of upsetting someone you loved?"

Mom stopped folding and studied me. "Chelsea, what's going on with you? You haven't been acting like yourself these last few weeks. You know you can always talk to me, right? I'll listen without passing judgment."

"I know, but I'm not ready to tell you yet."

"Is it serious?"

I shrugged.

"Do you want to talk to your dad about it? Maybe you should ask for some time off at work and drive up to see him."

*I wouldn't even need to take any time off at work.* "No, that's okay," I said.

"He'd love to have you visit him," Mom continued. "I know he misses having you on the holidays. You could take your sewing machine with you and work up there for a couple of days. Maybe that would take your mind off whatever is bugging you."

I folded a soft red jersey knit blouse with a button-tie front. "I'm fine here."

"Or you could call your sister if you're not comfortable talking to me."

"Thanks, but I don't need to talk to her." I could never admit to Christina that I'd been hungover and lost my job. She wouldn't understand. I loaded all of my folded clothes into a basket. "I'll go put these away."

Mom frowned. "I'm worried about you, Chelsea."

"I'll be fine. Thanks, Mom." I carried the basket upstairs while silently chastising myself. I'd had another perfect opportunity to tell my mother the truth, and I'd let it slip by.

*You're a coward, Chelsea Grace Morris. She deserves to know the truth!*

I put my clothes away and sat down in front of the sewing machine where Frenchy's jacket waited. I looked at the small wooden cross hanging above my bed. My nana had given it to me on the day I was baptized.

I closed my eyes and prayed:

> *I know you're disappointed in me, Lord. I feel like I've gotten in too deep, and I don't know how to get out. I don't know who I am or where I belong. But I know one thing for sure, God. I miss my close relationship*

*with my mom and Todd and you. Please lead me back to you. Amen.*

I sewed the rest of that afternoon until my mother called me downstairs for dinner. I let my brothers do all the talking during the meal, and I continued thinking about Dylan's advice and my prayer. After I helped clear away the dinner dishes, I sewed some more until I couldn't see straight, and then I flopped into bed with Buttons by my side.

I heard my phone buzz from across the room. When I retrieved it from my purse, I found a missed call and a voice mail message from Emily. I listened to the message: "Hey, Chelsea. It's Em. I just wanted to make sure you're okay. You didn't seem like yourself at lunch today. It was kind of odd to see you with Dylan. I hope everything is going well with you two." She paused for a moment. "Anyway, give me a call. I'll be happy to listen anytime. Bye."

I deleted the message and considered calling her back. Instead, I put the phone back in my purse and climbed into bed. Emily could never understand how I felt. I was better off just keeping my problems to myself.

# chapter fifteen

On Wednesday morning I smiled as I put the finishing touches on Frenchy's Pink Ladies' jacket. I'd followed Dylan's advice and pretended to go to work each day. I left the house before seven and drove around town until I was certain my parents were at work and the twins were at day camp. I then returned to the house and sewed until they came home from work. I had supper ready each night, and my mother was delighted. She had no idea I wasn't working, and despite my guilt, I'd found the time alone at home to be very productive.

Three of the Pink Ladies' jackets were now complete—Rizzo's, Marty's, and Frenchy's. I just had to finish Jan's.

I was placing the last sequin on the back of the jacket when I thought I heard the front door open. My stomach dropped, and I tiptoed to the top of the stairs.

"Chelsea?" Jason's voice sounded from somewhere downstairs. "Chelsea, are you here?"

I swallowed and slowly walked downstairs. My stepfather was standing in the hallway with a scowl on his face.

"Hi, Jason," I said, trying to sound casual. "What are you doing home?"

"I was just going to ask you the same question, but I already know the answer."

"You do?"

"Yes, I do." Jason gestured widely. "I had a meeting scheduled for nine, so I decided to stop somewhere for a cup of coffee first. Since I wasn't far from the center of town, I thought I'd pop in at the Fork & Knife and see you too."

*Oh no* ... My throat went dry.

"It's funny, though, Chelsea." He pointed to me. "You weren't there."

I held my hands up in defense. "I can explain."

"Oh, I'm not done yet. I can explain too. I asked Trudy Hughes why you weren't there, and she looked at me as if I were insane. She said she fired you last Friday." His brown eyes narrowed. "That was five days ago. Why didn't you tell your mom or me that you got fired?"

"I wanted to, but I was afraid."

"What?" Jason shook his head.

"But I can't stand the idea of her being disappointed in me. I don't want to let her down."

"Let me get this straight." He tapped a finger against his chin. "You mean to tell me that instead of disappointing your mom by telling her the truth about getting fired, you've pretended to go to work for three days in a row? Does that make sense to you, Chelsea?"

"No. Not when you say it like that." My voice was as tiny as I felt—just a few inches tall.

"You're a very smart girl." He looked stunned. "This doesn't seem like you at all. What's going on, Chelsea?"

"I don't know," I said. "I've been trying to figure that out."

"Here's what's going to happen. I'm not going to call your mother at work and tell her about this now. It will just ruin her day." He wagged a finger at me. "However, I will tell her about this when she gets home."

"Okay."

He glanced at the clock in the kitchen. "I have to run now. But this isn't over." He started toward the door.

"Jason," I called after him. He paused and looked over his shoulder at me. "For what it's worth, I am sorry."

"We'll talk more later." He slipped out the door, and regret filled me. I'd done exactly what I feared I would do—broken my parents' hearts. Now I had to face the consequences.

A feeling of foreboding haunted me as I climbed the stairs. But I couldn't spend time thinking about what might happen now. I had to finish Sandy's black velvet catsuit for the finale.

♫

Later that afternoon, I headed to the playhouse with the three finished jackets and the velvet catsuit. Carrying the items on hangers, I was walking toward the backstage entrance, being careful not to drag the legs of the catsuit through the grass, when I spotted Todd talking with P.J. on the stairs. My heart jumped into my throat. I couldn't stand the thought of seeing Todd after his parents had fired me.

When Todd saw me heading their way, he jumped up and held the door open. "Do you need help carrying that stuff to the dressing room?" he offered.

"No, thanks." I shook my head. "I'm fine."

"Are those the Pink Ladies' jackets?" Todd asked, his eyes wide and curious.

"Three of them, anyway. I'm still working on Jan's." I held out one of the denim jackets so he could see it better.

Todd took the hanger from my hand and examined the jacket from all sides. "Wow, Chels. This is amazing." He motioned for P.J. to take a look. "Check out this jacket. She made it."

"You made this?" P.J.'s wide-eyed expression mirrored Todd's.

"I had to. I couldn't find a ready-made one that I liked or could afford to buy. I found the material at a discount fabric shop, and the pattern was free online."

"Wow." P.J. grinned. "Chels, you're really talented."

"I already knew that," Todd said proudly as he examined the *Pink Ladies* lettering on the back. "Check out the sequins, P.J. Chels, did you sew those on by hand?"

"I did," I admitted. "It wasn't a big deal."

Todd shook his head. "You shouldn't sell yourself short. This is amazing. Mr. Muller is going to love it."

"I hope so." I took the jacket back from him, and we stared at each other for a moment. "Thanks." *I miss you.*

"You're welcome." His expression was intense, and my heart thumped in a crazy rhythm.

"Chelsea!" Kylie's bellow broke my trance.

"I'd better go," I said. "Excuse me."

Todd nodded, and I headed down the hallway to where Kylie was standing with Britney and Marni. I was floored by how nice Todd was being to me. I didn't deserve his kindness. He was a better person than I was.

"You finished the jackets!" Kylie jumped up and down like a child on Christmas morning. "I can't wait for the girls to see them! I'll go round them up."

"I'll come with you." Britney followed Kylie down the hall.

Marni took two of the jackets from my arms. "Kylie gets excited, doesn't she?"

I rolled my eyes. "That was nothing. You should hear her talk about Jimmy. She practically does backflips."

"How are you doing?" Marni asked as we walked into the dressing room.

"I'm not doing too well." I hung the jackets and catsuit on the rack. "My stepdad went by the restaurant to see me this morning."

"Oh?" Marni looked confused.

"I hadn't told my parents that I got fired on Friday."

Marni grimaced. "Oh dear."

"Wait until you see these jackets!" Kylie burst into the room with the five actresses trailing her.

"Your names are written on the inside," I said, gesturing toward the jackets.

The girls gasped as they inspected them.

"I'm still working on yours, Jamie. Britney, I need you to try on the velvet catsuit for the finale." I handed Britney the suit.

The actresses tried on the jackets, and they fit perfectly. I breathed a sigh of relief. Britney stepped out of the bathroom in the velvet jumpsuit, and it fit her like a glove.

*Thank you, God, for guiding my hands and my sewing machine.*

"You're amazing," Britney said. She stood in front of the full-length mirror and admired her reflection. "This is fantastic."

"I love my jacket!" Natasha, the girl playing Rizzo, squealed.

"I know!" Elena, who was playing Marty, agreed. "I love the sequins."

Amelia, who was playing Frenchy, chimed in, "I want to keep my jacket after the production. This is just so fabulous."

Jamie, who was playing Jan, nodded with enthusiasm. "I can't wait to get mine. The others are way cool."

"What is way cool?" Mr. Muller appeared in the doorway, and I felt my body stiffen.

"Check out our jackets," Amelia said. "Aren't they amazing?"

Mr. Muller crossed the dressing room and peered at them closely. "Fantastic job, Chelsea." He turned toward me. "Very nice."

"And my catsuit?" Britney twirled around. "Nice, huh?"

"I see only three pink jackets. Where's the fourth one?" Mr. Muller's expression hardened.

"I'll have it done in two more days," I said, hoping I could keep that promise.

"You'd better have it done." Mr. Muller left the room, and I blew out the breath I'd been holding.

"You did great." Kylie patted my back. "Do you want help with the last one?"

"No, I've got it down now." I smiled at her. "You just make sure the cast keeps their costumes straight, okay?"

"Sure." Kylie hung up the jackets in their proper places.

Britney changed back into her clothes and hung up the catsuit. Then she and Kylie followed the rest of the girls out of the dressing room.

"So things are bad at home?" Marni asked once we were alone again.

"They aren't bad yet, but they're going to be." I lowered myself onto a cold metal folding chair. "My stepdad is going to tell my mom I was fired as soon as she gets home from work. I can't even imagine what she'll say."

Marni pulled up a chair across from me and sat down. "What are you going to do?"

"I have to come clean. I have to tell them everything, and then I have to face the consequences. I was really stupid to let things get this far, but I was following Dylan's advice."

"Dylan told you to lie to your parents?"

I nodded. "He said it wasn't bad to simply omit the truth if it kept peace in the house."

Marni burst out laughing. "Are you serious? Is that how he deals with things in his house?"

I felt stupid as I listened to her laugh.

"I'm sorry. I'm not laughing at you. I'm just surprised he

gave you such bad advice." Her smile faded. "I wish you had called me. I would've given you better advice than to pretend you weren't fired."

"I was dumb enough to do what he said." I slumped in the chair. "I can't believe how badly things have turned out. I lost Todd, I lost my job, and just when I thought things couldn't get any worse, they have. Now I'm caught in a huge lie. It's like I'm sinking, and I can't swim. I'm a walking *Titanic*."

"It will get better. Just face the consequences like an adult. Tell your parents you're sorry. Explain that you'll do anything you have to do in order to make it better."

"You're right." I sat up straight. "I'll do that. I don't know why I thought this other way was a good plan."

"You were scared. And I think Dylan can be very convincing when he says things. It's those blue eyes. Girls are mesmerized by him." She frowned. "Did I just offend you? If I did, I'm sorry. I know you like Dylan."

"It's okay." I leaned forward. "Can you keep a secret?"

"Sure." She smiled. "What's your secret?"

"I went to church with Dylan on Sunday, and then he took me out to lunch. When he drove me home, he actually kissed me."

Marni gasped. "Oh, then I'm really sorry. I didn't mean to insult him. Or you."

I waved off her comment. "Don't worry about it. What I was going to tell you is that the kiss wasn't a big deal."

Marni tilted her head. "I'm listening ..."

I paused, contemplating my words. "Todd's kisses are better."

"Wow." Marni sat up straight in the chair. "I don't think Dylan is the one for you then. If you don't feel anything when he kisses you, he can't be the one. It sounds like— "

"Todd was the one." I finished her thought.

"Well, what do I know about love? I'm only eighteen."

I considered how nice Todd had been to me earlier when I was carrying in the costumes, and I wondered if he was the one. Or if he wasn't the one, then was he still someone who was meant to be in my life—a special person God had put in my path, but I've disregarded him like trash?

Marni looked at her watch. "You'd better get home. It's after five o'clock."

I felt my body tense. "I don't want to go home."

"You know you have to." Marni stood. "You're stronger than you think, Chelsea. Go home, and get it over with. You'll feel better once it's all out in the open. Just keep telling yourself that you're an adult now, and you're ready to face the music. Right?"

"Right." I picked up my bag and gave Marni a long hug. "Thank you. You're a wonderful friend."

"You're welcome." She patted my back. "Now go home and make me proud. Call me if you need someone to listen."

"If I still have a phone, I will do that," I promised, hiking the strap of my messenger bag onto my shoulder.

"I'll be thinking of you," Marni said as we made our way into the hall.

I walked out to the parking lot and spotted Todd standing next to his car. He was talking with Molly Adams, a pretty blonde who was a member of the chorus. Jealousy nipped at me, and I pushed it back down. I had no right to be jealous if Todd had met someone else. After all, I'd been partying with Dylan for weeks, and I'd even let him kiss me on Sunday. What claim did I have to Todd's heart? I felt honored that he would even talk to me today after the way I'd spoken to him and treated him.

I climbed into my car. As I drove past him and Molly, he

lifted his hand and gave me a little wave. I waved back wishing I could rewind time and start the summer over.

I mentally prepared an apology speech as I drove through town and made my way toward home. By the time I pulled into the neighborhood, I had rehearsed the speech three times. When I pulled into the driveway and saw both of my parents' cars there, however, I forgot every word of it.

I entered the house and dropped my bag on the dining room table. My parents were sitting at the kitchen table. When they heard me walk into the room, they both looked up.

"Hi," I said, feeling foolish and guilty all at once.

"Have a seat." Mom pulled out a chair between her and Jason. "We need to talk."

"Yes, ma'am." I sat between them and mentally recited Marni's advice—*I am an adult. I will take my punishment like an adult. I can do this.*

An awkward few moments of silence passed as the three of us stared at each other. I wanted to say something, but I didn't know what to say. I didn't know if I should apologize or let them talk first. What was I supposed to do? What was the mature thing to do?

"Chelsea," Mom finally began, "I'm trying to figure out your logic. Did you really think you could spend the rest of the summer pretending you still have a job?"

"I don't— " I started to say, but she cut me off.

"Let me finish." Mom's voice rose. "How could you chat with me on Sunday as if nothing had happened? I felt like we were having a heart-to-heart discussion while we folded the laundry." She motioned toward the laundry room. "But in reality, you were trying to figure out whether or not you should lie to me."

"I didn't lie. I just didn't tell you the whole truth." The stupid statements leapt from my lips before I could stop them.

"That's still lying!" Mom's voice boomed.

"Audrey." Jason's voice was amazingly even. "Calm down. Don't get yourself all upset."

"How can I not get upset?" Mom nearly shouted. "My daughter lied to me. She lied to *us*, Jason. She's never done this before." She turned her scowl on me. "I trusted you, Chelsea. Now I don't know if I can trust you at all. You've gone through a transformation this summer. I guess you're going through your rebellious period later than most teenagers. Your sister never went through this, so I have no idea how to handle your behavior. How should I punish you, Chelsea? What will get you to realize that you can't behave this way?"

Shame rained down on me, and I stared at my lap. "I'm sorry, Mom." My eyes flooded with tears. "I didn't mean for this to happen."

"Well, now it has happened, and we have to deal with the consequences. You've now lost a major amount of income that we needed for your college expenses. We were counting on that money to pay for gas and books." She tapped the table for emphasis. "I called your father, and he agrees you need to be punished for this. We're not going to just hand you the money that you were expecting to make."

I wiped my eyes. "I agree. I need to be punished. I messed up. I was immature and thoughtless."

"You're right." Mom nodded. "You were immature and thoughtless. You also were irresponsible."

I braced myself for the punishment.

"First of all, you're grounded for the rest of the summer," she said. "That means you are to go to the playhouse and come straight home. No parties, no coffeehouse visits, no lunches out, nothing." She counted off the items on her fingers.

"The rest of the summer? How can you ground me for that long?" I looked at Jason, but his expression was impassive. "That's unreasonable."

"You think that's unreasonable?" Mom held out her hand. "If you think that's too much, then give me your phone too. I can completely cut you off from your friends. And you deserve that after your blatant disregard for Jason and me. I was going to let you keep your phone in case you needed it during the musical. I know sometimes Mr. Muller may have to reach you to discuss rehearsal times and things like that. But if you want to argue with me, I'll take your phone and completely cut you off from everyone."

"Fine." I threw my hands up in surrender. "I'm grounded for the rest of the summer. I will accept the punishment."

"That's not all." Mom shook her head. "That's only the beginning. Since you aren't making the money you were supposed to make, our budget will be tight. That means we can't afford everything we'd planned for the boys."

"What are you saying?" I looked at Mom first and then my stepdad.

"We were going to keep the boys in that day camp until you were finished with the musical. But once the production was finished and you were headed off to college, we were going to put them in a cheaper camp with shorter hours. Jason was planning on working from home until the boys go to kindergarten anyway." Mom folded her hands on the table. "But now—to save money—we're going to pull the boys out of that day camp starting tomorrow." She pointed to me. "And you're going to babysit full time. This way we can make up the money that you can't earn now that you've lost your job."

"What?" I stood. "You have to be kidding me. How can I sew if I have to chase two five-year-olds?"

"You'll figure it out," Jason said.

"Sit down, Chelsea," Mom snapped. "We're not done talking."

"This is crazy." I tapped the table. "Just let me find another job. I'm sure I can find something part-time. I'll go to the mall tomorrow morning and fill out applications for every job opening. Whitney's boyfriend works at the bookstore. Maybe he can help me find something."

"No." Mom shook her head. "You're not getting off that easy. You're going to face the consequences. You're going to babysit your brothers until you go to school. That's it. End of discussion."

"But, Mom, please," I begged with folded hands. "Just let me find another job. Maybe I'll find one that pays even better than the restaurant."

"That's it, Chelsea. We've already decided. I'm done talking about it." Mom stood. "I'm going to get the boys in the bath." She left the kitchen, and I started after her.

"Chelsea, stop." Jason grabbed my arm. "Just let her go. She's not in the mood to talk anymore right now. She's really upset."

"I want to tell her I'm sorry." My voice broke on the last word.

"Let her go. She's crushed that you lied to her, and I think it's better if she calms down a bit." He gestured toward the refrigerator. "Why don't you make yourself something to eat?"

My stomach roiled at the thought of food. "I don't think I could eat a thing. I'm going to my room." I dragged myself up the stairs and threw myself across the bed. Burying my face in my pillow, I sobbed. I felt trapped in a horrible nightmare that kept swirling like a tornado, tearing up my life and destroying all of my relationships in its path.

*God, how am I going to fix this? How am I going to make my mother believe me when I say I'm sorry? Help me, God. Lead me back to the right path, God. Please!*

I felt a wet nose on my arm and heard purring in my ear. I rolled over and spotted Buttons snuggling up to me.

"Hi, Buttons," I whispered, rubbing his chin. "I'm glad you still love me."

He closed his eyes, enjoying the feel of my touch, and purred louder.

"I don't know what to do." I continued rubbing his chin. "I have to apologize to my mother."

I glanced across the room at the partially finished denim jacket for Jamie. "I guess I should get some work done."

I walked over to the sewing machine and stared at the jacket. I had no ambition to work on it, but I needed to keep my mind busy. All I could think about was the hurt in my mother's eyes. And I hadn't even told her about sneaking out and the drinking parties yet. How would she look at me if she knew that getting fired wasn't the worse thing I'd done this summer? I had to get the image of her look of betrayal out of my mind.

I worked until my stomach growled with hunger pains. It was almost eight o'clock. I walked downstairs and found Mom sitting at the kitchen table with a cup of tea.

"Hi, Mom," I said, walking to the refrigerator. I pulled out a package of turkey lunch meat, cheese, lettuce, tomato, mustard, and mayonnaise. Then I grabbed the loaf of bread and brought everything to the table.

Mom kept her eyes focused on the latest issue of a magazine while I made myself a sandwich. I waited for her to acknowledge me, but she continued staring at photos as if I weren't even there. I took a bite of the sandwich, wondering what to do.

"Mom," I said again.

She finally looked up at me, and her brown eyes were full of disappointment. “What do you want, Chelsea?”

“I want to say I’m sorry.” My voice was thin, but the meaning was deep. “I know you’re angry, but I want you to know I’m really sorry. I messed up. Please forgive me.”

“I know you’re sorry, but it’s going to take a while for me to get over this. I never expected to have problems with you.” She stood. “I’m heading to bed. Good night.” She stopped in the doorway and faced me again. “I expect you to be up and ready to take care of your brothers by six thirty tomorrow. I need to leave for work no later than seven.”

“I will.” I nodded as she left the kitchen.

# chapter sixteen

The following morning, I dragged myself out of bed at six and was dressed and making breakfast when my mother entered the kitchen.

"Your eggs are almost ready." I placed two pieces of toast on a plate and set them at her usual spot at the table.

"Thanks." Mom sat in the chair as I poured coffee into her mug.

I placed the coffeepot back on the base. "I'll put the boys' pancakes in the microwave."

"They're still sleeping." Mom added sweetener to the coffee. "You can get them up when you're ready."

"Okay." I scraped a pile of scrambled eggs out of the skillet and onto her plate, then swiped two eggs from the carton for Jason's breakfast. "Are you working late today?"

"Yes," she said simply. "It's Thursday."

I placed two pieces of bread into the toaster and pushed down the lever. After beating the two eggs with a fork, I poured them into the pan. The sizzle of frying eggs filled the kitchen. I tried to think of something to say to fill the chasm between us.

"Dress rehearsals start today." I stirred the eggs with a rubber spatula. "I have to go to the theater today."

"You'll have to take your brothers with you," she said.

"I know." I glanced back and saw she was perusing the newspaper. "They might get a kick out of it. Of course, that's only if I can get them to sit still."

Mom continued staring at the paper. I turned back to the pan and flipped the eggs.

"Good morning," Jason said cheerfully as he entered the kitchen. He leaned down and gave my mother a quick kiss, a gesture I'd witnessed nearly every day for the past decade. He turned toward me. "Breakfast smells delicious, Chelsea."

"Thanks." I scooped his eggs onto a plate just as the toast popped. I handed him his breakfast. "Here you go. Enjoy."

"Thank you." He smiled at me.

I tried to smile back, but it felt more like a grimace. He bowed his head in a quick prayer and began eating. Jason and Mom made small talk about their schedules while they ate. I stood by the counter waiting for the bagel that I'd stuck in the toaster for my breakfast.

After taking one last sip of coffee, Mom stood. "I have to run."

I swiftly retrieved her plate and mug. "I'll do the dishes."

"Thanks," Mom said without looking at me. She left the kitchen, and I placed her dishes on the counter.

My bagel popped, and I tossed it onto a plate. I sat across from Jason while I smothered the bagel with peanut butter.

"Chelsea." Jason's voice was warm and full of empathy. "She still loves you."

I nodded while studying my bagel. A lump was swelling in my throat, and I didn't want to cry. I'd cried enough tears in the past week to fill Dylan's swimming pool.

"Chels." Jason touched my hand, and I looked up to meet his sympathetic gaze. "It will get better. Just keep doing what you're doing."

"What do you mean?" My voice was thin.

"This." He gestured around the kitchen. "You're picking up the slack around here. You'll do a great job taking care of the twins today. I know you can show us how responsible you are. Your mother wants to know she can count on you and trust you."

"She can." My voice was strong again. "I can do this."

"Good." He patted my hand and ate the last bite of his toast. "I need to go too. Call me if you need me, okay?"

"I will."

He started to exit the kitchen.

"Jason," I called after him. He turned to face me. "Thanks."

"You're welcome. See you later." He smiled at me and then disappeared into the hallway.

♫

Later that morning I stood in front of my twin brothers like a drill sergeant, while they fidgeted on the living room couch. "Here's the deal. I need to sew today." I pointed toward the stairs. "That means I need both of you to behave. No fighting, no yelling, and no wrestling." I counted off the list on my fingers. "You can play in here or in your room. Do you understand?"

Justin scowled. "I don't want to play here. I want to see my friends. Why can't we go to camp?"

J.J. nodded. "Yeah, I want to see my new friend Rusty. He promised to play Army with me on the playground."

I rubbed my temples. *If only I'd gotten to work on time last Friday* ... "I'll make you a deal," I said. "If you guys behave and let me finish the jacket I'm working on, then I'll take you to the park tomorrow. Sound good?"

"Tomorrow?" J.J. whined.

"We want to go today!" Justin yelled. "Can't Todd take us to the park today?"

The question hit me in the gut.

"Yeah," J.J. continued whining. "We want to play with Todd."

An idea hit me like the final curtain at the end of a play. "We have to go the playhouse this afternoon. You'll see Todd there. How does that sound?" I gave them a big smile to help seal the deal.

"Can he take us to the park then?" J.J. asked.

"I don't know. Maybe we'll ask him if you're super good." It was the best I could do at the moment.

"Okay." J.J. linked arms with Justin. "Come on, let's play a video game."

"Great idea! I'm going upstairs to sew. Remember the rules, all right?" I waited until they were involved in their game before I slipped upstairs.

Less than an hour later, I was working on the jacket sleeves when I heard footsteps stomping up the stairs.

"Chelsea! Justin hit me!" J.J. bellowed.

I braced myself and said a silent prayer for patience.

"He hit me hard!" J.J. yelled again, now from the top of the stairs. He jerked a thumb over his right shoulder. "Tell him to leave me alone!"

Justin appeared behind him on the stairs and smirked. "He started it."

"No, I didn't!" J.J. stomped his foot.

"Yes, you did." Justin folded his arms over his chest.

"Guys, guys." I waved my arms like a referee. "I don't care *who* started it, but I want it to end *now.* J.J., go get your DS. You can play a video game up here with me. Justin, you can go back downstairs and play in the family room."

"No!" J.J. stomped his foot again. "I want to use the PS3!"

"Oh boy," I muttered. I needed a bribe. I glanced at the clock and saw it was only nine o'clock. How was I going to make it through the morning without losing my mind? I spotted my television on the other side of the room, and an idea popped in my head. "Should we plug in the PS3 up here?"

J.J.'s face lit up. "That's a great idea! Then I can lie on your bed with Buttons and play."

I looked at Justin and he smiled in agreement. "Okay."

Thirty minutes later, we had the PS3 up and running in my room. I tried in vain to tune out their commentary and cheers while they played their game and flopped around on my bed. Buttons, who was napping on my pillow, was somehow unaffected by all the noise. I, on the other hand, had difficulty concentrating on the jacket.

After an hour, Justin threw his controller on the bed. "I'm hungry."

"Yeah," J.J. chimed in. "Me too."

I rubbed my temples again. "It's not even noon, guys."

"But we're hungry!" they whined in unison.

At that moment, I had the utmost respect for their serene camp counselors. I stood. "Let's go make a snack."

After feeding the twins crackers and cheese, I managed to sneak in thirty more minutes of sewing while they played video games in my room. By noon, however, they were back to arguing, and I was ready to get out of the house.

"Let's go to the theater," I said. "Go grab your DS and some games, and then get in my car."

"What about lunch?" Justin asked, pulling on his shoes.

"Yeah," J.J. agreed. "I'm hungry too."

I grabbed my purse and phone from the dining room table. "We'll stop at the drive-through on the way."

"Burger World?" they asked in unison.

"Yes. I'll get you anything you want if you'll just cooperate right now and get in the car." They grabbed their handheld game systems, and I guided them toward the car. I blew out a sigh of relief when we were finally on the road.

After a quick stop at the drive-through, I drove the rest of the way to the playhouse. The greasy smell of burgers and fries filled my car, causing my stomach to growl. I parked at the back of the lot, and my pulse raced when I spotted Todd's Focus parked a few spots away.

"Can we eat now?" Justin lunged at me and tried to grab the bag of food as we made our way to the theater.

I held the bag up high and out of his reach. "I'll find a quiet place inside where you two can sit and eat, okay?"

The boys followed me up the stairs and into the theater. A few of the female chorus members said hello to the twins and grinned as they passed us.

"Let's go in here." I led them to a small, empty dressing room and motioned for them to sit. I set out their food and handed them napkins. "Just sit here and be quiet while you eat your food."

The boys began devouring the fries, and I hoped the food would keep them busy for at least a few minutes.

"Miss Morris." Mr. Muller glared at me from the doorway. "What's going on here?"

I smiled through my panic and decided to pretend that he didn't look like he was about to blow a gasket and scream at me.

"Hi, Mr. Muller." I made a sweeping gesture toward my brothers. "These are my little brothers, J.J. and Justin." I glanced down at the twins. "Boys, say hi to Mr. Muller."

The boys grinned and waved, their mouths full of fries.

"I have to watch my brothers this afternoon, so I thought I'd bring them with me." I smiled despite my anxiety.

Mr. Muller gestured for me to follow him out into the hallway, where actors and chorus members rushed by in preparation for the dress rehearsal. I thought I spotted Todd in my peripheral vision, but I kept my eyes focused on the director.

"Are we running a babysitting service now?" Mr. Muller's face burned a bright crimson. "A dress rehearsal is not a place for little kids. There are day care centers that are equipped to handle them."

"I know, and I'm sorry. My mom needed me to help her today. I had no choice."

"Yes, you did have a choice. You could have chosen to keep them at home where they belong. They do *not* belong here!" Mr. Muller raised his voice, causing the knot of people in the hallway to stop and stare.

I wanted to evaporate into the wall.

"Mr. Muller, I will do my best to keep them quiet. I'll see if Marni can help me." I had a feeling that my dear friend Marni would assist me in any way she could.

"I need Marni out on the stage with the rest of the chorus members." He pointed toward the auditorium. "And I need you to put on your headset and get ready for the dress rehearsal."

"I'm ready to do my job." I rubbed my sweaty palms on my jean shorts. "I'll see if Kylie can help then. I'm sure we can tag team with the costumes."

"That's not Kylie's job either." His expression was steely. "If babysitting is your priority, then you need to take those boys home. I'm certain Kylie is capable of handling the costumes if you can't, Miss Morris."

"Yes, sir." My voice was tiny compared to his.

He started to walk away and then stopped and turned to face me once more. "Did you finish the last jacket?"

"I'll have it done by tomorrow." I made the promise even though I knew it wasn't possible unless I duct-taped my brothers to the wall or stayed up all night and sewed—neither of which were plausible solutions.

"You'd better, Miss Morris." He marched down the hallway toward the auditorium, and I leaned against the wall and tried to take deep breaths.

After I'd steadied my frazzled nerves, for the most part, I looked inside the dressing room and found it empty. My brothers and their food were gone.

"J.J.?!" I yelled. "Justin?! Where are you guys?!"

Britney tapped me on the arm. "Are you looking for your cute little twin brothers?"

"Yeah. Have you seen them?"

She pointed down the hallway behind me. "I saw Todd take them that way toward the electronics storage area."

"Todd took them?" I asked, confused.

"Yeah." She headed toward the stage. "See ya later."

"Thanks!" I rushed down the hallway and stopped in the storage room doorway.

My brothers were sitting at a card table and quietly eating their food while Todd pointed toward the large flat screen TV fastened to the wall.

"So, when the rehearsal starts, you can watch it right there," Todd explained. "There's a camera pointed at the stage, and you'll see the play like it's being shown on television. The crew uses these screens so we know what's going on during the performance. We use it for our cues."

My brothers chewed their fries and nodded, captivated by Todd's explanations of what cues were. My heart warmed as I watched Todd interact with the twins. He was so thoughtful and kind. Even though he'd broken up with me, he was still spending time with my brothers. I inwardly kicked myself for letting such a special guy slip through my fingers. How could I have ever taken him for granted?

Todd turned toward the doorway and our eyes met, causing my heartbeat to flutter. "Hi," he said. "I was just giving the boys a lesson on the stage crew."

"That's great." I looked at my brothers. "See? I told you we'd get to see Todd today."

Todd raised an eyebrow. "They wanted to see me?"

"Yeah." I stepped into the room. "They ask about you all the time."

"Do they?" His intense expression caught me off guard, and I quickly turned my eyes toward the screen.

"I guess the rehearsal is about to start." I pointed to the image of Mr. Muller lecturing the keyboardist and drummer from the stage.

"I'd better go." Todd leaned down and swiped one of J.J.'s fries. "It was good seeing you guys. You behave for Chelsea, okay?"

"We will," they said in unison.

"See you guys later." Todd mussed their red hair.

He moved toward the door, and I had the sudden urge to stop him.

"Todd," I said. "Wait."

He faced me. "Yeah?"

"Thanks for helping me today." I gestured toward my brothers. "I was stuck today, and Mr. Muller was giving me a hard time. I really appreciate it."

"Yeah, I saw him hassling you." He crossed his arms over his chest. "You're welcome." He paused for a moment, and we shared an awkward silence that made me hold my breath. "I'm sorry my mom fired you."

"It was my fault." I managed to say. "As you can see, this is my punishment." I pointed toward my brothers again. "I have to prove to my parents that I'm responsible."

"I hope it goes well." He waved to my brothers. "See you, guys!" He started down the hallway, and I stared after him, wondering if I could ever fix what I'd broken between us.

Kylie and I took turns watching my brothers during the dress rehearsal. We both wore headsets so we could hear the stage manager and director give instructions and feedback. Each time Todd's voice sounded through the headset, my pulse quickened. His voice was so warm and comforting. I missed him so much that my heart ached, and I silently begged God to guide me on how to get him back.

After the dress rehearsal ended, I rushed back to the electronics storage area where my brothers were engrossed in their handheld game systems.

"Were they okay?" I asked Kylie.

"They're fine." Kylie pointed toward the boys. "Those portable video games are the best inventions ever."

"I agree. I hope I can get them to continue playing them at home so I can finish that last jacket." I picked up the boys' wrappers from their lunches. "Let's go home, guys." I looked at Kylie. "Thanks for helping me today."

"You're welcome. Are the costumes all okay?" she asked.

"Yeah, they looked good. I think Mr. Muller is happy."

Kylie gave me a thumbs-up. "See you later. Call if you need me."

"I will." I tossed the food wrappers in the trash and led the boys toward the door. We stepped out into the hallway as Dylan approached.

"Hey." Dylan grinned at me. "I haven't had a chance to talk to you." He gave my brothers a once-over. "Who are the rug rats?"

"Dylan, these are my brothers, J.J. and Justin." I tapped my brothers on their shoulders. "Guys, this is my friend Dylan."

The boys said hello, and Dylan barely gave them a half smile before turning to me. I stared at him, wondering why he couldn't give my brothers the time of day.

"Listen, I'm having a party tonight. It's going to be our last bash before the performances start." He rubbed his hands together. "My parents are out of town until tomorrow night, so I have free rein of the house. What do you think?"

"I don't think so."

"Please." He touched my arm. "I want you there. I thought we were, you know, sort of going out."

"I'm grounded."

"Again?" he asked with disgust.

"Yeah, my mom found out I lied about losing my job. Your advice totally backfired on me." Out of the corner of my eye, I saw my brothers dart down the hallway and head for the back door. "I have to go. The *rug rats* are leaving." I enunciated his dismissive nickname for the twins.

Without waiting for a response, I followed my brothers out to my car.

# chapter seventeen

I was working on the jacket collar when my phone rang at eleven thirty that night. I glanced down and read "Dylan's Cell" on the screen before pushing the phone away. I couldn't stop thinking about the stark difference between Todd and Dylan. While Todd had gone out of his way to help me keep my brothers occupied at the playhouse, Dylan had blown them off as if they were as bothersome as gum on the heel of his shoe.

The phone stopped ringing, and after a few minutes, it chimed, alerting me that Dylan had left a voice mail.

When the phone rang again, I finally picked it up and answered. "Hello?"

"Chelsea." Dylan's voice was surprisingly humble. Muffled voices and music reverberated in the background, and I imagined him standing inside his house near the sliding glass door overlooking the deck.

"Dylan, I can't talk to you right now," I said. "And like I told you, I'm grounded."

"Wait!" He sounded urgent. "Please don't hang up on me."

"What do you want?"

"I want to apologize. I was a real jerk earlier."

My eyebrows raised. *Dylan has a conscience?* "I'm listening."

"I'm sorry I called your brothers *rug rats*." He paused. "Will you forgive me?"

"Yes." My lips turned up in a satisfied smile. "I forgive you."

"Awesome." He sounded relieved. "Can I come pick you up now?"

"No," I insisted. "I really am grounded."

"That didn't stop you before."

"I know, but it's different this time. I broke my mom's heart when I lied to her about my job. I can't risk making this mess a whole lot worse." I leaned back in my chair and studied the jacket while I spoke.

"What she doesn't know won't hurt her. I promise I'll have you back in time to get some sleep."

"Dylan, I can't." I ran my finger over the edge of the table. "I'm sorry."

"Please, Chelsea? Pretty please?"

"Why is it so important for me to be there?"

"I told you: This is our last party before opening night. This is like our last chance to cut loose and celebrate how far we've come this summer." He paused. "And I really like you, Chelsea. I want you here with me. Is that so bad?"

"No, it's not bad." Temptation crept into my mind. "I guess I could come for a little bit. Maybe an hour or so."

"Great! I'll pick you up in ten minutes." He disconnected the call.

I stood and stretched, and my eyes moved to a photo frame that I'd recently laid facedown on my dresser. I picked up the frame and studied the photo of Todd and me at the senior prom. We looked so happy. Todd's arm encircled my waist, and I proudly wore the wrist corsage he'd given me. Things were so easy back then. Why had I let our relationship get so off course?

I pulled my hair up into a ponytail, and I stared at my reflection. My inner voice kept telling me not to go to the party but to stay home and finish the jacket instead—to keep my promise to Mr. Muller.

*But it's one last party, one last hurrah before opening night.*

I gave in to the second voice and changed into denim shorts and a peach cotton-lace-trimmed tank top. I slipped on matching peach bangle bracelets and earrings before sneaking out of the house.

I was standing on the corner when Dylan's yellow Camaro thundered around the corner. The sports car came to a stop in front of me, and I hesitated for a moment. The first inner voice that warned me not to go, voiced its opinion again: *You don't want to hurt Mom this way. You can still go back to the house.*

Dylan leaned over and opened the passenger door. "Are you getting in or what?"

"Yeah." I slipped into the seat.

"What was that all about?" he asked with a look of disdain.

"Nothing." I shook my head as I buckled my seat belt.

"You sure?" He stared at me.

"I'm fine. Let's go." I gripped the door handle as he sped toward the neighborhood exit and roared onto Main Street.

He cranked the volume on the radio, and hard-rock songs serenaded our ride to his neighborhood. When the Camaro raced onto his street, I immediately noticed that the driveway and the street in front of his house were clogged with cars.

"How many people are here?" I asked.

"Everyone." He drove his car onto the grass next to the driveway and put it in park.

"Everyone?" My heartbeat accelerated. *Is Todd here?*

"All of the important people, anyway. No losers." Dylan turned off the car and yanked his keys from the ignition. "Let's go get you a drink."

I climbed out of the car and met Dylan in front of the hood. He stumbled a little as we made our way toward the gate. I touched his arm. "Are you okay?"

"Me?" He laughed. "Chels, I am fine. I feel fantastic!" He opened the gate and motioned for me to enter. "Let me get you that beer."

"No, thanks," I said, but he'd already moved on to speak to another group of friends.

"A familiar face." Marni sidled up to me and spoke over the blaring music. "I thought you were grounded."

"I am." I kept my eyes focused on Dylan as I spoke. "Dylan called and begged me to come."

"*Begged* you?" Marni looked surprised. "I guess he's really into you, huh?"

"I'm not so sure about that," I said, watching him hug an unfamiliar girl. The hug turned into a kiss, and I frowned. "I guess he's just a flirt, huh?"

"Just a flirt?" Marni shook her head. "Chelsea, he's worse than a flirt."

"I know. He's a player," I said. "Turns out all of the people who warned me about him were right, including Todd and my friend Whitney."

Marni touched my arm. "Are you okay?"

"I'm fine." I looked at her. "But I could really use a diet soda."

Marni raised her eyebrows. "No beer?"

"No, not for me." I shook my head.

"Let's get you that soda." She fished two cans out of a nearby cooler, and we sat at the table that was the farthest away from the blaring speakers. "I don't know who half these people are."

"Some of them look vaguely familiar. They may be from Dylan's class at CHS." I opened the can and took a long drink.

"I guess news travels fast when you're having a party while your parents are out of town."

"I guess so." Marni grimaced. "Oh dear."

"What?" I asked.

"Look." She pointed toward the group on the other side of the pool. I followed her stare and found Dylan dancing closely with the girl he'd been kissing. He drank and danced, rubbing his body against the girl's. Kylie and Jimmy danced in a similar fashion next to them.

My mouth formed a thin line as I wondered why I had risked sneaking out to come to this party. I didn't belong with these people. Marni was the only real friend among the large crowd of drinkers.

While I watched the group dancing and drinking, my thoughts turned to a sermon Pastor Kevin had given a few weeks ago. He'd spoken about living a life that emulates Jesus Christ. Chapter one verse twenty-two from the book of James suddenly popped into my mind: "Do not merely listen to the word, and so deceive yourselves. Do what it says."

"Oh no." The urge to flee gripped me. *I need to get out of here*. I longed to go home. I wanted to confess to my parents everything I'd done, and then call Todd and apologize to him too.

I had to make things right, and I wanted to do it immediately.

"Chelsea?" Marni touched my arm. "Are you okay?"

"No, but I will be soon. Do you have your car here by chance?" I asked.

"No." She shook her head. "I hitched a ride with Natasha." She pointed toward one of the girls dancing and drinking. "I'm stuck until she's ready to go home. And from the looks of it, I may be the one driving instead of her. She's getting awfully drunk."

"Oh." I glanced around the crowd. "Do you happen to know where the bathroom is?"

"Yes." Marni pointed toward the deck. "Go through the sliding glass door, and it's the second door on the right, just past the kitchen."

"Great. Thanks." I walked around the pool and up the stairs to the deck. I moved through a knot of people drinking and eating and slipped through the sliding glass door.

I stepped into the kitchen and silently marveled at how spacious it was. There was an island with plenty of storage, a nook containing a large table and chairs, plenty of cherry cabinets, marble counters, and a Spanish tile floor with a blue-and-white-lace pattern. My mother would flip over a kitchen that large and beautiful. I absently wondered if Dylan or his parents even appreciated the beauty of their home.

I made my way to the bathroom and was thankful to find it empty. I locked myself inside and sat on the lid of the toilet while I stared at my phone. I needed to find a quick and safe ride home, but I wasn't sure whom to ask. After all, I was stuck at a party that I'd snuck out to attend while I was grounded. I was embarrassed to admit I'd agreed to come to the party and now I wanted to go home.

Truthfully, I wanted Todd to swoop in and rescue me before we drove off together, talking and laughing as if nothing had gone wrong between us. I knew the talking and laughing part would take some time. But just getting him to come and get me would be a start.

I took a deep breath and began typing a text to Todd: I'm sorry I hurt u. I was wrong about everything. I'm trapped at a party at Dylan's, and I want to go home. Pls come get me. I know it's a lot to ask, but I'll make it up to u. Pls give me a chance. Thx.

I hit Send and closed my eyes.

*Please, God. Please forgive me for all of my many sins. Please soften Todd's heart toward me. I was wrong to hurt him, and I was wrong to lie and sneak around. I acknowledge my mistakes, and I will do better. Amen.*

I waited a few more minutes and then texted Emily: Em! Help! I'm trapped at a party at Dylan's. Can u come get me? Pls? Thx!

I waited a few more minutes and then wondered if I should call my parents. I clicked through to my home number and almost hit the Send button. I stopped when I considered how furious my mother would be if I called her from a party after she'd grounded me. I knew it would be better if I got home first and then confessed my mistakes to her. Asking her to come get me would only make it worse.

A fist pounded on the bathroom door, and I jumped with a start.

"Hey!" a voice boomed. "Are you done yet? I gotta go!"

"I'll be right out." I opened the door, and an unfamiliar guy glared at me. "Sorry."

I pushed past him and weaved back through the crowd on the deck. I marched over to where Dylan was kissing that same girl, and I poked him on the shoulder repeatedly until he turned toward me.

"Hey, Chels." He grinned. "You want a kiss too?"

"No!" I had to shout to be heard over the music. "I want to go home!"

"Why?" he demanded. "You just got here."

"I don't belong here, and I want to go home." I jammed a finger in his chest. "I want you to take me home right now."

"Now?" He shook his head. "Oh no. I'm having fun. I'm not leaving now."

He looped his arm around the girl's waist, pulling her to him. She giggled. I realized then that Dylan had never liked me.

He'd just used me, or maybe he'd enjoyed manipulating me into doing what he wanted, such as sneaking out to go to his parties.

"Yes, you *are* going to leave this party!" My voice rose even louder, and I noticed the crowd was watching us now. "I want to go home *now*, and *you're* going to take me. You talked me into coming here, and now you can just take me back home." I folded my arms over my chest in an effort to stop my body from quaking with white-hot fury.

I felt a hand on my shoulder. "Calm down," Marni said in my ear.

Dylan's smile faded. "I'm busy. You can wait until I'm ready to take you home."

Marni grabbed my arm and pulled me away from Dylan. "Let it go. We'll find someone to take you home. You're not going to get into a car with him now. He's been drinking."

"Yes, I am." I pulled my arm away from her as angry tears filled my eyes. "He brought me here, and I'm miserable. He can take me home." I checked my phone, hoping to find a text from Todd or Emily, but the screen was blank. I went to unlock the phone, and it buzzed, indicating I had entered the wrong code. "I'm so stupid. The code is five, five, three, three. How hard is that to enter?" I finally unlocked the phone and found there weren't any new messages. "Emily and Todd haven't texted me back, so Dylan is going to take me home. I'll *make* him take me." I slipped my phone into my purse.

"He's drunk, Chels. I don't want you or anyone else getting in a car with him. It's not safe." She led me over to our table. "Just sit. I can call my parents."

"No, that's not necessary." I sat next to her and stared over at Dylan. "He's going to take me home." I tapped the table for emphasis. "He insisted on bringing me here, and then blew me off like I didn't matter. He owes me a ride home."

"I don't think that's a good idea." Marni shook her head. "He can't even stand up straight, so he shouldn't get behind the wheel."

"It's not that far to Rock Creek. Maybe I should walk home."

"It would take you probably an hour to walk home, and it's not safe to walk home alone at night."

"What if we walked together?"

"Chelsea, let me call my parents, okay? They promised they will come and get me, no questions asked." She pulled her phone out of her pocket.

"I would hate for you to leave early on account of me." I pushed her phone away from her ear. "I'll be fine."

Dylan made his way over to us and gestured toward the gate. "Come on. Let's get this over with."

I looked at Marni. "I'll see you tomorrow, okay?"

Marni shook her head and grabbed for my arm. "Please don't go. I'll walk home with you."

"No, it's okay. Really, I'm fine." I followed Dylan toward the gate.

Kylie and Jimmy joined us.

"Where are you two going?" Kylie asked with a beer in hand.

"I'm taking her home." Dylan frowned and pointed at me. "I'll be right back."

Jimmy looked at Kylie. "Are you ready to head out too?"

"Sure." She grinned. "My parents aren't home. You can come to my place."

"We'll follow you," Jimmy said.

"Fine." Dylan started out the gate, stumbled, and then righted himself. The car keys jingled as he pulled them from his back pocket.

Marni's warning about Dylan's intoxication echoed through me. I had to speak up now before I climbed into that car.

"I don't think you're in any condition to get behind the wheel," I said calmly, despite my growing feeling of anxiety. "How about I drive?"

His eyes narrowed to slits. "No one drives my car but me," he said as he jammed a thumb toward his chest. "Now get in."

I reached for the door handle and hesitated. My inner voice told me not to get into the car, but I really wanted to go home. I glanced over to where Jimmy and Kylie were standing by Jimmy's black Dodge pickup and wondered how many beers Jimmy had consumed. If he was sober, did they have room for me in their truck?

"Are you getting in, or are you walking?" Dylan's voice was laced with irritation. "You bugged me to take you home, and now you're standing here like a statue. What's the deal, Chelsea?"

I climbed into the car.

"This is ridiculous," he mumbled, jamming the key into the ignition. "I'm missing my party because you decided you have to go home."

I buckled my seat belt and sent up a silent prayer for safety.

The car rumbled to life, and he punched the car into reverse before roaring off the grass and onto the road.

I gripped the dashboard and stared at him. "Was that really necessary?"

He ignored me and slammed the car into drive after revving the engine.

Jimmy's truck pulled up on the left side of the Camaro, and Kylie rolled down the passenger side window. Dylan lowered his window too.

"Do you want to race?" Jimmy asked, leaning around Kylie.

Dylan gave him an evil grin. "You'll regret it because I'll have all the bragging rights."

"Oh yeah?" Jimmy revved his truck's engine. "I've got a Hemi."

"No!" I yelled as my body quaked with horror. "Take me home before you race!"

"Hold on, Chelsea," Dylan warned.

Dylan slammed his foot on the accelerator, and a scream tore from my throat. The Camaro plunged forward, and I gripped the door handle as the stop sign at the corner came closer and closer. A sedan approached from the cross street, and icy tendrils of fear gripped my spine. I closed my eyes.

I felt the car jerk hard to the right and then pitch to the left. The screaming squeal of tires and the smell of burning rubber filled my nose just before the deafening crash.

My body bounced forward like a rag doll, and I heard my head crack against something hard and metal.

And then everything went black.

# chapter eighteen

I awoke with a thunderous headache coupled with excruciating pain radiating from my right ankle. The pain was horrific, and I sucked in a breath. I wished those blaring sirens would stop. They sounded like they were surrounding me. I wanted to move, but my body felt like it was strapped down, and my neck was restricted too. I couldn't turn my head. My body jostled about, and when I finally opened my eyes, I saw a white metal ceiling above me.

"Hey." A young man in a white uniform peered down at me. "How are you feeling?"

"Where am I?" My voice was hoarse, like I'd been screaming at a concert for two hours.

"You're in an ambulance." He touched my arm. "My name is Jake, and I'm an EMT."

"EMT?" I tried to remember what had happened, but everything was fuzzy.

"You were in an accident." He kept his tone even as he talked over the wailing siren.

I wished someone would turn off that siren. It was starting to give me a headache. Or maybe I already had a migraine. I couldn't tell which had come first—the ankle pain or the migraine. And then there was that burning sensation on my face.

"What's your name, sweetheart?" Jake asked. He had a kind face.

"Chelsea Morris."

He asked me some more simple questions, and I recited my birthday and address for him. The ambulance came to a stop, and the board slid forward, causing the neck brace to strangle me for a moment. Jake quickly leaned over and adjusted the board, and I blew out a deep breath.

"Sorry about that." Jake gazed down at me with concern. "How are you feeling?"

"My head and my leg hurt." Tears filled my eyes. "Where are we going?"

"We're on our way to the hospital. We're almost there." He touched my hand. "Do you remember what happened?"

"No." I tried to shake my head, but the brace prevented me from moving.

"You were a passenger in a yellow Camaro. Your friend ran a stop sign and then overcorrected when he saw oncoming traffic. Do you remember your friend's name—the young man who was driving the car?"

The details started to come back into focus. Dylan's party. Dylan kissing that girl and ignoring me. The text message I sent to Todd. Trying to find a ride home. Jimmy and Kylie. Drag racing.

"Dylan McCormick," I said as the tears began to flow. "Dylan was driving the car."

"That's right." He rubbed my hand.

"How is he?" I asked.

"He's fine. He said he was a little sore, but he refused to go to the hospital. He was talking to a police officer when we left. Don't worry about him, okay?"

I couldn't stop my tears. Soon I was crying with deep shuddering sobs.

"It's okay, sweetheart. We're almost at the hospital. Just one more light."

"Did someone call my mom?"

"Yes. One of your friends found your phone in your purse and called your parents. I spoke to your mom. She's on her way."

"It must have been Kylie. She was there."

"Kylie?" Jake looked confused. "That name doesn't sound familiar, but there was a lot of chaos. Quite a few people came running when they heard the crash. One of the girls called nine-one-one. I think she called your folks too."

My eyes began to close involuntarily, and Jake's voice and the siren started to fade.

"Stay with me, Chelsea." His voice was urgent. "Do you have any pets?"

"I have a cat." I tried to keep my eyes open, but they fought to close.

"What's your cat's name?" he asked.

"Buttons."

"Buttons?" He laughed. "And what does Buttons look like?"

"He's a big orange cat."

"Wow. Buttons is a funny name for a big orange cat."

"I like to sew."

"Really?" he asked. "What do you like to sew?"

I babbled on and on to this total stranger about costumes while the ambulance sped on toward the hospital. I had a feeling he was trying to keep me awake. Did I have a concussion? I'd once heard that people with concussions weren't allowed to go to sleep.

Soon the siren died, and the ambulance came to an abrupt stop.

"We're here." Jake stood. "We're at the hospital. Bob and I are going to lower you down. You just sit tight."

"I don't think I'm going anywhere strapped to this board," I muttered.

"Hold on to that sense of humor, Chelsea." Jake grinned at me.

Jake and the other EMT unloaded the gurney from the ambulance, and then I started a journey through doors and down hallways. I was restricted to staring at the fluorescent lights and listening to the chatter of voices around me. The sterile aroma of bleach and other disinfectants permeated my nose.

Finally, a pretty blonde in a white coat stared down at me. "Hi, Chelsea. I'm Dr. Caren Strout. How are you feeling?"

"Sore." My voice was thick. "My ankle, my face, and my head hurt."

"From what I've heard, you're a very lucky girl." She touched my hand. "You had an angel on your shoulder tonight." She wrote something on a clipboard. "I want to send you for a few tests. But first I'm going to go see if your parents are here yet." She squeezed my hand.

"Are you leaving me?" Panic seized me as a tear trickled down my face.

"I will be right back, sweetie. I promise."

"Okay." My voice croaked, and more tears flowed. If I'd listened to my inner voice tonight, I'd be sleeping in my own bed with Buttons snuggled up next to me. Why did I have to sneak out? And why hadn't I listened to Marni? If her parents had come to get us, I'd be at home now, talking to my parents and getting everything off my conscience.

Pain surged from my ankle, and I swallowed a groan. I wanted my mom. I wanted my bed. I wanted to start the summer over again.

"Chelsea!" Mom's voice rang out. "Oh, Chelsea."

"Mom." My voice cracked as I started to sob. "I'm so

sorry for sneaking out. I'm sorry for lying to you. I'm sorry for everything."

"Shhh." Mom pushed my hair back. "Don't worry about that now. We'll talk about it later."

"No, Mom." I insisted through my tears. "I've been so wrong about everything. Please forgive me. Please, Mom."

"Shhh, baby. Of course, I forgive you." Tears shone in her brown eyes. "You just concentrate on getting better."

"I'm Dr. Strout," the doctor said.

"I'm Audrey Klein, Chelsea's mother." Mom's voice was thin and ragged. "How is my daughter?"

I strained to hear their conversation but couldn't. They must have deliberately moved away from me. Lost in my own thoughts, I alternated between trying to stop the pain in my ankle with the force of my will and wishing I was back home in my bed listening to Buttons purr.

"We'd like to run some tests, so I need you to sign a few forms," Dr. Strout said, then lowered her voice again.

I reached up and wiped the tears from my hot cheeks while I waited.

"Okay, Chelsea." Mom took my hand in hers. "The doctor wants to run a couple of tests. If the results are okay, then you can get off that board."

"When am I going for the tests?"

"As soon as the nurse gets here to take you. The doctor is ordering the tests now."

"Oh." I tried to make sense of it all, despite the fog in my brain.

"Your dad is on his way down here now. He should be here in about an hour."

"Daddy is coming?" I asked. "How did he know?"

"I called to tell him you were in an accident. I also called

Christina, and she's very upset. She wants to know if she should catch a flight home. I told her to wait and see what the doctor says."

"She doesn't have to come."

"Well, we'll see. Jason is at home with the twins, but he sends his love." She pushed my hair back from my face. "My heart stopped when I got that phone call."

"Mom, I'm sorry. I never should've gone out tonight. Please forgive me."

"Shhh. It's going to be okay. Let's just concentrate on praying for your tests." She paused and played with my hair some more. "I'm just glad you're talking. When Marni said you were unconscious, I thought I was going to pass out."

"Wait a minute." I stared at her as the words registered. "Marni called you?"

"Yes, that's right."

"Not Kylie?"

"No, Marni called me." Mom shook her head. "Marni is out in the waiting room right now. She introduced herself to me and gave me your purse and phone. She must be a good friend. I'm glad you met her."

"Yeah," I said slowly. "Me too." *But where is Kylie?*

"Hi, Chelsea. I'm Evan." A young man wearing blue scrubs smiled down at me. "I'm going to take you for a few tests. Are you ready?"

"Sure," I said.

Mom squeezed my hand again. "I'll be waiting right here when you get back, okay?"

"Okay."

Evan chattered on about the weather while he pushed the gurney through the hallway. His words only served as background noise to my own thoughts. I couldn't stop wondering why Marni had called my mother. Why hadn't Kylie made the call if she'd witnessed the accident? From what I recalled, the accident happened within a block of Dylan's home. If Kylie had been nearby, why wouldn't she have made the call?

"We're going to do an MRI to make sure your bones aren't broken. Is that okay?" the nurse asked, breaking through my thoughts.

"Yes."

"I'm going to put you inside this machine, and you need to lie perfectly still. Are you claustrophobic?"

"No."

"Great." He pushed the gurney into a long cylinder.

I closed my eyes and tried not to think about how I was inside a giant, metal coffin. Instead, I began to pray:

> *Thank you, God, for protecting me from the accident. Thank you for saving Dylan too. Please lead Dylan and me back to the right road. Please bless my family. Please help me bridge the chasm between my mother and me. Please help me mend my broken relationship with Todd. Thank you for my life. In Jesus's holy name, Amen.*

I repeated the prayer over and over until the machine stopped humming. Once the test was complete, Evan guided my gurney back to the small treatment room where my mother and a policeman were waiting.

"Mom?" I asked as the policeman walked over to the gurney.

"Hi, Chelsea. I'm Officer Young." The middle-aged man smiled down at me. "How are you feeling?"

"Sore."

"I'm sorry about that." He held a small notepad and a pen. "I need to ask you a few questions about the accident. Is it all right if I talk to you now?"

"Sure," I said.

"Good. Your mom said she'd like to stay while I talk to you. Is that all right with you?"

"Of course."

"Great. Do you remember what happened tonight?"

"I think so." I cleared my throat. "I went to Dylan's house for a party."

"What is Dylan's full name?" he asked. "And how do you know him?"

"His name is Dylan McCormick. We're both working on the community theater production of *Grease*."

"How did you get to the party?" Mom chimed in.

I explained I was working on the jacket when Dylan called and pressured me into going. I said Dylan had picked me up and then ignored me once we got to his house. I explained that I'd wanted to go home right away, but I couldn't get my friends to text me back after I texted them and asked for a ride.

"Was everyone at the party drinking?" the officer asked.

"I can't say everyone was, but most of the people were."

"Were you drinking?" he asked.

"No. Marni and I were drinking diet soda. Marni warned me not to get in the car with Dylan, but I was stupid. I just wanted to go home so badly that I wasn't thinking straight." My eyes filled with fresh tears. "I'm sorry, Mom. I never should have gone to the party, and I never should've gotten into the car with him."

"Where were his parents?" Mom asked. She looked pretty shocked by what she'd heard so far.

"He said they're out of town."

"I can't believe he was serving alcohol at the party," Mom continued.

"What happened when you got into the car?" Officer Young asked.

I explained that I'd offered to drive his car, but he'd refused. I then told how Jimmy had challenged Dylan to a race, and I'd begged him not to do it while I was in the car.

"He was street racing?" Officer Young raised an eyebrow.

"Yes, sir."

"Who was in the other vehicle, and what kind of vehicle was it?"

"Jimmy French was driving his black Dodge pickup truck. His girlfriend, Kylie Buchanan, was in the passenger seat."

"That's very interesting," the officer said. "There were only two vehicles at the scene: Dylan's and the one he swerved to miss. Dylan didn't mention that he was street racing."

"What?" I said. "Jimmy and Kylie left the scene?"

"It appears that way."

"They left?" I asked again. "I can't believe it. I thought Kylie was my friend."

"It's okay, Chelsea." Mom touched my hand. "Don't get upset."

The police officer asked a few more questions about the accident, and then he asked my mother for follow-up phone numbers.

"I will be in touch, Mrs. Klein." He looked at me and said, "You take care of yourself, Chelsea."

Mom stood by my bedside and held my hand after the officer left. "You could have called me to come get you. If you're ever in a situation like that again where you feel threatened, you can *always* call Jason and me. We'll come and get you, no questions asked."

I realized then that I should have trusted my parents to help me. Just like Marni had said about her parents, deep down I knew my parents would have come in a heartbeat. "I should've called you. I'm sorry, Mom."

"Shhh." Mom rubbed my arm. "Stop apologizing."

"You should ground me until I'm thirty," I continued. "I need to be punished."

"Hmm." Mom looked as if she was having difficulty hiding her smile. "I think that would be hard to enforce while you're at college. Are you saying you want to skip college?"

"No, but I deserve to be in trouble for a long time. I've let everyone down."

"You just stop worrying about that right now. There will be plenty of time for punishment after you're out of the hospital."

"Chelsea." I heard my dad's voice. "Oh, baby. What happened?"

"Daddy!" I reached for him and tried to remove the tethers from around my throat. But the tethers were stuck, and I couldn't move. "Daddy, you came."

"Of course, I did. I jumped in the car as soon as your mother called me." Dad stood over me. "What happened?"

Mom gave him a brief overview of the accident while Dad listened with his mouth open.

"Where is this Dylan McCormick kid?" Dad demanded. "I'd like to have a word with him. How dare he drive drunk, especially with our daughter in the car."

"I had the same thought." Mom shook her head. "I can't wait until his parents come home from their trip. We can visit him together."

"That's a good plan," Dad agreed before touching my hand. "How are you, honey? What hurts?"

I described my aches and pains.

"I'm sure the doctor is going to take good care of you," he promised.

Soon Dr. Strout reappeared. "I have good news. Your leg and ankle aren't broken. I think the ankle pain is from a bad sprain. We'll get it wrapped up and give you a pair of crutches and some pain-killers. You do have a mild concussion, so I'd like you to hang out here a little longer just so we can observe you. After we're sure you're okay, we'll send you on your way. Sound good?"

"Yes." I groaned. "Just get me off this board."

"Absolutely," Dr. Strout said.

A few moments later, a nurse came in and removed the suffocating straps. He and Dad helped me get off the board and into a much more comfortable hospital bed. I could finally sit up and see something other than fluorescent lights and white ceiling tiles. Dad took a seat in the chair next to my bed

Another nurse came in and showed me an elastic bandage. "We're going to wrap your ankle with this." She looked at my mother. "Do you want to watch how I do this so you can rewrap it after she showers?"

"Absolutely." Mom stood next to the nurse to observe. Dad held my hand.

I sucked in a breath as the nurse gently moved my foot into position and tightly wrapped the bandage around my foot and ankle. She placed the wrapped foot on top of a pillow and set an ice pack on it.

"How's that?" the nurse asked.

"It's okay," I said in spite of the shooting pains that were still radiating from my ankle.

She pointed toward the controller next to the bed. "Hit the button if you need anything."

"Thank you."

Mom leaned over and pushed my hair off my forehead. She ran a hand down the side of my face while I took a long drink of ice water from a pink plastic cup. My hand shook as I reached up and touched my face where it was sore and throbbing. "Is my face bruised or cut?"

"Yes, both." My mom nodded. "I think that's from the air bag."

"I'm sure it is." Dad's expression was solemn. "You're lucky it wasn't worse."

Dad offered Mom the chair next to my bed while he moved to stand in the doorway.

"I'm sorry for putting you both through this." I ran my hand down my sore face, wondering how bad I looked. "You can take away my car, my phone, anything. I know I was wrong."

"We'll discuss that later." Mom rubbed my arm. "All that matters now is that you're okay."

"Exactly." Dad walked over to the bed and rubbed my left foot, which wasn't injured. "Don't worry about getting punished. Only worry about getting better."

"Excuse me." The nurse stepped into the room. "There are a few folks out here who'd like to see Chelsea. Is it okay if Emily, Marni, and Zander visit?"

"Yes." I nodded.

A few minutes later, the three stepped into the small room.

My mother introduced my friends to my dad, and Zander shook Dad's hand.

Mom said to Dad, "How about we give the kids some time alone to visit? We can go to the cafeteria and talk a bit."

"Sounds good." Dad smiled at me. "We'll be back soon."

"Thanks, Daddy," I said as they left the room. I tried to shift my weight to a different position in the bed, but the pain from my ankle prevented me from finding a comfortable spot.

Tears streamed down Emily's face as she rushed over to the hospital bed. "I'm so sorry I missed your text. Zander and I were watching a movie at his house, and my phone was in my purse. I never heard it ring." She hugged me. "If I'd gotten your message, we would've come over right away to get you."

"Absolutely. We would've been there in a heartbeat." Zander stepped toward the bed. "How are you?"

"Sore." I pointed at my ankle. "My ankle is sprained. It hurts like crazy, but at least it's not broken."

"I'm so sorry." Emily wiped her tears, and Zander placed a hand on her shoulder. "When Marni called me, we were on our way to my house. We turned around and came right here. I wish I'd been there to help you. Then you never would've gotten into his car."

"It's okay, Emily. Don't cry. I'm fine. It's my fault for going over to that jerk's house in the first place." I looked over at Marni who was standing by the door. "Thank you for calling my mom and Emily."

"You're welcome." Marni moved toward the bed, and her bottom lip quivered. "I had such a bad feeling when you got into that car. And then when I heard the crash ..." Her voice trailed off as she began to cry.

Emily touched Marni's arm. "I know what you mean. I had the worst feeling when you told me about the crash. I was so worried that she was ... you know ..."

Marni nodded. "I ran up the street after the accident, and when I saw her unconscious in the passenger seat, my heart was pounding and I thought I was going to faint. I immediately thought the worst. I'm so thankful I was wrong."

They hugged each other, and I was overwhelmed by their instant friendship. They were crying because they'd been worried about *me*. My heart overflowed with love and regret as I studied my two friends.

"I'm sorry for being such a lousy friend to you two." I sniffed. "You both have been so good to me, and I was so focused on being one of the cool kids that I didn't realize what I had right in front of me."

"Oh, Chelsea." Emily hugged me.

Marni came around to the other side of the bed and made it a group hug.

The three of us wiped our tears.

Emily glanced over at Zander and chuckled. "Do you want to join in?"

"No, thanks." He held up his hands and grinned. "I'm just fine over here in the corner."

Emily picked up a box of tissues and passed it to Marni and me.

"Thanks," I said, wiping my nose. "I've had such loyal friends all along, and I was too blinded by Dylan's nonsense to see it. I've hurt a lot of people, including Todd." My voice cracked as I said his name. "I've gone against everything I've been taught since I was little, and I'm so sorry. I'm embarrassed I haven't been the person I've always tried to be."

"We all make mistakes," Marni said as she took a seat in the chair next to the bed. "None of us are perfect."

"That's why we need Jesus. Chelsea, you need to remember that Jesus's sacrifice means we can always ask God to forgive us when we mess up. No believer is perfect, but we are forgiven and loved by God." Emily looked over at Zander. "Right, Zander? I know I've messed up before."

"We all have." Zander moved a chair to the other side of the bed and motioned for Emily to sit. "We're all forgiven, Chelsea, so stop beating yourself up."

"You're right. Thanks for reminding me." I glanced at Marni and thought back to the accident. "How did you know where to find my phone?"

"I watched you put it in your purse at the party." Marni leaned back in the chair. "Remember when you couldn't get the phone to unlock so you could check your messages?"

I tried to concentrate through my headache and the lingering haze inside my head. "Oh right."

"You were so frustrated, you said the code out loud. Well, for some reason when I found your purse and phone, I remembered the code. I brought your purse to your mom," Marni said.

"Thanks," I said.

Marni continued, "When I got to the scene of the accident, Dylan was already talking on his phone with someone. I don't know who he was talking to, but I called nine-one-one. After that, I called your mom, and then I called Emily."

My thoughts turned to Kylie. "Was Kylie there?"

"Was Kylie where?" Marni asked.

"At the accident scene. Did she and Jimmy help?"

Marni looked confused. "No. Why would they be there?"

"Jimmy and Dylan were racing," I explained. "That's why Dylan ran the stop sign and almost collided with that other car."

"Dylan was street racing?" Zander's voice had an edge to it. "They were street racing in *my* neighborhood?"

I nodded.

"I only saw Dylan's car and the BMW he almost hit. He swerved and hit a power pole instead of the BMW." Marni demonstrated with her hands. "The Camaro was here, the pole was there, and then the BMW was about one hundred yards away. There were skid marks on the street from where the Camaro slid. But that's it. Jimmy's pickup wasn't anywhere in sight."

"They must have fled the scene," Emily said.

"They left me." I shook my head. "They didn't even stick around to see if I was still alive."

"You don't need them." Emily's expression was serious. "You have us, right, Marni?"

"That's right." Marni gave an emphatic nod. "From what you've told me, Kylie wasn't much help with the costumes anyway."

"The costumes." New worry filled me as I covered my face with my hands. "Saturday night is opening night, and I'm still not finished. What am I going to do?"

"What do you need?" Marni moved her chair closer to the bed.

"I haven't finished Jan's Pink Ladies' jacket yet." I looked at Emily. "The others are done, but I just have this last one to do."

"Oh wow." Emily frowned. "I can fix a car, but I can't sew."

"I can finish it for you. I'll come over tomorrow morning, and you can lounge while I sew," Marni said.

"Are you sure?" I asked.

"It's no problem," Marni insisted. "I'll stop by the theater in the morning and grab one of the other jackets to use as an example. You can bark orders, and I'll do the work. Piece of cake."

"You're the best, Marni."

My parents appeared in the doorway with two drink carriers.

"I have cola and diet cola," Mom said. "Who's thirsty?"

Marni grabbed two diet sodas and handed one to me.

"Let's have a toast." I held up my cup. "To my amazing friends and family. God is good."

"Yes, he is," Emily said.

As I sipped my drink, I thanked God for blessing me with special friends and a wonderful family.

# chapter nineteen

"Chelsea!" Mom's voice called. "Good morning! Actually, it's almost afternoon now. It's after eleven."

I moaned and stared at the ceiling. My parents had brought me home from the hospital after three in the morning, and I'd spent most of the night trying to get comfortable. The painkillers did little to stop the pain in my foot or the rest of my body. My whole body ached from the impact of the accident. My back and neck and hips were sore, and I felt as if the Camaro had run over me.

"Are you hungry?" Mom carried a tray of food toward the bed, and the smell of scrambled eggs filled my room.

"Oh wow." My stomach growled. "That smells so good." I tried to sit up.

"Wait. Let me help you." Mom set the tray on the floor and shooed Buttons away from the food. She grabbed my bright purple bed pillow off the floor and held it up. "Can you scoot back without hurting your ankle?"

I gingerly sat up, and Mom set the pillow behind me. "Thank you," I said, leaning back with a sigh.

"Here's your pain pill." She handed me a small white pill and a glass of chocolate milk.

I took the pill, and she set the breakfast tray over my legs. "Thanks, Mom."

"You're welcome." Mom stood by the bed while I ate. "I don't know if you heard the phone, but it's been ringing most of the morning."

"I did hear it a couple of times." I scooped eggs into my mouth. "Who called?"

"A better question would be who *hasn't* called."

I sipped the milk. "What do you mean?"

"Your sister has called a few times. I convinced her she doesn't need to come home. She's going to call you later." Mom counted off the people on her fingers. "Emily and Marni are on their way over to see you. Janie Cavanaugh from the restaurant called. She's coming later today. She said she has something for you. Also, your dad called to say he made it home safely. He's going to come visit you Sunday."

"Wait." I held up my hand. "Emily and Marni are coming here now?"

"Yes." Mom looked toward the digital clock on my nightstand. "They should be here soon. Marni said she's going to finish sewing that jacket, and Emily wants to do anything she can to help."

"Doesn't Marni have practice?" I asked.

"She said she got special permission to miss it. She explained the situation to Mr. Muller, and he was supportive."

"Really?" I blinked with surprise. "Wow."

"Emily said I could go to work if I need to, but I told her I want to be here with you. But she still insisted she wants to come help. She's worried about you." Mom moved my sewing chair next to the bed and sat down. "I am too. I think we need to talk."

"Where are the boys?" I asked suspiciously. "It's too quiet."

Mom laughed. "Jason took them to the park for a while. He's going in to work later today."

"Oh." I scooped more eggs into my mouth.

"When I talked to your sister this morning and told her what happened, I asked her if I'd done something wrong." Mom crossed her legs and rested her arm on her knee. "How did I let this happen to you?"

"Why would you blame yourself for the bad decisions I made?"

"I'm your mother, so I feel like I pushed you to sneak out and party. Did I do or say something that made you feel like you didn't matter to this family?" Her eyes filled with worry. "Do you feel ignored because the twins take up so much of my time and effort?"

"No." I shook my head. "No, it's not that at all. I don't resent them. I love them. You know that."

"I know you love them, but your life changed tremendously when I had them. You have to feel a little bit of resentment," she said. "I realized that I overreacted when you were late picking them up from camp that one day. Grounding you for your first offense was too much. You're eighteen and you deserved more respect and trust than I had given you. I'm sorry that I lost my temper. I've just been so stressed out about work, and I'm sorry for taking it out on you. Also, making you babysit them was too much on top of your obligations with the musical."

*This is it. It's time to come clean and tell her the whole truth.* I set the fork on the tray. "Mom, last night wasn't the first time I'd snuck out."

Her eyes rounded. "It wasn't?"

I shook my head. "No, I'd done it a few times before that. And I also drank beer at three of the parties. That's why I was late to work twice. That's why Mrs. Hughes fired me."

Mom stared at me. "I had no idea."

"I never should have snuck out, and I never should've drank

alcohol. I don't even like beer, and despise how I feel when I'm hungover." I moved the eggs around on my plate while I thought about what I'd say next. "I was irresponsible, and I went against everything you've ever taught me about being a good, responsible adult."

"Why did you do it?" Mom pleaded. "Were you trying to fit in?"

"Yeah." I traced the edge of the tray with my finger. "I wanted to be cool like Dylan—and the other members of the cast. Dylan is in college, he's handsome, and he showed interest in me. In the end I realized he wasn't a good friend at all. I mean, he didn't even come to the hospital after the accident, and he hasn't called to check on me."

"He never should've gotten behind the wheel. Your father and Jason and I are talking to a lawyer about that."

"You're right." I nodded. "And I never should've gotten in the car with him. Marni warned me not to. In fact, she begged me not to. She was the smartest one at the parties. She never had one drop of alcohol. She constantly told me I didn't have to drink to fit in. She's a really good friend." I thought about Kylie. "Has Kylie called?"

"No." Mom shook her head and frowned. "I bet she's afraid to since she and Jimmy left the scene of the accident. The police are looking into that too." She rubbed my leg. "You should finish eating."

I picked up the bagel and took a bite. "Has Todd called?" I had been wondering that since I first heard the phone ring.

"No." Mom continued to rub my leg. "I'm sorry."

"It's okay." I shrugged as if it weren't a big deal, even though it was breaking my heart. "I can't expect him to act like nothing happened."

"Did you and Todd break up because of your partying?"

"Yeah. That's what came between us. I didn't realize what a colossal mistake I was making until it was too late." I chewed a bite of bagel.

"Don't give up on him. The Lord tells us to forgive. And from what I've seen, Todd is a good guy and a solid Christian." Mom smiled. "I have a feeling he'd forgive you if you showed him how much you still care about him."

I wiped my mouth with a napkin. "I hope so." I cleared my throat and finally worked up the courage to ask the other question that had been on my mind. "Have you and dad decided on my punishment for sneaking out?"

Mom crossed her arms. "Your father and I were discussing that last night while we were in the hospital cafeteria. We bounced around some ideas, but I thought I might try something different."

"You're going to try something different?" Concern filled me. "What were your ideas? Are you sending me to military school?"

Mom laughed. "That actually wasn't one of our ideas, but I can suggest it to him."

I pointed to my foot. "I don't think I'd make it through basic training."

We both laughed. And the sound of her laughter was a comfort to me after she'd been so upset with me for so long.

"On a more serious note," Mom said, "we're thinking you need to be grounded for the rest of the summer for sure. That means no cast parties after the performances."

I held up my hands. "I completely agree. I'm done with cast parties."

"I don't want to cut you off from your friends completely, though, so you can have a few close friends over here, if you want to," Mom said. "And after what happened last night, we'd like you to speak to the youth at church about the dangers of alcohol. When you're feeling better, we can talk to Pastor Kevin and the youth minister about how to put that together. You need to share your experience with the youth and help them realize how much worse it could've been."

"That's a great idea. God can use my experience to help others and maybe save a few kids from making the same mistakes."

"Exactly."

I waited for her to continue, but she remained silent. "That's it? You're grounding me and making me tell the kids at church not to drink?"

She smiled. "Did you want a stiffer punishment?"

"No, but I'm surprised."

"Chelsea, I'm just so glad you're okay." She pointed toward my right foot. "You won't be driving anytime soon, so you're essentially losing your car privileges anyway. Once you show me that you're responsible, you'll get your freedom back. Right now I just want you to rest and get better."

"Am I still allowed to go to opening night tomorrow?" I asked before finishing off the last bite of bagel.

"Of course you are. You've earned that."

The doorbell rang downstairs, and Buttons rushed toward the first floor.

"It looks like we have company." Mom stood. "Is it all right if I send them upstairs?"

"Yes." I pointed toward my dresser. "Can you bring me my handheld mirror?"

"Sure."

I cautiously peered at my reflection and gasped at the sight. My right cheek was puffy and red, and small cuts peppered both of my cheeks and my forehead. "I look like a train wreck. Would you hand me my brush?"

"You look fine, Chelsea. Don't worry about it." She handed me the brush and picked up the food tray. "Just relax."

I brushed my hair back and smoothed my hands over my pink polka-dotted pajama top.

Mom started for the stairs. "Do you need anything else?"

"No, thanks."

"I'll send them up."

"Mom," I said, and she turned to face me. "Thanks for everything. I love you."

"You're welcome, and I love you too." Mom disappeared down the stairs.

I heard loud voices in the front hall, and within a few minutes, footsteps echoed on the stairs as Emily and Marni burst into my room.

"Chelsea! I brought you a surprise." Emily held up two DVDs. "We're going to eat popcorn and watch *Grease* and *Grease* 2! Your mom started making the popcorn for us." She walked over to my television and turned on the DVD player. "Get ready to sing."

"Thank you." I shook my head and laughed. "How did you get the day off work?"

"My dad *is* the assistant manager." Emily turned on the television and hit the Mute button. "He gave me the day off and sends his love. He hopes you feel better soon. Whitney sends her love too."

"While you two enjoy the movie, I will be finishing that jacket. I'm ready to work." Marni held up one of the denim jackets I'd already finished. "Mr. Muller said I'm excused from rehearsals today so I can finish Jan's jacket."

"How did you manage that, Marni?" I asked.

"I talked to his wife first. Mrs. Muller is much less strict." Marni moved the sewing chair closer to the table and sat down.

"She said I've done well during rehearsals, and she agreed that you needed the help right now. She also said she was sorry to hear about the accident."

"Thanks. What about Kylie?"

"I haven't heard from her or seen her," Marni said. "When I spoke to Mr. Muller, I told him I've been helping my mother with sewing projects for years, and I can get the job done today. I suggested he let Kylie handle the costume changes during the rehearsals." She grimaced as she looked at the jacket. "Let's hope I can."

"If you need me to, I can waddle over there and help," I offered.

"No, it looks like you were almost finished." Marni held up the jacket. "You already got the sleeves in, and that's the hardest part." She grinned at me. "I can do this."

"You're amazing," I said. "You can sing, dance, act, and sew."

Marni held up her finger. "Don't give me all the credit yet. The jacket may not come out the way you want it to, and Jan may have to share Rizzo's jacket."

"I have complete faith in you," I told her.

As Marni examined the unfinished jacket, my eyes landed on the sewing machine from Dylan. Mom's advice about returning it to him echoed through my mind. After the way he'd treated me, I definitely wanted to return it—the sooner, the better!

Emily slipped the DVD into the player and sniffed the air. "I smell popcorn! I'll be back in a minute with popcorn and sodas."

By the end of the afternoon, I'd watched both *Grease* and *Grease 2* and Marni had finished the jacket while Buttons napped on the floor under the sewing table. And Emily catered to my every whim, even escorting me down to the bathroom whenever I needed to go.

After five o'clock, I hobbled down the stairs behind my friends to the front door.

"Thank you so much," I said, hugging them both. "I'm so thankful for each of you."

Emily waved off the compliment. "It was fun! I'll see you at the performance tomorrow night?"

"You're going?" I asked.

"Are you kidding?" Emily laughed. "I wouldn't miss it for the world. Zander and I are going with Whitney and Taylor. We're super excited."

"I'll take these to the playhouse for you." Marni held up the two completed Pink Ladies' jackets.

"I can't thank you enough," I said. "You did a fantastic job. You're a lifesaver."

"I'm happy I could help." Marni looked over at my mother standing in the kitchen doorway. "Good-bye, Mrs. Klein."

"Thanks again you two." Mom came over and hugged each girl. "We appreciate you both."

Emily and Marni turned and waved as they hurried out to Emily's car parked on the street.

"I'm going to start supper," Mom said as she headed toward the kitchen. "You can go sit with the boys if you want."

I started hopping down the hall on my crutches when the doorbell rang. "Who can that be?" I hobbled back to the door and was surprised to find Janie standing on the porch with a vase full of flowers.

"Janie," I opened the door. "Come in."

"Hey, Chelsea. I don't have much time. I have to get back to the restaurant." Janie stepped into the foyer. "But I heard about what happened last night, and I wanted to stop by and make sure you're okay."

"Thank you." My eyes moved to the vase of flowers.

"Oh, these are for you." Janie held up the vase. "My cousin didn't have the guts to come here himself."

"Those are from Todd?" My heart thudded in my chest as I examined the colorful bouquet of peach long-stemmed roses, white daisy poms, green button poms, and blue delphinium embellished with a variety of greenery. He knew peach roses were my favorite, and he cared enough to send them despite our breakup.

Janie grinned and shook her head. "Todd is a big chicken."

"Wow." I spotted a card among the flowers.

"My aunt and uncle send their love," Janie continued. "They were sorry to hear about the accident too." She gestured toward my foot. "Are you okay?"

"Yeah, it's just a bad sprain. I'm sore, but I'm fine."

Mom walked out of the kitchen. "Hi, there."

"Janie, this is my mom, Audrey Klein," I said. "Mom, this is Janie Cavanaugh. She works at the Fork & Knife. She's Todd's cousin."

"It's nice to meet you." Janie handed the flowers to my mom. "I wanted to deliver these and say hi to Chelsea. But I have to get back to work now."

"These are gorgeous." Mom smelled the flowers. "Thank you, Janie."

"Oh, they aren't from me. I'm just the delivery girl." Janie stepped toward the door. "I have to run, but you take care, Chelsea."

"Thank you." I closed the door behind Janie and followed my mom into the kitchen. "Would you hand me the card?" I sat down at the table.

"Here you go." Mom gave me the small white envelope and set the vase in the middle of the table. "They're lovely."

My pulse quickened as I pulled out the card. The note card

was decorated with flowers. Printing across the top said Get Well Soon. I immediately recognized Todd's messy cursive handwriting as I read, *Chelsea, I was sorry to hear about the accident. Hope you feel better soon. Todd.*

"What does it say?" Mom asked.

My eyes filled with tears as I handed the card to her.

Mom gasped as she read it. "Chelsea, these beautiful flowers are from Todd?" Her eyes lit up. "Do you know how much flowers like these cost?" She handed the card back to me.

"I imagine it was expensive."

"You should call and thank him."

"No, I can't." I cleared my throat and wiped my eyes.

"He's reaching out to you. It's only right to thank him." She retrieved the cordless phone from the base and handed it to me. "Call him. He obviously cares about you or he wouldn't have sent the flowers."

I placed the phone on the table. "If he cares about me, then why didn't he answer my text last night when I asked him for a ride home?"

"Maybe he didn't see the text until this morning. Maybe his phone was dead. It was the middle of the night, after all." Mom shrugged. "There are a million reasons why he may not have gotten the text, but he's reaching out to you now. You should take that opening and call him."

"I can't." I studied the flowers. "I don't know what to say."

"You could just call and say thank you. That would be a great conversation opener."

"I saw him talking to a pretty girl in the parking lot the other day, so he probably already has another girlfriend." I slipped the note card into my pocket. "I'm going to go sit with the twins."

"I'll call you when supper is ready," Mom said.

As I slowly made my way toward the family room, I hoped my mother was right when she said the flowers were Todd's way of reaching out to me. If so, then I hoped I could find the right words to say when I saw him opening night.

# chapter twenty

On Saturday evening, my mother steered her minivan into the parking lot of the Cameronville Community Theater. The lot was buzzing with performers and patrons. My heart fluttered when I spotted Todd's car parked at the back of the lot. Without thinking, my hand moved to my neckline and touched the necklace he'd given to me. I'd retrieved it from my jewelry box and put it on before we left home tonight. It may have been a silly notion, but I hoped it would help me feel connected to Todd again.

I'd considered calling him several times last night and again today; however, I'd chickened out. I was both excited and nervous about seeing him at the show.

Mom stopped the van by the stairs leading to the stage door and glanced in the rearview mirror. "Oh no. There's a line of cars behind me. Why don't you wait by the stairs? I'll help you navigate them after I park the van."

"Okay." I slowly climbed out of the van with my crutches and hobbled over to the building. I grabbed the stair railing and tried to pull myself up the steps, but I couldn't manage it without putting weight on my ankle.

The stage door opened and closed with a loud thump. I glanced up just as Todd rushed down the stairs to assist me.

"Chelsea." He held out his arm. "Can I help you?"

"Sure." My face burned with embarrassment. "Thank you."

"How are you feeling?" Holding my crutches in his left hand and supporting my left arm with his right hand, Todd helped me hop up the stairs.

"I'm pretty sore." I tried to concentrate on balancing, but the scent of his cologne mixed with the clean scent of soap distracted me to the point of almost tripping. "And I had no idea how exhausted I'd get from using these crutches."

"I've heard they're tiring." His strong hand was just the balance I needed to reach the top of the steps. "Are you all right?" he asked when we reached the stoop.

"Yeah." I heaved a deep sigh as I tried to catch my breath. "Wow. I'm worn out now. I could really use a nap."

Todd grinned, and my heart turned over in my chest. He was so handsome in his black jeans and black fitted T-shirt; I feared I might melt right there on the pavement. "Maybe you should sit out this performance and try again next weekend when you're feeling better." He handed my crutches to me.

"Are you kidding?" I asked. "I've worked too hard this summer to miss opening night."

"Chelsea," my mother called from the bottom step. "Are you okay?"

"Yeah." I smiled down at her, and her smile caused the tips of my ears to burn with embarrassment.

"Hi, Mrs. Klein," Todd said with a wave. "I'll make sure she gets inside okay."

"Thank you, Todd," Mom said. "It's good to see you."

"You too." Todd pulled the door open.

"Chelsea, I'm going to wait for Jason and the twins in the lobby. I'll see you after the show. Good luck." She winked at me.

"Thanks, Mom." I hopped through the door and stepped into the chaos of opening night as actors, actresses, chorus and crew members buzzed around backstage. I looked up at Todd and longed to pull him into a quiet room to talk. "Thanks for your help."

"You're welcome."

"I wanted to call you last night to thank you for those beautiful flowers," I said. "That was really sweet of you. But I wasn't sure— "

"Chelsea!" Mr. Muller interrupted our conversation. "I'm so glad you made it!" He touched my arm. "We have a chair set up for you just offstage so you can oversee the costumes before the actors go on. Let's get you set up before it gets too close to show time."

Todd squeezed my hand, and my fingers warmed at his touch. He leaned close to my ear and whispered, "We'll talk later."

Mr. Muller nudged me toward the auditorium before I could respond, but a spark of hope ignited in my soul as I started down the hallway. Cast and crew members greeted me as I hobbled past. I spotted Dylan talking with a few girls across the way. He met my gaze and nodded. I thought he might walk over to ask how I was and apologize for the accident, but he continued his conversation instead.

"Louise and I have been concerned about you," Mr. Muller said.

"Thanks," I said. "I was determined not to miss this performance."

I made my way to the chair Mr. Muller had set up for me near the stage entrance.

He handed me a set of headphones. "You take it easy. If you don't feel well, you let someone know. We'll take you back to one of the lounges so you can relax in peace."

"Thank you," I said. "I appreciate it."

I was getting situated in the chair when Kylie rushed over to me.

"Chelsea!" Her eyes sparkled with tears. "Oh, Chelsea, I'm so glad you're okay. I've been so worried about you!"

"Really?" I couldn't help but snort in disbelief. "If you were so worried, then why did you and Jimmy leave the scene of the accident? Why didn't you come visit me in the hospital? And why didn't you call me at home afterward?"

"Oh, well ... I was just ... well ..." Kylie stammered. "I was scared."

"Why?" I demanded. "You weren't involved with the accident."

She squatted down in front of me. "Jimmy was afraid he'd be arrested because he's been caught driving drunk once before. He's also been in trouble for street racing." Tears trickled down her face. "I wanted to call you, but the police came to my house on Friday. They said I could get in trouble for leaving the scene."

"You definitely *should* be scared after leaving the scene of an accident. But a real friend wouldn't have been more worried about getting in trouble than she was about her friend who got injured." I was on a roll. All of the hurt and anger that had been pent up inside of me came flowing out. "A real friend would have been worried about how *I* was doing. My real friends came to see me in the hospital. And it helped me see that you've never been a real friend. You've always been more worried about yourself."

Kylie wiped away more tears. "I'm so sorry, Chelsea. I *am* your real friend, and I've been so worried about you. The accident was terrible. I *have* been thinking about you." She pointed at my foot. "How are you?"

"I'm in pain, but I'll be fine." I glanced behind her to see

Marni watching and smiling. "The musical is going to start soon, and we have work to do. I need you to go to the laundry area and grab the sewing basket. We need to be prepared to make last-minute alterations. I'm sort of limited as to what I can do, but I can sit here and give you instructions."

"Okay." Kylie hopped up. "I'm really sorry, Chelsea. And I really am glad you're okay." She hurried back toward the laundry room.

Marni walked over and hugged me. "I heard what you said," she whispered in my ear. "Good for you."

"Thanks. I had to get it off my chest."

"How are you doing?"

"I'm okay. Just sore and exhausted from using these stupid crutches."

"Have you seen Dylan?" Marni asked.

"I saw him from a distance. He didn't speak to me though. He hasn't called me or anything. I was wondering if I'd get an apology, but I haven't heard from him at all."

Marni scowled. "He should be in jail for drinking and driving and racing. But I heard that his uncle sprung him. His uncle posted Dylan's bail Thursday night since his parents were out of town." Her expression brightened. "Oh! But I've been dying to tell you something. You missed quite a show earlier."

"Really?" I asked.

"Todd told off Dylan right in the middle of the hallway." She kept her voice low as people rushed past us. "It nearly came to blows."

I gasped. "Are you serious?"

"Todd marched right up to Dylan and got in his face. He told Dylan he had no right getting behind the wheel of the car when he was drunk, and especially not when you were with him." Marni's face was animated as she recounted the story.

"Dylan called Todd a loser, and Todd said Dylan is the real loser because he uses people and thinks he can't have fun unless he's drunk. Then Todd said, 'Unlike you, I know how to treat a special girl like Chelsea.' Dylan said something like, 'Well, if you know so much, then why was she with *me* that night?' Todd went to punch Dylan, but P.J. pulled Todd back before he could. It was intense." She bumped my arm with her fist.

"I can't believe he did that." I touched my necklace again. "Todd asked his cousin to bring me flowers yesterday." I pulled the card from my pocket. "This was with it."

Marni read it over my shoulder. "Oh, Chels. Todd really does care about you."

"Places, everyone!" Mrs. Muller stage whispered.

"I'll see you after the show," Marni stood.

"Break a leg," I said with a laugh.

"No, thanks. I don't have the upper body strength to use crutches." Marni laughed as she walked away.

♫

When the show began, I lost myself in the excitement of the performance and the costumes. Kylie and I worked together, helping the actors change quickly and mending a few last-minute rips and missing buttons.

During the performance, I heard Todd's voice over the headphones a few times while he was talking to the stage manager. I couldn't stop smiling when I recalled Marni's story about how Todd defended me to Dylan. I prayed that I'd have a chance to apologize to Todd and convince him I cared for him. In fact, I suspected I may even love him.

When the show ended, the crowd clapped, cheered, and hooted as the cast members took their final bows. After the curtain dropped, the cast members traded high fives and rushed back to the dressing rooms.

Mr. and Mrs. Muller approached as I pushed myself up out of the chair and grabbed my crutches.

"Chelsea, the costumes were superb!" Mr. Muller said. "I think we're going to be nominated for an award this year. Great job!"

"Really?" I beamed. "Oh, that's fantastic."

"Wonderful job," Mrs. Muller said as she hugged me. "I'm glad you're doing okay after your accident. I was so worried when I heard about it. Do you need help?"

"No, I'm fine." I smiled. "Thank you so much."

"Hey!" Marni came up behind me. "How did things look from your point of view?"

"It looked great. I think Jan's Pink Ladies' jacket was the best."

"I think you're just saying that." She reached for my purse. "Let me help you with that."

"Thank you."

"Where are we headed?" she asked as we slowly made our way down the hall.

"I want to go outside, but I'm not sure which exit is best. I don't know if I want to do those stairs again, but the handicapped exit leads out to the lobby. I'm sure that part of the building is a mob of people right now. I guess I'll just take my time on the stairs."

"That sounds good. I'll help you."

We made our way to the backstage exit, and Marni held the door for me as I hobbled out. By the time I made it to the bottom step, I'd spotted Emily, Zander, Whitney, and Taylor approaching.

"That was awesome!" Emily hugged me and then Marni. "Great job!"

"The costumes were fantastic, Chels!" Whitney hugged me next. "How are you doing?"

"I'm tired but okay," I told her.

"Chelsea!" My brothers ran up to me with my parents in tow.

"Hey, little buddies." I leaned down and smiled at them. "Did you like the show?"

They both nodded.

"Oh, Chelsea. It was wonderful." Mom hugged me next.

"Your mother is right." Jason touched my arm. "You are one talented seamstress. I'm so proud of you, Chelsea."

"Thank you," I said. "I appreciate that."

"We were talking about going out for ice cream," Emily said to Marni and me. "Would you two like to join us?"

"Oh, no thank you." I looked at my mom. "I'm way too tired for that."

"You can go," Mom said. "You've earned it."

"Thanks, but I really am exhausted, Emily. Those stairs did me in," I admitted. "Thank you for coming. It means a lot to me."

I said good-bye to Emily and the others, and they headed out.

"I'm going to head out too." Marni hugged me and whispered in my ear, "Todd is on his way over here now. I want to hear all the details tomorrow!" She said good-bye to my family and then crossed the parking lot.

My heart fluttered as Todd walked up to us.

"Todd!" My brothers ran over and high-fived him.

"Hey, guys." Todd looked over at my parents. "Hi, Mr. and Mrs. Klein."

"How are you, Todd?" Jason shook his hand. "We were just telling Chelsea how fantastic the show was."

"Yeah, it was." Todd looked at me. "The costumes were the best part."

"Nah," I joked. "I thought the lighting stole the show."

He laughed. "I was serious about the costumes. You have some amazing talent."

"Thank you."

"Are you going to the after party?" Todd motioned toward a group of crew members standing by the back door. "They're all going to the diner."

"You can go, Chelsea," Mom said with a smile.

"Can we go?" Justin asked.

"I want ice cream!" J.J. chimed in.

"Thanks, but I'm too exhausted." I adjusted my hands on the grips of the crutches. "I'm ready to change into my pajamas."

"Oh, okay." Todd looked disappointed. He turned to Mom and said, "Would it be all right if I gave Chelsea a ride home?"

"Sure. I think that would be nice."

Todd turned to me. "Is that okay with you?"

"Of course." My thoughts twirled with excitement as my heart hammered away in my chest.

"Great." Todd looked relieved. "I'll go get my car." He waved to my family. "It was good seeing you."

"Take care, Todd," Jason said.

"Don't be a stranger," Mom added, as the twins yelled, "Bye!"

As Todd jogged across the parking lot, Mom touched my arm. "Have fun, and take your time."

"Why are you relaxing the terms of my grounding?" I gave her a confused look. "I thought I wasn't allowed to go anywhere except to the theater and then home. But you kept trying to get me to go out for ice cream or out with my friends."

She nodded toward Jason. "We talked about it, and we want you to enjoy your last few weeks of summer before college starts—within reason. No parties like the ones you've been sneaking out to, but quiet gatherings are acceptable."

Jason rubbed Mom's back. "You've been through a lot, but we know you've figured out some tough life lessons, Chelsea."

"Thank you." I hugged my parents.

# chapter twenty-one

Todd's red Focus came to a stop by the sidewalk. He hopped out, jogged around the car, and opened the passenger door for me. Taking my hand, he helped me climb in and then stowed the crutches in the trunk.

Todd climbed in next to me and closed the car door. As he steered through the parking lot, my heart turned over in my chest. Sitting next to him in his car felt like coming home. I was finally back where I belonged—with Todd.

Yet it wasn't that simple. I still had to apologize and try to get him to understand how much I appreciated him even though I'd treated him so badly.

As he merged onto Main Street, we both started talking at the same time.

"I'm sorry," I said. "What were you going to say?"

"No, ladies first."

"I insist, Todd. What were you going to say?"

"Do you remember our first date?" he asked with a sideways glance.

"Of course I do. We ordered milk shakes from the drive-through at the Dairy Barn, and then we parked in the back of the lot, drank our shakes, and talked for hours."

He slowed and then stopped at a red light before angling

toward me. "What do you say we go to the Dairy Barn for old time's sake?"

"Yes, but on one condition."

"You name it."

I pointed toward my bad ankle. "Don't make me get out of the car and hobble over to a table."

"I promise." He slapped on the turn signal. "What were you going to say?"

My palms began to sweat as I tried to remember the mental apology I'd been practicing. I rubbed my hands on my jeans and took a deep, ragged breath.

"Todd, I'm sorry," I began, my voice quivering. "I've treated you like garbage ever since the production started, and you didn't deserve that. I've made a lot of mistakes this summer, and I hope you can forgive me."

The light turned green, and he merged onto Lynnhaven Parkway. When he didn't speak, I felt like I needed to fill the quiet, so I began pouring out my heart to him.

"When Dylan started paying attention to me, I lost my mind. For the past twenty-four hours, I've been trying to figure out why I let him have that kind of power over me, and it finally clicked yesterday."

"What clicked?" he asked, keeping his eyes focused on the road.

"Emily and Marni came over to visit me yesterday, and Emily made me watch *Grease* and *Grease 2*." I touched my necklace as I spoke. "Well, I finally realized that I've been acting just like Sandy in *Grease*."

"What?" Todd laughed.

"Just like Sandy, I thought I needed to be someone I'm not in order to fit in with Dylan and his friends," I explained. "But by the time I was finally accepted into their group, I no longer felt like myself because I'd gone against everything I believe in: I snuck out of the house, and I drank alcohol." I turned toward him. "But worst of all, I took you for granted. Aside from my family, you're the most important person in my life."

Todd stopped at another red light and faced me. His gorgeous brown eyes were soft and full of empathy.

"I'm not proud of what I did." My voice was thin and shaky again. "And you have every right to hate me."

He shook his head. "I couldn't hate you if I tried."

"You *should* hate me. I lied to you, and I was thoughtless." Tears filled my eyes. "I feel like God allowed me to be tested this summer. And as soon as I saw temptation, I grabbed it and ran with it. Yet through all of my mistakes, I realized what was most important to me, and I figured out who I really am. I also realized who my true friends are: Emily, Marni, Whitney, and you. I never want to stray from the right path again."

A tear trickled down my cheek, and Todd wiped it away with his finger.

The light turned green, and he merged onto Holland Road. Silence filled the car, and I tried to think of something else to say. My body trembled with anticipation while I awaited his response to my confession and apology.

"I've missed you," he finally said. "And I've realized a few things too. Part of this was my fault."

"No, it wasn't. It was all me."

"Let me finish," he said gently. "I wasn't listening to you when you told me you wanted to spend time with me. I should have given you more attention and been more willing to do the things you wanted to do. Maybe if I'd gone with you to one of Dylan's parties, you and I wouldn't have drifted apart." He glanced over at me. "And I'm sorry for not responding to your text on the night of the accident."

"You don't have to apologize. I had a lot of nerve texting you after the way I'd treated you."

"I'm glad you texted me, but I'm sorry I missed it." He slapped on the blinker and pulled into the Dairy Barn's parking lot. "When you texted, I didn't have my phone on me. I'd left it in the cup holder in my car. I didn't see the text until the next morning." He steered into the drive-through and stopped behind an SUV parked in front of the menu board. "When I got to work that morning, Janie asked if I'd heard that you'd been in a bad car accident. Later she told me she was going to go visit you, so I asked her to take the flowers for me."

"Which are gorgeous, by the way," I said.

Todd grinned. "I'm glad you like them. Janie told me I was a chicken for not taking them to you myself."

"Well then, we're even because I was a chicken for not calling to thank you for the flowers." I studied him. "Why *didn't* you bring them to me yourself?"

His smile faded, and he paused to consider his response.

"May I take your order?" a tinny voice blared through the speaker beneath the menu.

He turned to me and asked, "Large strawberry shake?"

"Yes, please." I rubbed my hands together in anticipation.

"Anything else?" he offered. "It's my treat."

"No, thanks."

"Would you share an order of fries with me?"

"Sure." I grinned, enjoying the feeling of being part of a couple again.

Todd spoke into the menu board, "I'd like to order a large strawberry shake, a large chocolate shake, and a large order of fries, please."

The tinny voice confirmed the order and Todd pulled the car forward.

"Thank you," I said.

"You're welcome." He pulled his wallet from his back pocket and retrieved a twenty-dollar bill.

We sat in comfortable silence while we waited for the order. After Todd paid for and received our food, he parked his car in a spot at the back of the lot.

I took a long drink of my shake and smiled. "This is pure heaven."

"I was just thinking the same thing." His eyes moved to my collarbone. "You're wearing the necklace I gave you."

I touched the heart-shaped stone. "I missed it."

He nodded slowly.

"You never answered my question before." I took a fry out of the cardboard container Todd had stuck inside one of the cup holders. "Why didn't you deliver the flowers yourself?"

Todd took a long drink of his shake, and I wondered if he was avoiding the question. "I didn't want to risk seeing you with Dylan."

"What do you mean?"

"Janie told me you'd been in an accident in a yellow Camaro. Her EMT friend said the pretty redheaded passenger was taken to the hospital, but the driver was fine. I know who owns a yellow Camaro, and I know who the pretty redhead is." Todd ate a fry. "I didn't want to show up at your house and find Dylan there. If I'd brought you flowers while your new boyfriend was taking care of you, I would have felt like the big loser he's always claiming I am."

I snorted. "Dylan was never my boyfriend. In fact, he never came to the hospital or called to make sure I was still alive after the ambulance took me away."

Todd's eyes narrowed. "He is a complete and total lowlife." Todd leaned against his door. "So why were you too chicken to call and thank me for those flowers?"

"I didn't know what to say, and I was afraid you'd found someone else to date."

"If I'd found someone else, then why would I send you flowers?"

I wagged at fry at him. "You have a point. But I saw you talking to that girl Molly in the parking lot after practice last week."

"Molly?" he asked.

"You know Molly. She's one of the girls in the chorus. A really pretty blonde."

"Oh, Molly Adams? She asked me if my parents were hiring at the restaurant. I told her to stop by sometime and talk to my mom about filling out an application." Todd suddenly grinned. "You were jealous of Molly!"

I smiled. "Yes, yes I was—just like you were jealous of Dylan."

We drank our shakes in silence for a moment.

"Marni told me P.J. had to pull you off Dylan earlier today," I said shyly.

Todd looked embarrassed but smiled. "Yeah, that wasn't my finest hour. I'm surprised Mr. Muller didn't kick me off the production."

"It means a lot that you did that. Thanks for defending me." I reached over and touched his hand.

"You're welcome." His expression clouded over. "I was furious when I heard Dylan had been drinking and street racing with you in the car. I can't imagine putting anyone in that kind of danger."

I suddenly thought of the sewing machine. "Would you do me a favor?"

"Of course." He ate another fry. "What do you need?"

"After you take me home, would you mind taking Dylan's

mom's sewing machine over to Castleton and leaving it on his front porch?"

Todd lifted his drink. "I'd be glad to do that."

"Thank you." I cleared my throat as emotion surged through me again. "Todd, I'm so sorry I hurt you. I've tried to figure out how I can show you how much you mean to me." My eyes filled with fresh tears. "My mom said God puts special people in our lives for a reason. You're the most special person I know, and I've been racking my brain trying to figure out how to win you back. I don't know what I can say to prove to you that I miss you. I want to make things right between us."

Todd leaned forward and kissed me, sending my stomach into a deep dive. His sweet lips tasted like chocolate mixed with french fries. My pulse raced, and I savored the familiar feel of his lips.

He rested his forehead against mine and stared into my eyes. "Chelsea Morris, would you be my girlfriend again?"

"Yes." My voice was a thin whisper as I tried to catch my breath.

"Good." He pulled me close, and I rested my head on his shoulder. "I'll do my best to make time for you from now on. My dad hired another cook, so I promise I won't be tired every night. We can hang out as often as you'd like."

"And I promise I won't take you for granted. Thanks for giving me another chance." I ran my fingers through his thick, dark hair.

He kissed the top of my head. "It's so good to have you back."

"It's good to be back."

# *Miles from Nowhere* discussion questions

1. When Chelsea snuck out to go to the parties at Dylan's house, she was defying her parents and going against everything she once believed in. Chelsea was bowing to peer pressure in order to fit in. If you were Chelsea, would you have given in to peer pressure just so you might be considered popular? Why or why not? Have you ever given in to peer pressure? If so, how did that situation turn out?
2. Chelsea loves to sew and dreams of designing costumes for professional stage productions one day. Is there a hobby you feel passionate about? If so, have you ever shared your dreams with anyone?
3. Chelsea hung out with Marni during Dylan's parties. Chelsea eventually gave in to peer pressure and drank, but Marni never did. In fact, Marni told Chelsea she didn't need to drink to prove she's cool. Have you ever felt pressured to do something you didn't want to do? If so, how did you handle the situation? If you were Chelsea's friend, what advice would you give her about peer pressure?
4. Kylie witnessed Chelsea's car accident and fled the scene because she was afraid of getting in trouble. Although she was worried about Chelsea, she didn't contact her the next day. If you were Kylie, what, if anything, would you have done differently at the scene of the car accident?

5. Marni and Emily tried to offer Chelsea advice and to be good friends to her while she was going through a difficult time in her life. If you were Chelsea's friend, how would you have tried to help her cope?
6. Chelsea believed God led her through a difficult time to help her build up her faith and figure out who her true friends were before she went to college and started making new friends. Have you ever felt like God was allowing you to be tested? If so, what did you learn?
7. Todd felt betrayed by Chelsea when he found out she'd been sneaking out to parties and spending time with Dylan. Have you ever felt betrayed by a friend or significant other? If so, how did you handle that betrayal? Did you work out your problems with that person or did the relationship end? Looking back, would you have handled the situation differently?
8. When Chelsea wanted to leave that last party, she got in the car with Dylan—even though she knew he'd been drinking. Then, just as Marni predicted, the ride ended badly. How do you think Chelsea should have handled getting home that night? If you were Chelsea, what would you have done differently? In real life, do you have an emergency backup plan if you should ever wind up in a bad situation and need a quick way out?
9. Chelsea felt terrible about the way she'd treated Todd. So she tried to figure out a way to regain his trust and friendship. Have you ever hurt someone who meant a lot to you? If so, did you try to mend that broken relationship? How did that situation turn out?
10. Chelsea used prayer to help her find the words to apologize to her parents and to Todd. Do you pray regularly? What kinds of things do you discuss with God? How does prayer help you?

# Acknowledgments

As always, I'm thankful for my loving family, including my mother, Lola Goebelbecker; my husband, Joe; and my sons, Zac and Matt. Thank you, Mom, for always letting me bounce ideas off you. You're my best plotting partner!

This book was so much fun to write, and it was also a trip down memory lane for me. I have to thank Christine Ricciardo, my best friend since kindergarten, for my love of the movies *Grease* and *Grease* 2. Those weekly sleepovers were the best!

I'm more grateful than words can express to my patient friends who critique my writing for me—Nancy Hardy, Amy Lillard, Janet Pecorella, Lauran Rodriguez, and, of course, my mother. I truly appreciate the time you take out of your busy lives to help me polish my books.

I'm also thankful to my friends who helped me with theater research, including Diane Adams, Mary Blythe Chapman, Austin Mejia, Beth Miles, and Pam Young. Thank you also to Rebecca Coffman and Sandra Handy.

Special thanks to Mary Gaertner, who introduced me to Bud Simmons, director of operations with the Charlotte Symphony Orchestra. I really enjoyed our special guided tour of the Knight Theater. I learned so much and had a blast spending time with you!

Thank you to my wonderful church family at Morning Star Lutheran in Matthews, North Carolina, for your encouragement, prayers, love, and friendship. You all mean so much to my family and me.

To my agent, Susan Brower—I am grateful for your friendship, support, and guidance in my writing career. Thank you for all you do!

Thank you to my amazing editor—Jacque Alberta. I appreciate your guidance and friendship. I'm grateful to each and every person at Zondervan who helped make this book a reality.

To my readers—thank you for choosing my novels. My books are a blessing in my life for many reasons, including the special friendships I've formed with my readers.

Thank you most of all to God, for giving me the inspiration and the words to glorify You. I'm so grateful and humbled that You've chosen this path for me.

# Roadside Assistance

*Amy Clipston*

A very bumpy ride. Emily Curtis is used to dealing with her problems while under the hood of an old Chevy, but when her mom dies, Emily's world seems shaken beyond repair. Driven from home by hospital bills they can't pay, Emily and her dad move in with his wealthy sister, who intends to make her niece more feminine—in other words, just like Whitney, Emily's perfect cousin. But when Emily hears the engine of a 1970 Dodge Challenger, and sees the cute gearhead, Zander, next door, things seem to be looking up. But even working alongside Zander can't completely fix the hole in Emily's life. Ever since her mom died, Emily hasn't been able to pray, and no one—not even Zander—seems to understand. But sometimes the help you need can come from the person you least expect.

*Available in stores and online!*

# Reckless Heart

*Amy Clipston*

Slipping. Lydia Bontrager's youngest sister is frighteningly ill, and as a good Amish daughter, it falls to Lydia to care for her siblings and keep the household running, in addition to working as a teacher's assistant and helping part time at her grandmother's bakery. Succumbing to stress, Lydia gives in to one wild night and returns home drunk. The secret of that mistake leaves Lydia feeling even more restless and confused, especially when Joshua, the only boy she's ever loved, becomes increasingly distant. When a non-Amish boy moves in nearby, Lydia finds someone who understands her, but the community is convinced Lydia is becoming too reckless. With the pressures at home and her sister's worsening condition, a splintering relationship with Joshua, and her own growing questions over what is right, Lydia could lose everything that she's ever held close.